QUIET
NO
MORE

Nikki Barthelmess

Mendota Heights, Minnesota

First Edition
First Printing, 2020

Book design by Sarah Taplin and Jake Nordby
Cover design by Sarah Taplin and Jake Nordby
Cover images by AaronAmat/Getty Images, Engin_Akyurt/Pixabay, ractapopulous/Pixabay, Fotocitizen/Pixabay

Flux, an imprint of North Star Editions, Inc.

Library of Congress Cataloging-in-Publication Data (pending)
978-1-63583-063-7

Flux
North Star Editions, Inc.
2297 Waters Drive
Mendota Heights, MN 55120
www.fluxnow.com

Printed in the United States of America

For Hadley

CHAPTER
ONE

'm smiling as I pack up my bag to leave class. Smiling—I actually do that now. Last year, that would have been unthinkable, when even graduating high school and making it to college seemed like it might never happen for me.

But I made it happen.

I wouldn't let my father take that from me too.

My English 101 professor just spent the last ten minutes waxing poetic about Sherlock Holmes and how the detective doesn't get enough credit in literary circles. I chuckle, knowing my Holmes aficionado boyfriend will eat up everything Tessa said.

In the cacophony of noise—backpacks zipping, people talking, feet thudding on the floor, everyone rushing to get outside and experience the early September warmth—I feel someone staring. Lana, who sits a row ahead of me, nods as she walks through the open classroom door.

I want to respond, maybe suggest we study together for an upcoming test or something, but the words evaporate on my tongue. With Kale still back in Silver Valley, and Christina and Jess busy with dorm life at each of their new schools, I haven't spent much time with my friends. Making new ones hasn't been easy either. Lana's the secretary for the advocacy club that fights against sexual harassment and assault on campus.

Students Against Sexual Assault and Harassment. SASAH. I started attending a few weeks ago, but we haven't spoken much outside of meetings. I shoot a text to Kale telling him about the Sherlock Holmes stuff and slide my phone into my back pocket before pushing through the double doors and walking into the Reno sunshine.

The wind blows a piece of my fiery hair into my face. I spit it out as I head toward the grassy area in front of Truckee Meadows Community College. The sun glitters over the still-snow-dotted Sierra Nevada mountains off in the distance. Sure, it's not the quad at UNR, where Jess and I used to plan on hanging out in between classes. But it'll do. I put my legs out in front of me as I sit on the grass. Stare at the kids walking around. Some are sitting under a tree nearby, laughing together like they've been friends for years. Maybe they have been. My phone buzzes in my pocket—Kale texting back—and I smile as I reply with several heart face emojis. I sigh at the now familiar pang in my gut. I miss him. Sitting outside texting Kale for the few minutes between class and the SASAH meeting has become a Tuesday ritual for me.

I found the group on the school's website when I was looking for clubs to join. A way to get involved. Maybe meet some new people. The old Victoria, who I was last year when I was trying to hide from everything that happened with Dad, would have never joined a club, any club, especially not one that focuses on preventing sexual assault.

I breathe deeply. That's not the only reason why I joined the club. Sure, I want to make friends, but there's more to it than that. I want to help others from becoming victims—no, *survivors*—of the kind of abuse I went through. I want to do something positive to make what happened to me mean something. To show myself that what Dad did didn't break me.

Because I won't let it.

A laugh trills behind me, from a girl catching a Frisbee before one of her friends wraps their arms around her and takes her down. I swallow. This year isn't going to be like last year. Pushing people away, keeping secrets—it only hurt me.

And my stepsister, Sarah.

There are other Sarahs out there, other people who have been hurt, who will get hurt. That's why I go to the meetings, even if it's hard being in a room full of people who constantly talk about assault and how to prevent it. Ripping the Band-Aid off every time I hear the word *victim* or *survivor* or *perpetrator*. But I keep going.

Sarah and I generally avoid talking about my dad since he pled guilty to battery with the intent to commit sexual assault on a minor, on both of us, his daughter and stepdaughter. He beat his wife, too, and Tiffany ended up pressing charges. But we don't ever hear her talk about it. The DA's office gave him the plea deal for a lesser charge (intent, rather than admitting to sexually assaulting Sarah and me), since they didn't want to drag out the case and we didn't have any proof anyway. He says/she says kind of thing. This way, he'll for sure get jail time. Five years to life with the possibility of parole. He could have gone free if it had gone to trial.

Still, five years to life is a big range. Sentencing doesn't happen for a couple of months, and that's when Sarah and

I will have our chance to give victim impact statements in front of the judge, to see if what we say will affect sentencing.

I pull out my notebook and look at what I have so far.

Victim Impact Statement, it reads.

My dad hurt me, and now he's in jail. I'm glad he's there so he can't hurt me and my stepsister anymore, but

I never finished the sentence. I can't bear to write what I was thinking when I wrote it. To finish the thought, *but I don't want to hurt him.*

I resist the urge to crumple the piece of paper. I won't go back to where I was last year, trying to protect my father. All it did was cause pain, and not just to myself, but to Sarah too.

I try to force the thought from my mind. The date of the hearing hasn't been set yet. It could be months away. I have time.

Thinking about what my dad did to me, and my chance to tell the judge who is sentencing him about it, makes my stomach clench. My hands sweat. It's like I'm scared or running from something, but nothing's here with me. Just school. Not Dad.

I can't escape him. Instead of letting the dread take hold of me, I do what I can do. A trick I learned from reading an article about coping with trauma and stress. Change the channel in my mind. Move toward a distraction, something productive. Something that can help other people, people who suffered like Sarah. Or me. Better yet, maybe the efforts of SASAH can help keep stuff like that from happening in the first place.

I head for the meeting in the building behind me. Inside,

at the front of the single long table, which is always set up for club meetings, there's Lana. I wave enthusiastically and then drop my hand, embarrassed.

Lana's pale face splits into a smile. "Come on over, the seat next to me is open."

I usually sit near the back, but Lana's invitation, possibly brought on by my ridiculous waving, emboldens me. Lana makes room by pushing several boxes of pizza away from her, into the middle of the table, near a few liters of soda, paper plates, all the stuff the club usually provides for meetings. Poor college students love free food, and free weekly lunches are one of the perks of joining this club.

Jasmine, the club president, puts her slice down the second she spots me. She stands, wipes her hands on a napkin, and reaches her dark, copper-toned hand out to me. "Good to see you again, Victoria."

I laugh awkwardly at her formality and shake her hand. "Glad to be here," I say, before taking a seat a few chairs away. With a swing of her long black-and-red-streaked braids, Jasmine returns to her spot, leaning over the podium. I wave to Candace and Lance as they rush in, and the room fills up with the usual twelve to fifteen people. Some sit in chairs along the wall, behind the table.

Trey glides through the open door, heading toward us. He waves at Lana and me.

Tall, fit, with dirty blond hair cut short on the sides but long on top, Trey looks like he could be in a punk band. When we first met, his friendliness immediately disarmed me.

I scoot my backpack out of the way, in case Trey wants

to sit with us. Instead, he joins Jasmine up front, like usual. My face warms because I'm not sure why I thought he would sit here. Of course he'd sit up front. He's the club vice president, after all.

Trey stands and squares his shoulders as he readies to address the room.

"Great turnout." Trey projects his voice without fail. "Come up and grab some food, talk amongst yourselves for a bit, and the meeting will officially start in about ten. Sound good?"

Everyone eats pizza. I ask Lance about how he keeps his long, curly black hair so shiny. Not the tangled mess my red waves turn into at the drop of a hat. "Conditioner, baby," he says, before Candace pipes in, "Seriously, this guy spends more on hair products than anyone I've ever met. It's ridiculous."

I laugh into my pizza, feeling less alone than I did before.

Jasmine clears her throat, standing at the whiteboard, marker in hand. "Let's get started, shall we? I've got some bad news. Hope House, the battered women's shelter across town, is officially closing their doors. The city council voted against increasing the funding for all shelters in town, and Hope House was already hanging on by a thread."

The room goes eerily quiet. Because we've talked about this before. Without Hope House, there will be dozens more assault survivors on the street or returning to their abusers because they have nowhere else to go.

"That's it?" Lana asks from beside me. "There's gotta be something we can do to help keep their doors open!"

Lance, Candace, and several others murmur in agreement. Jasmine's eyes turn down. "Unfortunately, that ship has sailed. Hope House owed the city money for several months of back taxes. They've been evicted. What we need to focus our efforts on now are the people who are affected. We need to make sure they get the resources that they need."

My thoughts turn to my stepmother, Tiffany, and how she put up with my dad beating her because she thought he loved her. How she was afraid to leave him because she didn't have a job or anywhere to take Sarah.

I sit up straighter. "You said the city council has denied increasing the funding for all the shelters, right?"

Jasmine nods at me.

"Well, then we should try to do whatever we can to keep other places open."

I take a breath as I realize all eyes are on me. I just stated something obvious, but I don't have a solution. My palms start to sweat, but Lana gives me an encouraging smile.

I think quickly. "Could we do a fundraiser or something? I mean, they need the money already if they're asking city council for more. They probably need it now more than ever, if any of the women and children who used to go to Hope House are seeking help from the other shelters. There were only two battered women's shelters in town, and now it's just the one, the Women's and Children's Domestic Violence Shelter. That makes sense, right?"

I pause, feeling my face redden. I'm not used to speaking up in class, much less in meetings like this. And I'm new to the club, so who am I to try to come up with ideas?

Lana nods vigorously, putting me at ease. She pushes her plastic cup full of Sprite aside. "Victoria's right." She stares at me for a second, quietly, as though she's forming a plan, before looking back to Jasmine. "The women's and family shelter wanted to build a new wing. Isn't that what you said a few weeks ago, Jasmine? When you went to the city council meeting to listen to the executive director speak during open comment?"

Jasmine nods, and I can see in her eyes that she and Lana are thinking the same thing.

Lana looks at me. "Like Victoria said, we should help another shelter stay open, but I think we should do more than that. We can help them build so that they can take the people who would normally go to Hope House, keeping them off the streets."

A guy with a black faux hawk at the end of the table closest to the door claps loudly. "I'm in. Let's do this!" He hoots as a few others clap.

Jasmine smiles. "Love the enthusiasm, Steve." She taps the podium with the tips of her manicured nails. "Lana, Victoria, I think you're onto something. The women's and family shelter only has thirty-five beds and they have to turn away hundreds of people every month. We could raise money for them, so they can build that new wing. Or buy more beds or whatever they need." People murmur in agreement all around us.

Trey chimes in. "I think that's a great idea."

The club brainstorms for the next few minutes before Jasmine tells us all to think it over and bring our best ideas to the next club meeting. She goes on to pass out literature about sexual harassment and assault on campuses around the country and what we can do about it. "Let's keep our recruiting efforts up. The more people we can get in a club like this, the more people we have on our side to dismantle rape culture."

Jasmine appears behind me and leans forward so Lana and I can hear her. "I'm so glad you're here, Victoria." She smiles at me. "Thanks for participating with ideas—it can be hard to get new members to do that. This club means the world to so many of us. It's the only place on campus that's a safe space for survivors to be proactive and help others."

Instinctively, I stiffen when Jasmine says the word *survivors*. Her dark eyes hold mine for a second before she hurriedly adds, "You don't have to be a survivor to care about the mission of this club, of course."

Lana meets my eye, and I give her and Jasmine a tentative smile. "Happy to be here."

———————

"Do you want a ride home?" Lana asks me as she, Trey, and I walk out of the meeting together. I should say yes, wanting to make new friends and all, but after all that activity, meeting new people, not to mention the topic at hand—sexual assault—I really just want to be alone.

I force a smile. "No, thanks. I've got a lot of homework to do and sitting on the bus helps me think."

Lana makes a face at Trey then smiles back at me. "Whatever you're into."

I say my goodbyes and then head for the bus stop, feeling emotionally drained but proud of myself for coming up with the idea to help another shelter in need. It's better to be proactive than to let the news of something bad crush you. Like a shelter closing.

Or like having to write a victim impact statement about how your dad hurt you. Because—even if he deserves it—telling the truth will hurt him. And he's still my dad. The guy who raised me and taught me how to ride a bike and who was so happy when we played beach volleyball with Mom at the lake before she died.

I still love him, though I can't admit that to anyone else.

Because they would look at me like I lost my mind. How could you love someone who did something so awful to you?

It's better to join a club that helps victims than focus on how I am one.

My bus ride home is always a little longer than necessary, as we go out of the way to stop downtown. The bus squeaks to a halt on a corner surrounded by casinos, high-rise buildings that sparkle and shimmer at night but look gray, dirty, and overall depressing in the light of day. Lots of my fellow bus riders wear card dealer uniforms or the short, low-cut getups the casinos make the women cocktail servers wear.

I scoot over, making room for an older lady and her overflowing tote bag. She reeks of stale cigarettes and starts coughing heavily, rummaging in her purse and pulling out a tissue as she sits next to me. I lean toward the window and try not to breathe as the bus starts rolling again. I could buy a bike and avoid this, but I'm saving for a used car. I haven't spent everything I got from financial aid; I keep it in the bank for food and other expenses. It's only September, so I'm hoping that after this first semester ends in a few months, I'll have a better feel for how I'll handle my coursework, and I'll be able to get a part-time job.

Once the bus leaves me at my stop, I'm off, walking the couple of blocks to my place. The faded red, brick apartment building isn't much to look at, but it's home. My upstairs neighbor, Ray Pérez, is starting his car in the parking lot. I catch his eye, and he rolls the window down. "Have you seen that mangy cat running around?" he begins without preamble. "I'm starting to think it's a stray. You've been feeding it?"

I nod. I've left water and sandwich meat outside my door a few times. "It's so skinny."

"But if it has an owner, I don't want it to keep coming back to us," Ray says. I roll my eyes at him because I know he's been leaving food out for the cat too. Suddenly, the aforementioned stray meows loudly from the other side of the parking lot. I stare as the striped tabby meows loudly again, its green eyes staring right at me as it does.

"I'm starting to worry no one is going to claim it, especially as the nights start getting colder," I tell Ray.

Ray scratches his head, ruffling his short black hair. "Maybe I should call animal control."

As if the cat understands, it darts away from us, running into the bushes where the lot meets the sidewalk. "I wouldn't want to go to the pound either," I say.

"You're a big softie," Ray says, but the way he watches

the area the cat ran to for a long moment makes me think he is too.

I smile at Ray. He's been nice to me since I moved in at the end of July. The first friend I made since leaving Silver Valley.

I wave goodbye and once inside, drop my keys on the end table before I plop down on the couch Tiffany bought me. The couch, two-person dining room table, bed, and small dresser—they're all courtesy of my stepmother, trying to make amends.

Buying me things will never do that. I'm not sure anything will.

Still, she's trying.

———————————

I pull my laptop out. Thinking of my stepmom and how she didn't protect me from my dad only makes me think of Sarah and how I didn't protect her. I can't fix that, undo what Dad did to her, but I *can* help others in a bad position: the women and families who would benefit from being able to stay in the shelter after it gets more beds or room or whatever.

I search online for ideas for fundraisers. Bake sales. Nope. Wouldn't raise enough money. Car washes. An image of me in a bathing suit with bro-like guys from school catcalling while I wash their cars comes to mind. Nope, nope, nope.

A few months ago, Mindy, my old social worker, told me there were alumni groups for former foster kids out there if

I wanted to make some friends who knew what I was going through. I never looked into any—I wanted to leave foster care in the rearview mirror—but Mindy did say they were all about raising awareness, kind of like SASAH wants to do, and that they had events and stuff. Maybe one of them was a fundraiser.

I look up foster care alumni groups, clicking through the pages of a website, and several pictures come up. The biggest is of a bunch of smiling faces wearing matching green shirts. It looks like they do a fundraiser every year, a walk for awareness to raise money for their efforts. We could do a fundraising walk too. I'm smiling big as I take out a notebook to jot some ideas down.

Kale texts me wanting to know if now is a good time to talk. But I've just gotten started with my fundraising research, and I don't want to stop now.

I'm slammed with school stuff. Can I call you later? Soon?

Kale, my ever-supportive boyfriend, agrees. And I get back to it.

———

I spend the next day continuing to finesse my ideas and how I'll present them at the next SASAH meeting. This feels good. Doing something.

It feels right.

After class Thursday, I approach Lana. "I have an idea for a fundraiser," I blurt.

She laughs. "Excited much?"

Trey strides toward us and the three of us walk out of class together.

"We could do a walk for awareness, have people pay to do it or sponsor others to do it. We could do it at a park nearby, make it fun, feed people burgers or something."

Lana's brown eyes twinkle. "That's an awesome idea, Victoria!"

Trey opens one of the double doors for us and Lana and I walk through it, heading outside. "Jasmine will love it," he says. "And what if we go door-to-door telling people around town about it? That way we could get community buy-in and not just from people at school."

Lana nods vigorously. "Yes!"

The three of us head toward the parking lot. My phone buzzes. A text from Kale. *Shoot.* I forgot to call him back Tuesday, and then yesterday, I told him I'd video chat with him when I got out of class. But that didn't happen either.

"I gotta run," I say, already heading toward the direction of the bus stop. "We can talk about all this more Tuesday."

I text Kale. *FaceTime in a half hour?*

He replies with several heart and smiley emojis. After I get off the bus and inside my place, I drop my backpack to the floor and park on the couch. Kale's face appears on my phone almost immediately after I call.

He's grinning. "I was starting to think you were ghosting me. Didn't take long for you to outgrow your old high school boyfriend, huh?"

Kale's smiling still, but my stomach plummets. That he's joking about this is so Kale, even though that was an issue for us last year: how we'd stay together when he would still have a year left of high school in Silver Valley while I'm away in Reno starting my new life.

I roll my eyes. "Way to kill the mood, junior."

Kale sits up in his desk chair in his bedroom and huffs faux indignantly. "You can't call me that anymore! I'm a senior!"

Behind Kale, posters of Benedict Cumberbatch from *Sherlock* decorate his walls. I laugh. "Okay, okay. Senior then. I'm glad we're finally talking. Sorry I've been so busy."

I fill Kale in on the SASAH stuff.

Kale's face lights up. "Look at you, you've only been there for a minute and you're already changing the world!"

My face warms. Kale's sincerity and overall support has always made me blush. He's great about those kinds of things. He's great about everything, really.

"I miss you." I sigh. Kale's only about an hour-and-a-half drive from me in Silver Valley, but sometimes it feels like he's light-years away.

Kale's bright blue eyes crinkle. "I miss you too. I want to come see you soon, maybe next weekend?"

"That would be great," I say, wanting nothing more in this moment than to be able to kiss him.

———————————

Tuesday, at the next weekly club meeting, Lana immediately tells everyone what we discussed, giving me credit for the walk idea. Jasmine's eyes crinkle at the edges as she smiles at us like we're little kids. "No one could say you three lack enthusiasm. Trey already told me. Texted me about it for days, actually."

Trey shrugs when Lana shoots a glare at him where he stands next to Jasmine. "I wanted her to be prepared with ideas so we could get started right away," he says.

"That he did," Jasmine adds. She coughs and then clears her throat. "Sorry, trying to beat this cold but I'm losing my voice." Jasmine rummages in the shelf under the podium and pulls a microphone out. She flips the on switch and says, "Testing. Testing." But her words aren't amplified. "Huh." She taps the microphone, trying again. But no luck.

Behind me, Candace stands, just as Trey is about to take the microphone from Jasmine. "Let me see if I can help."

Candace flips the switch on and off to test it again. Her big blue eyes glare at the still-not-working microphone. She unplugs the power cord from the wall and plugs it back in. Trey laughs at her as she whacks the microphone on the podium before Jasmine jumps in, "Whoa there. Easy. How about you send an email to tech support instead?"

"Fiiine," Candace says, returning to sit beside Lance, who is in the seat next to me. "But you know they hardly ever respond."

Jasmine clears her scratchy throat. "Before we move forward, does anyone else have fundraising ideas they'd like to share with the group?"

Lance's hair falls into his face as he speaks. "Honestly, those ideas are solid. Better than anything I thought of."

Candace pats his arm. "I'd be lying if I said I wanted

to see that car wash idea through." The girls around them laugh, and I crack a smile too.

"Quick vote then," Jasmine rasps. "All in favor of the walk, with canvassing to get the word out?" Everyone raises their hand, and I beam. "Good." Jasmine grabs a stack of papers to pass out. Lana takes one and hands the stack to me, before I do the same and hand it to Lance.

"Everyone will need to partner up," Trey says. "Never, I repeat *never*, canvass alone, whether on campus or in one of the neighborhoods. To lessen the risk of harassment, I'd prefer we partner up boy-girl, too, because though we all know anyone can be harassed, no matter their gender, I know the ladies and non-binary people get a lot more shit from your average dumbass, and I'd rather be safe than sorry. That work with everyone?"

Voices around me utter their agreement as Jasmine sips from the water bottle Trey just handed her. Lana turns to me and shrugs. "Sorry we can't partner up."

I take a deep breath. There goes being friends with my canvassing partner to make it less awkward.

Trey's eyes land on me. "Partner?"

I exhale and nod.

"Okay, since we have an odd number, Tara, if you want to partner with Lance and Candace that'd be great," Jasmine says. Next to Candace, the girl with wiry, curly brown hair agrees, and Jasmine keeps talking, making sure we each have a partner.

"Great." Jasmine turns to the board and starts writing days and times. "Here are the recommended options for door-to-door canvassing, but you can also choose to stay on campus and man a booth in the front of the Welcome Center. Talk to me if you want to do that. Otherwise, everyone sign up for two to three slots over the next month, please, so that we can start getting the word out. And over the next few meetings, we'll start talking about the big walk for sexual violence awareness. First, we'll need to get a permit in place and permission from student government."

Lana stiffens next to me. "You know that could be a problem," she tells Jasmine.

"Which is exactly why we won't have *you* ask Blake."

"Who's Blake?" I look from Lana to Jasmine. A hush falls around the table.

Lana grits her teeth. "The student body vice president. He's the biggest . . ." She stops and takes a deep breath. "We don't get along."

"I'll do it," I say. "Where do I start?"

"I'll give you the paperwork," Jasmine says, "and you just have to set up an appointment with the student body leadership to tell them what we want to do and get approval. I'll come with you; I just don't have time to take care of the logistical stuff."

"Got it, no problem," I say. Or, rather, new *proactive* Victoria says.

The rest of the meeting, Trey takes over talking for Jasmine, presenting from a PowerPoint she made about ways to effectively communicate about a cause. At the end of the hour, after Jasmine calls the meeting to a close, a few of us stay behind to clean up.

Trey catches up to me on my way back from dropping the empty pizza boxes in the trash.

"What days on the sign-up sheet look good to you?" He checks the calendar on his phone. "I'm free Monday afternoons mostly, here and there most weeknights, and all day on Fridays. What about you?"

I pull my phone out too. Though I don't need to check my calendar—I have my schedule memorized—it feels more natural to have something to do with my hands rather than just stand here. "How about Friday night? Jasmine said nights are when people are home from work and that's a good time to knock on doors, right?"

Trey shakes his head. "Not on Friday nights. People are exhausted from the week. Or out partying. How about Monday night? Or any other night, except Tuesdays; I have Poli Sci from five thirty to eight thirty."

My eyebrows shoot to the top of my head. "A three-hour class? Brutal!"

Trey sighs. "You're telling me."

I nod, thinking. "Maybe we should wait to go until after we've had a chance to practice, together at school or with the club?"

"Good idea," Trey says. "Can you put your number in my phone and I'll text you so you have mine?" He hands me his phone.

I put my number in and hand him his phone. Trey adjusts his backpack strap. "See you in English!"

He's walking away before I get the chance to say anything

else. Lana, computer bag strap around her shoulder, makes her way over to me.

"Trey's pretty cool—don't you dare tell him I said that, his head is big enough as it is—so canvassing should be a little less unbearable with him as a partner."

I don't say anything as Lana falls into step beside me. She lowers her voice. "I'm partnered with Faux-Hawk Steve."

I smirk. "What's wrong with Steve?"

Lana rolls her eyes. "As much as people claim to care about social justice, getting them to actually do anything rather than just post about it on social media, virtue signaling like the lemmings they are, is like pulling teeth." Lana shrugs. "But you'll see for yourself when you go canvassing."

I stare at Lana for a few seconds longer than necessary before answering. "Looking forward to it."

CHAPTER
TWO

Friday night, Kale pulls into the parking lot outside of my apartment. I meet him outside, the tall light near the street shedding an orange glow over Kale's dad's truck that he borrowed to come visit me. Even though Kale and I have been dating for months, I've only met his father once. He's out of town a lot, working as a truck driver, and when he is home, he and Kale often don't get along—mostly because of his dad's drinking and all the subsequent yelling he does at Kale's mom.

Kale's dad was nice enough when we met, albeit a little gruff, but it was hard for me to want to be around him after everything Kale has told me.

I reach for Kale's duffel bag, but he swings it out of my reach. "I've got it," he says, smiling, before unceremoniously dropping it at our feet and sweeping me up in his arms. I laugh as he dips me and plants a big kiss on my lips.

"I missed you too."

Inside, we go straight to my bedroom.

Later, lying in bed next to each other, I feel peaceful. This was our first time *together* when we didn't have to worry about when Kale's family would come home. It's always special with Kale, never expected by him or pushed, never any of the things I worried being with someone would actually be.

Sometimes, before *it* happened, I used to worry that

images of my dad's angry face would pop into my mind, like they did at the worst moments last school year.

But Kale is so sweet and loving and gentle, and so *Kale*, nothing like my dad, that all I have to do is look into his eyes and know that he would never hurt me. And I'm okay.

As I stare at my sweet boyfriend's kind and unassuming face, I wish he could be here with me all the time, not just on a weekend when he's allowed to borrow his dad's truck and his parents have given him gas money.

Kale seems to notice my dip in mood because his brows are furrowed in that way they get when he's worried. He softly pushes a piece of hair away from my eyes. "Is something wrong?"

I sigh and pull the blanket close. "I just miss you is all. And Christina. And Silver Valley, even." I chuckle. "Never thought I'd hear myself say that."

Kale scoots closer to me and I lay my head on his bare, lean chest. "We have a way of growing on people."

We lie in comfortable silence, and I wish I could hold on to this moment.

The rest of the weekend is spent bingeing TV shows— *Sherlock*, mostly—and taking Kale to TMCC to show him around campus.

Sunday night, Kale and I drive to my old house for family dinner with Tiffany and Sarah.

"Kale, how wonderful to see you!" Tiffany exclaims at the door. She wraps Kale in a fierce hug before he even gets the chance to walk over the threshold. Kale chokes on a piece of Tiffany's blonde hair that somehow ended up in his mouth. She must not notice, because she smiles at him warmly as she pulls away.

Tiffany has always felt grateful, indebted even, to Kale and Christina for helping us stand up to Dad that time we drove to Reno to rescue Sarah. She and I both.

"Great to see you too!" Kale peeks over her shoulder. "Is that spaghetti," Kale pauses and sniffs the air around us, "and marinara I smell?"

Tiffany and I watch each other for an awkward moment. Neither of us move to hug. She hugs me, sometimes, and I bear it. But it's not natural for me with her. It never was *before*, and it isn't now.

I shut the door behind me.

"How's cross country going?" Sarah appears behind Tiffany, looking comfortable in sweats, her hair wet from a shower. She ushers us all to come further inside. She's grown so much during her sophomore year. Sarah's all legs now as she leads us to the living room, where Kale and I sit on the black leather couch with her. "You think you're going to take state this year?"

Kale grins. "You know it!"

I smile and take Kale's hand in mine. He's so good with Sarah and Tiffany. With everyone, really.

In the kitchen, Tiffany opens the silverware drawer and grabs forks and knives. Kale heads over and takes them out of her hands. "I got it," he says, before walking around her and grabbing a stack of napkins.

"Suck up," Sarah says loud enough for Kale and Tiffany to hear.

Tiffany feigns outrage, her long face scrunching up. "Don't make fun of my favorite child that way, Sarah!"

The four of us laugh. Something I would never have done last year if Tiffany had made that joke. It was so clear that she favored Sarah, her own daughter, leaps and bounds ahead of me. When everything first went down, Tiffany refused to believe Dad ever laid a finger on me, but when Sarah couldn't take his abuse anymore, she told her mom what he'd done to her, and Tiffany was ready to throw him out and press charges.

It's easier to be near Tiffany when Kale's around and he can joke and charm his way out of awkwardness. My lingering hard feelings. Tiffany buying me things and complimenting me all the time to try to win my affection, to get me to forgive her. There's no mention of Dad. Not that we ever *really* talk about him.

Whenever thoughts of my victim impact statement intrude and I think of how it will hurt Dad, I look at Sarah and think of how he hurt her. How me wanting to protect him, like I always did, put her in danger. Keeping my mouth shut left her at home with him.

I have to remember that, every time my hand shakes as I try to write my statement. It's not just for me that I'm writing it. It's for her.

"Come on and eat." Tiffany sits at the head of the table. Sarah, Kale, and I join her, and we have a nice dinner. We talk about the club—not so much about the assault and harassment prevention, because the wounds are too fresh, but mostly about the walk and how I'm spearheading a lot of it. We talk about what Kale and Sarah are up to at their respective schools. Tiffany's job as an office assistant. And things are good. Normal. For us anyway.

I want to hold on to every moment with Kale. When I feel loved and supported, when I can be silly and free and not have to worry about some stupid victim impact statement I'm supposed to be writing.

That night, after we drive home from Tiffany and Sarah's, the dreaded time to say goodbye to Kale comes.

"I love you," Kale says as he leans against his truck. And a little piece of my heart cracks because I don't want him to go. I want to feel the ease I feel when we're together.

"I love you too."

Kale said it to me for the first time a few months ago and though it took me a while to be able to say it back, I eventually did.

Kale gives me the most massive smile, just like every time I say those three words. He pulls me into a hug and breathes in deeply.

I lean in and kiss his neck softly. "FaceTime soon?"

Kale pulls away and nods. "I'll text you when I get home tonight too."

As the truck drives away, I think about how happy I would have been last year if I knew I'd have gotten through foster care, gotten through all my secrets in Silver Valley. Things may be hard long distance, but Kale and I are making it work. Even if I don't get the butterflies in my stomach everyone says you get when you're in love, which if you ask me seems overrated. I feel good when I'm with Kale. Listened to. Respected. Safe.

And I'm grateful for that.

——————————

Monday afternoon, I'm sitting on my couch scrolling through Christina's Instagram feed. My best friend from Silver Valley has been posting pictures of all these amazing things in DC. The National Mall and other monuments, neighborhoods with old row houses that look straight out of the movies.

I want to visit her, but I don't have the money. I hope she comes here soon.

My phone buzzes. My stepmom's calling. Which doesn't make sense. Kale and I just saw her and Sarah for family dinner last night.

"Hey, Tiffany . . ." I trail off, dread washing over me. She usually texts, not calls. "What's up?"

My stepmother's voice comes out about an octave higher than usual, which is really saying something. "Victoria, are you busy right now? I'd like to talk to you, in person. If I could come over—"

My breathing hitches, and I clutch the phone as panic for my stepsister sets in. "Is everything okay?" I blurt. "Sarah, is she all right?" She and I have been through so much, and I can't help but feel like it's my job to protect her.

Tiffany exhales audibly. "Sarah's fine." But then she hesitates. "There's something I'd like to talk to you about in private, without Sarah. Soon. The sooner, the better. Before next family dinner."

What could be so important that it can't wait? My chest tenses. There are a million bad scenarios I can imagine, and the longer I'm in the dark about what's going on, the more nervous about everything I'll be.

"Come over now," I say. "If you can. I'm free."

Twenty minutes of anxiety later, I usher Tiffany into my apartment.

"Can I get you anything? Water?" I ask my stepmother.

Tiffany shakes her head as she sits on my light gray couch. She holds a blue throw pillow on her lap, tapping the edges with her fingers. I sit on the other end of the couch.

"Your father's been sending me letters, as you know, and I've been throwing them straight in the garbage, like I've told you," Tiffany begins, the light and warmth from last night's dinner with Kale replaced by hesitation.

My mouth goes dry. Dad. That's what she's here to talk about.

Sometimes we talk about my and Sarah's nightmares, but we don't talk about *him*. My father. It's like he's become some kind of bogeyman, like if we say his name, it'll make him a person rather than a monster.

Tiffany inhales deeply, reaching into her purse and pulling out a piece of printer paper. "This morning, I got this in my inbox. I can only assume she got my email address from your father. This woman says she's your dad's sister,"—Tiffany stammers, a piece of her blonde hair falling in her face—"your aunt."

I shake my head, quickly, like a fly is in my face. "I don't have an aunt. My dad is an only child."

"According to this email, that's not true. She says they've been estranged for years. They had an argument after their parents died, she says, which of course was before I met your father. It happened when you were just a toddler. And they haven't spoken since."

Jumbled thoughts race through my mind. This can't be right. If it's true, why am I just finding this out now?

"Let's pretend for a second she's not lying, then why—"

"I don't think she's lying, Victoria," Tiffany interrupts, still clutching the page. "I looked her up online. And I found your grandparents' obituaries, using her last name, not Parker. She explains in the email that your father changed his last name after their parents died." I'm shaking my head, but Tiffany presses on.

"Everything of his that I've seen—his college degrees, his birth certificate, and our marriage license—all say Parker on it. I'm embarrassed to say I didn't question your father about his parents much since he seemed to get so agitated when I did."

Tiffany's face is pinched, as though she's in pain. As though the man she thought she knew, the one she loved, seems like a complete stranger.

"I thought that was grief about losing them when he was young," Tiffany says. "The obituaries said they were survived by their adult children, Audrey and Jeffrey. I never thought your father would lie about being an only child. Who would? But I can see that there's a lot we don't know about Jeffrey." Tiffany gingerly puts the printed email in my hand.

I force myself to look at Tiffany. Her blue eyes are starting to water. Great. Another Tiffany crying session.

Tiffany gets emotional a lot, given that both her daughter and I were abused by my father under her nose and she didn't see it. Didn't want to see it. I stuff my anger down. I can't focus on that right now, not when Tiffany's just dropped this bomb on me.

"What does she want, Tiffany? Why is she writing you?" I push the message back. I can barely stand to touch this piece of paper right now, much less read it.

"She's in town. Your father wrote to her from jail. He told her he wanted her support when it came to sentencing." Tiffany blinks several times, a solitary tear trickling down her narrow nose. "She was out of the country until recently, she says, but I don't know much more than that. She writes that she's staying near the jail and visiting him regularly. She . . ." Tiffany pauses. "Audrey—her name is Audrey. Audrey says there are things we need to talk about, things I should know about their past. Things you should know about their—your—family."

Heat floods my body. "So what, is she here to talk us out of telling the truth? Like Dad didn't . . . like he didn't—"

I stand. Even though when I'm alone I feel sympathy for my father, the thought of this supposed aunt asking me to help him makes my blood boil. What right would either of them have after what happened to *me*?

I can never forget Dad didn't hurt just me; he hurt Sarah. And there are other people out there suffering for what's been done to them. That's why I work so hard in SASAH. If I stay in my head, I get so angry and sad and lost. I have to do something else. Help someone else.

It's a hell of a lot better than being here with Tiffany, talking about my dad and this person who claims to be my aunt.

Tiffany reaches up to touch my shoulder. I bristle.

Tiffany's face falls. She watches me with her blue eyes that look like her daughter's. Sarah. They're my family, *even Tiffany*, not this Audrey woman.

My mind flashes to my unfinished victim impact statement. I've struggled to write it because I've been afraid it'll further hurt my dad.

Tiffany takes a deep breath as she stands. "I'm not recanting about anything your dad did to me, and I would never ask you to do that. I would never ask Sarah to do that." As Tiffany tilts her head, her fine blonde hair falls into her face. She pushes it away. Again, I am reminded of Sarah, how I failed to protect her.

"Audrey wants to meet both of us, but to be honest, Victoria, I have no interest in meeting her. I thought you might. Either way, I wasn't going to hide it from you. You deserve to know what's happening."

I unclench my jaw. "Thank you," I manage. "I just need some time to think. Can you leave the message? I might want to read it. Later."

Tiffany picks the paper off the couch and hands it to

me. "Take your time, Victoria. There's nothing pushing you to do this, if you don't want to. And whatever you decide, I fully support you."

Slowly, she leans forward, and I know she's asking without saying the words if she can give me a hug. I nod and close my eyes as I feel her wrap her arms around me. She smells like citrus. I reach one arm around her and pat her back once before letting go.

"Does Sarah know about this?"

Tiffany shakes her head. "I figured you might want to read the message and talk to her about it." She offers what I guess is an attempt at a maternal smile. "What do you think?"

I nod.

"I know this must come as a shock. It was for me. I still haven't wrapped my head around it since this morning. Let me know if you want to talk once you've read it. I'm here for you, Victoria."

My jaw clenches again, instinct telling me not to believe her. I flash to the times Dad yelled at me and Tiffany said nothing. To the way she believed him after she caught him attacking me in my bedroom, when she believed I'd made a pass at him rather than the truth—that she'd walked in on him assaulting me.

I walk past Tiffany and open the door for her. "I'll let you know."

With Tiffany gone, I sit back on the couch and unfold the email. Better to read it alone, rather than being watched for any emotional reaction by my stepmother.

Dear Tiffany,

My name is Audrey BeeBee, and I'm Jeffrey's older sister. From what I understand from my brother, he never told you about me. Although we've been estranged for years, I must confess that I was pained to learn he kept my existence completely hidden from his family.

We had a terrible argument shortly after our parents died and haven't spoken, until recently. I called him and wrote him for years, when Victoria was young and Leah was still alive, but I found being ignored too painful, and I finally stopped trying.

I have missed so much since our parents died. Most regrettably, I have missed getting to know my niece.

I swear to you I knew nothing of what happened in your family last year. Jeffrey didn't tell social services about me. I was out of the country and hadn't heard from my brother in years. I had no idea that Victoria had been removed from his custody. I would have come. I would have liked to help. That is what I'm trying to do now.

Jeffrey recently contacted me, alerting me to his situation. I came at once and am staying in an apartment I've rented near the jail. I am so deeply sorry to hear of the suffering your family has endured. I make no excuses for my brother; what he has done is inexcusable. I was so sorry to hear that the cycle of abuse has continued in our family.

There is a reason my brother is so private, I'm afraid. There are things he's never wanted anyone to know, things he's lied to everyone about, including himself. We suffered as children at the hands of family. And I believe that is why Jeffrey has cut me out of his life. Seeing me, hearing from me, even acknowledging my existence, was a horrible reminder of our shared past. I certainly believe that if my brother had gotten the help he most desperately needed, if he had sought medical treatment or therapy as I have, I would not be writing this today.

I don't expect learning any of this to change the pain you and your family have endured. But I would welcome the opportunity to meet with you to talk about my brother. I really do think you'd want to hear what I have to say. And, if our meeting goes well, I hope that you might introduce me to Victoria. My phone number is below, along with the address for the rental I'm residing in for the foreseeable future. Please do not hesitate to call or come by, anytime. I very much hope to hear from you.

All my best,

Audrey BeeBee

P.S. You might be interested to know BeeBee is our family name. Jeffrey changed his name legally to Parker after our parents died, although I am sure social services could have figured that out if they were searching for relatives for Victoria. If he did, in fact, tell social services about me, I can only imagine what my brother said to keep them from seeking me out. But I assure you, whatever former feud I've had with my brother will be set aside for the well-being of his daughter.

I blink, several times, and stare at the words, as I try to make sense of them.

I lie down on the couch, clutching the page to my chest. How can I really have an aunt but have never known it? And my last name should be BeeBee?

My stomach squeezes. Someone hurt my father. It's obvious that's what Audrey is getting at. And my dad's been running from whatever happened—changing his name, lying about his past, disowning his sister. But he still became a monster.

I resist the urge to crumple the paper in my hands. Why does any of this matter now that Dad is in jail? What does this woman want from me?

I pull out my notebook and turn to the page of my unfinished victim impact statement.

Victim Impact Statement

My dad hurt me, and now he's in jail. I'm glad he's there so he can't hurt me and my stepsister anymore, but

I hesitate, holding the pen over the part I stopped writing mid-sentence. I didn't know what to say. Before, I didn't want my words to be the reason Dad got more jail time. But now, I feel like the statement is missing something important.

My dad hurt me, and now he's in jail. I'm glad he's there so he can't hurt me and my stepsister anymore, but maybe there's more to the story than I ever knew.

My pen writes the question circling in my mind.

What if someone hurt him first?

My phone, forgotten on the couch next to me, lights up with an incoming call.

Without thinking, I answer. "Kale." His name comes out shaky.

"Are you okay?" My boyfriend's tone is serious. He must hear how upset I am.

I clear my throat and force a smile because I read somewhere that people can hear you smiling through your voice. "I, uh, just woke up, actually. Was taking a nap."

Smile. Smile.

"Lucky!" Kale exclaims, clearly buying my lie. "Sleeping all day, the life of a college student. I, on the other hand, just had to sit through one of the longest lectures imaginable on . . ."

I stop listening to Kale and whatever class he's complaining about. My vision blurs as I stare long and hard at the email.

"So, I said . . ." Kale continues, his voice picking up, like he's excited.

I fold the email and walk down the narrow hallway to my bedroom. Inside, I shove it underneath a pile of clothes, at the very bottom of the lowest dresser drawer. But after a moment, I take it back out and put it on top of my dresser.

I could tell Kale about the letter. *I should tell Kale, but . . . But.*

He'll want to protect me. He won't want me feeling bad for my dad. He'll say my dad hurt me and deserves to be in jail. He loves me and so I'm sure he wouldn't want me going down this rabbit hole.

Maybe not, though. Maybe I could tell Kale and he'd understand that I still love my dad and I feel guilty for that and I'm scared because I don't know what to do. Because though my dad hurt me, I don't want to hurt him.

Kale keeps talking about stuff at school, *high school,* that seems so trivial and far away from the real problems I have. Problems he'd never understand.

I pinch the bridge of my nose, feeling even more guilty. That's not fair. It's not Kale's fault.

"And then the new girl Hannah says . . ."

I sit on the edge of my bed, the white down blanket scrunched up with me, and rake a hand through my hair. My thoughts jumbled.

This woman says she's my aunt.

If she is, my mom knew and never told me.

"Victoria, are you there?"

I wonder if Audrey is visiting my dad in jail right now. Does he know she reached out to Tiffany? Do they talk about me?

"Victoria!" Kale's voice rings loud in my ear. "Can you hear me?"

"Yes! I'm here. Sorry, Kale." I rush the words out. "I'm not feeling great. I think I need to lie back down. Can I call you later?"

"Do you need to go to the doctor?"

I smile, for real this time. My worried boyfriend. "I'm fine. Just need to rest."

"Call me when you feel better. And text me when you wake up, okay?" He pauses. "Love you."

I nod, even though Kale can't see me, and though I just saw him yesterday, that seems like a long time ago, knowing what I know now, but not enough time to make sense of it. I have to make sense of this. "Love you too," I tell Kale. "And will do."

I hang up and start pacing back and forth in front of my bed. My room's tiny. Other than the bed and the dresser, plus a small closet, there's no space in here for much else. I look out the window, at the mostly empty parking lot outside.

Suddenly, my apartment feels even smaller, stuffy, suffocating. I feel trapped.

My phone is still clutched in my hand. I could call Tiffany and ask her to meet with Audrey. But she said she doesn't want to.

Audrey's address is written at the bottom of the email. I could go.

What would I even say to her? *Hey, I'm your niece. I hear you've been visiting my predator father in jail. How's that going?*

My head jerks involuntarily.

It would be too weird. And anyway, I don't owe her anything. I don't even *know* her.

Suddenly, I'm exhausted beyond belief. My limbs feel heavy. My eyelids droop.

I slump on my bed. Curl into a ball. Close my eyes. See images of Dad as a kid, what I think he looked like, since he hasn't shown me many pictures. I never found that strange before. That Dad didn't want to talk about his childhood or his family much. He said his life was with me and Mom, before she died. Why live in the past?

But now, lying here in my bed, that's where I can't help but go. The slideshow in my mind shows me the most horrific things. Dad, a little boy, with some terrible person I don't know, the door closing behind them.

Dad, a man, closing my bedroom door behind him that night. Stalking closer to me.

I pull the pillow over my head and sob. *No, no, no.*

I can't go there. I won't.

Instead I think over my to-do list for SASAH stuff. There's

so much to do before the walk. Yeah, SASAH. That's what I'll think about. SASAH. Doing good. Doing something.

I drift off to sleep. When I wake up to my blaring cell phone alarm, I'm still in yesterday's clothes. My stomach growls. I didn't bother to eat dinner last night.

In the kitchen, I rub my sore eyes, staring into the fridge. Nothing looks good. Not the hard-boiled eggs I prepared ahead of time for the school week, or the fresh fruit I got from the farmer's market. Food, though I know I need it, doesn't appeal to me when I feel like a shell of myself. *Thanks for that, Audrey.* So instead, I shower and head to class like any other day.

My chair screeches when I take my normal seat in Intro to Biology, closest to the door. We don't have individual desks, but long metal tables facing the front where Dr. Burton paces. I laser focus on her lecture about cell theory, not just her words, but the way she pauses for a few seconds after saying something she believes to be extra important. I watch which students around me take notes at that moment and which don't. I notice the way Dr. Burton's glasses slip down her nose when she switches slides on the projector. I do everything I can to stay here, *in this moment*, and not think of my dad when he was a kid and whatever happened to him.

When the lecture ends, I'm up, going straight to my next class in the adjacent building. Following the herd. Watching my feet in front of me on the sidewalk, listening to other people talk about their weekend plans, joke and laugh with their friends as they open the double doors into the next building.

My hand clutches my phone. I have some unanswered texts from Christina and Kale. But I can't think about them right now, my friends who want to talk about their courses and see how I'm doing. What's in front of me—that's all I can handle. My next class, statistics.

At the end of the day, I'm exhausted, like I ran a marathon rather than only attended a normal day of school. Too nauseated to eat anything more than the granola bar I had in my backpack. I want to go home and curl into a ball and shut the world out again.

But instead I head to the library, with my statistics homework ready to keep me company. My old sanctuary in Silver Valley, that's what the library was for me. Maybe I can recreate that feeling here. Because I need to pull myself together. I need to focus on school, on making friends, on *me*. Rather than on my aunt, here out of the blue. Or my dad, rotting in jail.

Once inside, I exhale. Smile. Relieved for the distraction. Lana's here. Black hair in two buns, Princess Leia style, she's studying at a computer station, a binder open in front of her, with headphones on.

I stand awkwardly behind Lana, noticing the back of her Captain Marvel T-shirt. She didn't see or hear me approach. Maybe I should say something about comics. Maybe we can talk about Marvel movies. Except I don't read comics and haven't seen any of the films except the first *Iron Man*.

Lana turns with a start. "Oh!" she laughs, as she slides

her purple headphones down her beige, freckled neck. "It's just you. I thought I was going to have to backhand some creepy guy when I felt someone behind me. You'd think dudes would know picking up chicks with headphones on while studying is not a good idea, but then you'd be wrong."

Heat rushes to my cheeks. "Sorry!" I switch from foot to foot, looking at the empty desks around us. "Can I join you?"

Lana gestures for me to sit at the computer station beside her. I drop my backpack between us. "So, how are you liking freshman year so far?"

Lana shrugs. "It feels too much like high school. I went to Wooster, and a ton of people I'd rather never see again are here. I'm still living at home with my parents. Overall it's just one big suck-fest so far."

"That's rough," I offer, looking around to make sure I don't see any other familiar faces. A couple guys sit near each other, going over a slideshow. The girl at the front desk looks bored, her eyes fixed on her phone rather than the computer screen in front of her. "I guess maybe it's not such a bad thing not knowing anyone. Most people I knew from school are at UNR, or at least aren't here."

Except, when I think about it, I realize I noticed one of the senators in student government here was in my math class at my old school, and I've seen several other people walking around campus that look familiar enough. But we weren't friends and have never had any meaningful contact or anything.

"You're pretty much the only person I've talked to so far," I tell Lana. "That and, you know, other SASAH people."

I immediately look down at my hands, as if my interest in the club tells all my secrets.

Lana's dark brows knit as she watches me. She can probably tell how uncomfortable I am. But I don't want her to think it's about the club. I mean *it is about the club*, but I don't want her to get the wrong idea. I swallow. Woman up, as Christina would say. "I'm really happy to be a part of it."

Lana's smile reaches her whole face, and I can't help smiling too. "Tuesday, I don't want to drive home after English only to have to come back for the meeting," she tells me. "Do you have another class after, or do you want to hang?"

"That would be great," I squeak, my voice coming out higher than intended. A few people at the desks near us glare in my direction. I duck my head.

Lana smiles. "Cool," she says, seemingly not making an effort to lower her voice. "We can get coffee and kill time. Do homework or whatever."

I say goodbye to Lana a few minutes later. As I'm walking toward the library exit, I'm smiling. It feels like I just did something big, important, even though all I did was make plans to hang out with a new friend. Or someone I hope will become my friend.

Lana is strong. She fights for what she believes in. She wants to keep people safe from those who would harm them. To keep people from being assaulted, like I was.

The letter cuts through my thoughts.

Suddenly, I'm imagining my dad, what he looked like as a kid, and thinking about him being scared. Hurting.

I'm feeling bad for him.

Angry tears start to cloud my vision, blurring the other students studying in desks and chairs, the gray walls around us. I shouldn't care—I know I shouldn't. Not after what Dad did to me and Sarah. I want to scream. He assaulted me and *I'm* the one feeling bad for *him*?

It's ridiculous. Even from jail, Dad is somehow screwing up my life. But only if I let him.

I'm out the door, heading to the bus stop before I have enough time to talk myself out of it.

I clench my fists. I need to deal with this. I won't let putting off the inevitable, being in denial, or anything related to my father mess up my life like I did in Silver Valley.

Time to meet Audrey, figure out who she is and what she *really* wants, and then, hopefully, move on.

CHAPTER
THREE

The duplex where my maybe-aunt is living is well kept. There's a rosebush and a small grass patch behind a short wooden fence. I hesitate, my knuckles suspended in midair. I could still turn back. I don't have to meet Audrey; I could—

The front door opens, revealing a woman standing behind it. She's holding her keys and purse as though she's about to go out. I drop my hand.

Her eyes go wide as my breath catches. Both of us gaping. We're probably noticing the same things. Seeing ourselves in each other.

Our hair is different—I've got my mom's wild red waves and Audrey's is dark brown—but our eyes: they're the same green as Dad's. Our noses—we have the same button nose. Our mouths—they're slightly fuller on the top than the bottom. Her cheeks are rounder, though, as is the rest of her. And I can see she's a couple inches shorter than I am, now that she's closing the space between us.

"Victoria," she whispers. "You came. I hoped I'd see you, that we'd meet, but I . . . I . . ." She trails off before laughing softly.

"It looks like you're leaving." I gesture to her purse. "Maybe we can talk some other time."

The woman, *my aunt*, shakes her head quickly. "No, no.

The grocery store can wait. Will you come in?" She looks behind her, toward the open door. "We have so much to talk about."

My mouth is a desert. I nod slowly, but I feel unsure. What if she's some kind of serial killer or weirdo? But she looks like me. And she's staring at me and waiting, and I know I have to go in there and get answers. I pick up my feet, step by heavy step, as I follow her.

Suede couches and a glass coffee table meet us inside her loft. The stairs are slabs of shiny wood, leading up to a small space upstairs that overlooks where we are now.

"Sit, please. I'll go get you something to drink. Soda? Tea?"

"Water, thank you," I manage.

Audrey heads through the living room to the kitchen. Instead of a dining room table, her granite countertops serve as a bar and eating area, with four black stools for sitting.

"Nice place," I mumble, not knowing what else to say. There's no *What to Do When Meeting an Estranged Aunt You've Never Heard Of* guidebook.

Audrey sets the glass in front of me, condensation making it cool and wet against my touch. I sip, wet my chapped lips.

"What do you want from me?" I don't mean to say the words so abruptly, but they slip out.

Audrey's eyes widen slightly, but otherwise she shows no reaction. She's calm. Her tone sounds as though we're having a normal conversation, even though we aren't.

"I want to get to know you—"

"Don't." I cut her off, my voice sharper than I thought it would be. "You want something, you want me to know something, and I'm not sure why. But I think it would be better for both of us if you just come out with it, so we can be on the same page. I don't want lies. Or secrets being kept."

Audrey blinks several times. Her makeup and long eyelashes make her green eyes stand out. It's unnerving, sitting across from this stranger while knowing we have shared blood. Shared relatives, maybe even a shared history, in a way.

Audrey swallows and pulls her lips into a seemingly forced smile. "Fair enough. I suppose I should start from the beginning." She stares at her light pink, gel-manicured nails on her lap and sighs before continuing. "It'd been so long since I'd seen your father, before he called me from jail. I'd given up on hearing from him ever again. After our parents died in that crash, we had this awful argument and he never returned a single message, call, email, or letter."

"What was the fight about?" I'm surprised by my boldness, but I spent all last year without answers—all my life without answers in a way—and I'm over it. Time for the truth.

Audrey stares straight into my eyes, unblinking. "He said 'good riddance' when they died."

I blink. What a thing to say when your parents die. My dad didn't talk to me about my grandparents much, except the rare times he shared a story about his childhood. But I never thought he hated them. Not like you'd have to, to say a thing like that.

But then again, I never knew he had a sister either.

Audrey's lower lip quivers, but her voice remains steady. "I didn't take that well. I told him he was a selfish child who couldn't get over one mistake in our past and who made our parents suffer for the rest of our lives because of it. I told him he'd made them and me miserable."

She blinks back tears. Her voice comes out husky. "I was *wrong*. So, so wrong."

The tears are falling down her cheeks now, and I'm not breathing. Just watching. Waiting.

"I see that now," she says shakily. "Years of missing my brother, working on myself in therapy. I was so wrong. And I ruined everything with Jeffrey because of it."

"Why did he say 'good riddance'?" I ask quietly.

Wordlessly, Audrey stands and heads to the kitchen counter. She grabs a tissue box and returns to her seat, dabbing at her eyes. Tears still cling to her long eyelashes.

"Our grandfather, our father's dad, he"—she pulls her lips together and looks away—"he molested us. Both of us. Starting when we were toddlers."

My insides curl with disgust. Toddlers? His own grandchildren? How could anyone do that? "How . . . how could . . ." I shake my head, unable to find words. "How long?"

I wipe the wetness from my cheeks.

Audrey's shoulders slump, and she stares at the tissue balled in her hands. "Too long. It was Jeffrey, when he was eight years old, who told me we should tell. He said it wasn't right. He'd told Grandpa to stop, but Grandpa would get so mad. He'd yell and beat Jeff when he fought back. He said if Jeffrey told, no one would believe him, and he'd only go worse on me. That kept my brother quiet. Even though I was two years older and should have been the one protecting him."

"It wasn't your fault," I begin. Quickly, I take a drink of my water, because I'm not here to console Audrey. I'm here for answers. To listen.

Audrey's eyes light up with something. Hope, maybe? But quickly they darken, and she hangs her head.

"Not that part, you're right. But there's more," she says. "Finally, the beatings got so bad on Jeff that I had to say something. I told our parents. And they . . . they didn't take it well. At first, they said Jeffrey and I were misunderstanding. But when we told them all the details, even about Grandpa's birthmark, they finally believed us."

My mouth falls open. And I want to puke. To scream. To rage.

But Audrey continues, leaning forward, talking fast, like she has to get this all out before something stops her, before she changes her mind. "Dad confronted Grandpa, I think. Mom took us out of town for a few days. We went to Disneyland." She laughs bitterly. "The happiest place on earth. I'll always remember it as the place we went to get away from Grandpa. I was so scared that he'd hurt our dad. I felt terrible for leaving him."

"What happened next?" I ask, my words coming out shaky. Knowing that whatever it was, it couldn't have been good. I clutch my water glass in front of me.

"When we got back, Dad sat us down for a talk." Audrey sighs. "He said Grandpa wasn't going to live with us any-more. He got his father an apartment nearby."

I sputter. "That's it? He kicked him out but still helped him get a place? He didn't send him to the cops?"

I bite my lip, stopping myself from feeling . . . I don't know what. It wasn't my fault what Dad did to me. I finally realized that after months of torturing myself in foster care, after learning what he did to Sarah when I was gone.

It wasn't Dad's fault what his grandpa did to him either, but . . .

But.

Dad still hurt me, hurt Sarah. Even if his grandfather hurt him first.

Audrey shakes her head sadly. "He told us Grandpa was sick and needed our help. That we were a family and families stick together. He promised that we'd never have to be alone with Grandpa after that." She breaks off for a moment and looks away, her eyes glittering. "But every holiday that he came by, every family visit, I had to stare at my attacker. I had to see his lips curl when he watched me walk. Watched me eat. When he lingered for hugs."

A loud sob escapes from Audrey's lips and I flinch. Seeing so much pain in a stranger, yet understanding—it hurts me too.

"It was awful, but I didn't say anything." Audrey lifts her chin and meets my eye. "Jeffrey did. He raged at our father, threw things, ran away as he got older, only to get dragged back by the cops. He punched Grandpa in the face once, so hard that it put Grandpa in the hospital, and Dad gave it to him really good after that. Gave Jeffrey a black eye."

My chest tightens, thinking about my dad in that kind

of circumstance. All of that happened to him and I never knew. I want to tell him I'm so sorry he went through something so terrible. Even though I wasn't born yet, part of me wishes I could talk to that little boy. Tell him it wasn't his fault. Protect him.

But then in my mind that little boy morphs into a man, and I shudder. Because he's sneaking into my room and attacking me. His daughter. And now I know he knew exactly how it would feel to be me in that moment. And he did it anyway.

I ball my fists and squeeze them tight, so tight that my fingernails pierce my skin. How can I feel so many things at once? Audrey looks at me knowingly. With empathy. And that makes me furious, even though I don't know why.

"It was never the same with Dad and Jeffrey after that. And our mom didn't help much either. She just wanted to push things under the rug, to pretend we were a normal, happy family. Jeff got angrier and angrier. He tried to get me to run away with him. But I wouldn't. Where would we go?" Audrey's looking at me with pleading eyes. Like she's trying to convince me of something. "As we got older, he turned more inward. He stayed alone in his room all the time and became sullen. Angrier. It was like I was losing my brother right in front of my eyes."

Heat flashes across my face.

Jaw clenched, I manage a few words. "Why are you telling me this?"

Audrey leans forward, her eyes wide and pleading. "I don't expect you to forgive your father or lie about what happened," she says, as though reading my thoughts. "I've lost so much time with him. I wasn't the big sister he needed me to be . . ."

Audrey trails off. She's here for Dad. She wants to support him. Even if Audrey knows what I'm going through, how can I trust her when she wants to help him?

Audrey looks back at me. "I don't know what happened with you two. But I know he pled guilty to at least trying . . . with both you and your stepsister . . ." she trails off and looks away before coming back to me. "I'm here if you want to talk about it. I might be able to understand. And I'm so, so deeply sorry for what you've been through."

She's sorry, sure she's sorry. But not just for me, for him too. I leap out of my seat and stand, ramrod straight. "I should go."

Audrey's face falls. She stands too. "It's a lot. Everything I've told you. I expect you'll need some time to process." She walks to her purse on the kitchen counter and pulls out a card. "Here's my number. My cell's on the back."

I take it from her and glance at the job title on the front. "You're a consultant? What does that mean?"

Audrey smiles, as if me asking this puts us in safer territory. "I advise businesses on how to spend their money, about making budget cuts or changing things to make the company run more smoothly, more effectively. I do this in New York City, usually, but I was in London for the last year helping one of my clients after a merger with an international company." She pauses before taking a step closer to me. "But I'm here now, for as long as you need me. For as long as Jeff—"

I step back, cut her off. "Got it. I should get going."

I head for the door until I feel her behind me, and I whip around. Fast, eyes wide. Not meaning to, just reacting.

"Sorry! S-s-sorry!" Audrey stammers. Her tears have returned. "Please do call me, Victoria. I want to be here for you. I want to know you. We've missed so much."

My entire body tenses. "I'll think about it."

And that's it. I'm out the door, getting away, away, away, away, as fast as I can.

CHAPTER
FOUR

Next club meeting is all about practicing canvassing. We pair up and stand in front of the group as though we're talking to them at their houses. Lana's turn is first, and she kills it, as expected. Just completely shows us how it's done: says all the right statistics, why people in our community should care, and what we can do to help. I want to repeat everything she said, word for word, but I know even if I memorized it, I wouldn't be able to. Not with the way my body is rigid with nerves—how my throat is dry, and I feel the urge to vomit. I swallow.

Trey and I are up next, and I'm sweating as I stand in front of everyone. Watching us. Watching me.

My hand shakes the list of talking points I'm holding.

Trey begins, "Thanks so much for your time, for giving us the opportunity to talk to you about sexual harassment and assault. We—"

Jasmine interrupts. "Trey, sorry, but don't forget to open with who you are and why you're there."

Trey laughs. "Right, how could I forget? Aye, aye, captain." He gives Jasmine a salute. Lance and a few club members chuckle, and Jasmine rolls her eyes at Trey.

Trey smiles at the audience, and I stare at him, instead of watching everyone else looking at us. "We're students at TMCC, Victoria and I, and we're here to talk about what our club, Students Against Sexual Assault and Harassment, is doing on campus and in our Reno community—that's where you come in—to combat it."

Trey looks at me, giving me the opportunity to say something.

"Right," I squeak.

Trey waits a moment, but I don't say anything. I look at the paper, but it's taking too long to land on what I want to say.

Trey saves me. "Our club gathers research on sexual assault and harassment and hosts events to teach college students what consent looks and feels like, which I think we can all agree is very important." Trey looks at me again.

Jasmine, too, is staring at me expectantly. I feel sweat pooling on my forehead as Lana, Lance, Candace, and the others watch me.

"I . . . uh . . ." I look down at my paper again. "I'm in this club because I want to help keep others safe."

It's so quiet you could hear a pin drop. Everyone waits for me to say something else. I don't know why I said that. It's not like I'm going to tell them all my life story. The thought starts to strangle me, as I wonder what they're thinking. Are they imagining what's happened to me? That someone assaulted me?

Trey's eyes linger on mine for a second before he cuts in. "Exactly, Victoria," he says, in a voice that seems more practiced than his usual. "We believe it's our duty to help change the culture on campus that all too often favors silence and shame after harassment or an assault has occurred. Our group provides safety tips for protecting yourself on campus and off, and ways to help make sure friends stay safe."

Trey looks at his paper, and a few people in the crowd start to whisper to each other. We're losing them. Jasmine sees this and interjects again.

"Okay, that's good for now. Trey, great job talking about our club and Victoria, I'm glad you mentioned briefly that you felt it's your responsibility to help. Everyone should feel that way, including the people you canvass to. Our job is to make them see why."

My face reddens, my heart pounding. Lana catches my eye and nods encouragingly.

Jasmine continues, "So, we have a good start. If we add what Lana talked about in her presentation about why the community should care and what they can do to help our efforts, plus what Trey and Victoria said about our club, that's a great presentation. I think we can move on to the next pair now."

I slink back to my seat in shame.

"I'm terrible at this," I whisper to Lana.

She tilts her head and whispers back, "You did fine. You just need some practice."

———————————

All week I obsess over how terribly I did during the practice canvass session. I write out bullet points of my own for what I plan to say next time.

Thoughts of Audrey race through my head whenever I'm not careful. If I let my mind wander in bio or statistics or another class, I find myself sweating and back in my room that night with Dad. Or thinking about his grandpa.

Kale can tell something is bothering me, but I'm still not telling him. I don't want to hear what I'm just about positive he'll say. That I shouldn't let what happened to my dad affect what I write in my statement. Because even though Kale's right, I don't like hearing the disgust he has for my dad whenever he comes up in conversation. I feel like I should defend my father, now more than ever. And that just confuses and frustrates me because *I know* I shouldn't feel that way.

I should tell the truth; I know I should.

I imagine my boyfriend Kale lovingly holding my hand, sitting next to me on the couch, as I pull out my notebook.

Victim Impact Statement

My dad hurt me, and he knew what he was doing, and he did it anyway. What does it matter now that I know he was molested? It should have made him want to NOT hurt me, rather than the opposite. I'm the victim here, my stepsister Sarah's the victim here, not him.

The word *victim* makes me cringe as I read it over.

Staring at the statement, I know for sure I'll never let the judge have this. I tear it out and toss it.

I squeeze my eyes shut to keep the tears from coming. NO.

Enough self-pity, enough worrying. Enough.

After studying for statistics and doing a little bio homework, I fill out the paperwork Jasmine sent me for requesting student government permission for an off-campus event. If approved by the committee, the school will request a permit from the city for us, and hopefully soon we'll get a date so we can have our fundraiser.

The questions are easy enough to answer: why we want to have this fundraiser, how many people will be involved, what will happen at the event, and how much funding we'll need for it. I give estimates on the money we'll need for signage to advertise the event as well as food like hamburgers and hot dogs—Jasmine approved the idea of having a barbecue after the walk. So, after I bus to the grocery store to pick up food for the next couple of weeks, I take pictures of price tags, make the calculations, and send the form off to Jasmine.

Jasmine approves my proposal, thanking me for getting it done so quickly, and sets up a meeting for the two of us to present our case to the student government committee in charge of funding and permits for next week. It feels good to have done something positive, rather than just stewing about my aunt. I want to keep feeling proactive, so I text Ray. He's a senior at UNR, studying advertising. If anyone can help me craft a pitch, it's him.

You busy right now? I could use some help working on my talking points for raising money for the women's shelter I told you about.

About five minutes later, Ray replies. *Be right up.*

I let Ray in and direct him to my couch, offering a muffin I set on the end table for him. He sits cross-legged and looks up at me. "How do you want to do this? Am I supposed to ask you questions?"

I stand a few feet away with the sheet Jasmine emailed

us all about sexual assault and harassment statistics, plus my recent additions.

Ray's phone vibrates, and he frowns as he checks a text. "What is it?" I ask.

Ray shrugs noncommittally. "Just a guy."

I raise an eyebrow. "Just a guy? Or like a *guy* guy?"

Ray picks up what I'm getting at. "Yeah, Brian and I have gone out a few times but he's like, I don't know, clingy. I think I'm going to have to break things off with him."

"You don't think you two can work it out?"

Ray's eyebrows furrow as if he's thinking, like he just realized something. "I could tell Brian why I don't like how he's acting. So yeah, we could work it out . . . I just don't want to." Ray blinks, focusing back on me. "Where were we? Oh, yeah. So, do you want me to ask you questions like I'm a real person you accosted on the street, trying to sign me up for your event?"

Ray smirks at me.

I stifle a laugh and shrug. "Just listen, I guess, and tell me where you get bored. Or if something I say doesn't make sense."

Ray's purple collared shirt ruffles as he sits up, eyeing me attentively. "I'm all ears," he says.

I take a deep breath and look down at my fact sheet.

"Nuh-uh!" Ray claps his hands to get my attention. "You're supposed to be looking at me, not that paper."

I roll my eyes, even though I asked Ray up here for this very reason. "If I had known asking an ad major to help me practice a presentation would be such a headache . . ." I trail off with a smile.

Ray grins as though I've just complimented him. "You're welcome." He reaches for the poppy seed muffin on the end table and takes a big bite. "Go on," he mumbles.

I quickly peek at the sheet of paper, before flitting my eyes back to him. "According to RAINN, the Rape, Abuse & Incest National Network, every seventy-three seconds, an American is sexually assaulted." I swallow, hard, as I prepare to recite the next line. "Every nine minutes, that victim is a child." The paper shakes in my hands, and I open my mouth to continue, but Ray stops me before I get the chance.

"Wait a minute, wait a minute. You're canvassing to let people know about the walk to get them to help the shelter, right? So, what's all this for?" He waves a hand in front of me.

Heat floods to my face. "It's why we're doing it," I say. "It's why people need the shelter."

Ray puts the muffin down and sighs. "Okay, big picture stuff matters. But it's not going to be what gets people to come to your walk."

I sputter, "I'm getting there." I huff. "Just let me—"

Ray snatches the paper from my hands. He scans it quickly, making exaggerated sighs. "This does nothing for me. It doesn't talk about the shelter, and why we need the shelter to have more beds, *here in Reno*. Why should *I*, rando on the street, care about that? Tell me about the people the shelter helps." He stands, handing me the paper. "Tell me about them."

My shoulders slump as I look up at Ray, who is much

taller than I am. "This is all Jasmine gave us to work with." I added some stuff about why people should care about victims, because they're *people*, not just their sisters, or wives, or neighbors, or whatever. But that's it. "I . . . I don't know anything about the people the shelter helps, I guess."

Ray pats my shoulder. "Well, you better get on that."

I slump down to sit on the floor, across from Ray, who plops back on the couch. "How am I supposed to do that?"

Ray raises his thick black eyebrows at me. "Think about it: you could look online. You could—"

I interrupt him. "I could go to the shelter! Check it out for myself!"

Ray nods happily. "Exactly." He takes another bite of his muffin.

We're both silent for a moment. Ray has been nothing but nice to me. We chat when we meet outside getting our mail. Mostly small stuff about school or the stray cat. I realize I don't know a whole lot about Ray though.

I tear a loose piece of carpet at my feet. "So, Ray, you're from Vegas, right? Why'd you decide to move here? I mean, I know why I did. There's no college in Silver Valley. But Las Vegas has UNLV."

Ray puts his arm up to rest on the side of the couch. "I needed a change," he says.

That's it.

That's not very forthcoming for my normally chatty friend. I don't want to pry though.

Ray smiles at me. "You're not going to ask why?"

I chuckle. "Sure, yeah. Why did you need a change, Ray?"

Ray sets his muffin on the end table but fingers the edges of the wrapper. "I had a lot of friends in high school. It's not hard when you're on the football team and, you know, have my winning personality and looks."

I laugh at Ray's bravado.

"But there was more to me than that. I just didn't know how to tell my parents. So, it was a long time, not until my senior year, actually, that I came out. Because I was afraid my parents would hear, and I'd disappoint them."

I drop the thread. "That must have been hard," I say.

"Yeah, my parents are traditional. They had a lot of expectations for me, their only kid. Their golden boy. They wanted a dutiful son, one who would become a lawyer or a doctor, marry a nice girl, and give them grandchildren. But by the time I was a teenager, it became pretty clear to me that dream wasn't going to happen. It wasn't who I was."

Ray smiles at me, and a dimple appears on his round face. It makes me smile too.

"But I finally told them, and you know, it wasn't easy." Ray looks away wistfully. "It was so awkward, to be honest. But they came around. And with their support, I told my friends. And they were great. Everyone accepted me, as they damn well should."

I stare at Ray, feeling like there's more to the story. "So why did you need a change, then?"

Ray takes one last bite of muffin and chews thoughtfully for a moment. "People were *accepting*, but they were still hella weird. Like, I wanted everyone to be cool, act like it wasn't a big deal, *because it isn't*, but all of a sudden, all my female friends wanted style or guy advice. And then some of my dudes went way out of their way, like ridiculously so, to talk to me about who I was dating or gay rights or stuff they normally didn't care about. They went overboard."

I remain quiet. I don't know what I could add to the conversation. But I'm intrigued. By Ray, by his story.

"So anyway," Ray continues, "I told them they didn't need to be so extra and yeah, a few people pulled back. But then it just felt like I wasn't Ray anymore; I was *gay Ray*. Because everyone who knew me thought they knew one version of me and then went and overcorrected when they realized they didn't. I just wanted to be Ray, you know? And it felt easiest to get a fresh start by moving."

I'm nodding before I realize I'm even doing it. "I get that."

Ray arches an eyebrow at me, and I laugh. "Not like, the whole coming out part, but wanting a fresh start. Wanting to go somewhere else where people don't know you, so you can decide who you want to be. How you want to be seen."

Ray scrunches the muffin wrapper in his hands and looks at me appraisingly. "I had a feeling about you, V," he says. "I knew you were cool."

I laugh. *Cool.* I don't know about all that, but I like that Ray felt comfortable enough to tell me his story. Maybe one day, *definitely not today*, but one day, I'll be brave enough to tell him mine.

That night, after Ray leaves and as I'm snacking on dark chocolate and tackling homework, my phone dings. Christina is video chatting me.

"Hey, chica!" Christina beams. Her smile is bigger than usual, and her eyes are a little glazed.

"Fun night?" I laugh as Christina sways happily. Behind her, I can see the rest of her dorm room. Two beds, the frames wooden with drawers in them and space for storage underneath. Her roommate must be out tonight. Christina, phone in hand, does a sloppy twirl, before flopping back on her bed.

"Went to a party thrown by the Latinx Student Association," she drawls. "The student body president is also a member, so we have that in common. I want to get on her good side because she's awesome and also I want to be her."

Christina narrows her eyes for a second as if thinking. "Except I don't want to get elected when I'm a senior. A sophomore, yeah, I'll run for president next year. I'll have to look up the student body constitution to see if that's legal." Christina raises a finger and perks up dramatically. "Which means I better get elected freshman class president this year. I've got my team in place already, my platform is going to be . . ."

Christina ticks off on her fingers the changes she wants to make at Georgetown and I'm wildly impressed this is where her mind goes when she's wasted. When she's finished, I clear my throat.

"I have something to tell you too," I begin. I consider telling Christina about my aunt and what she told me about my dad, but Christina's drunk and seems really happy, and I don't want to bring her down. "You know that club I told you about? I'm trying to help set up a fundraiser for the women's shelter in town. I'm actually presenting to student government with the club president next week to ask for approval and money." I don't mention my failed canvassing practice, because I'll do better next time. I haven't looked up the shelter yet because part of me wants to put it off. It would be a good thing to see what it's like there and to meet some of the people they're helping, but with Audrey's appearance still pressing on me, it just seems like a lot. I'll check out the shelter, I will, I just need some time until I'm ready. And anyway, I've got my hands full with the upcoming funding meeting Jasmine and I have to present at.

Christina's eyes widen, and her beautiful thick black curls fall in front of her face as she springs up in bed. "That's ah-ma-zing, Victoria! You're a rock star!"

I blush and look away. My best friend is the real rock star, but getting her approval on this feels good.

We brainstorm on Christina's campaign for freshman class president—she's already secured a campaign manager she met in one of her political science classes—and she advises me on making a good impression in the upcoming funding meeting.

"Make it impossible to say no," Christina says, before yawning. It's three hours later her time and she's been out partying. I'm shocked she's still upright. "Show them all the work you've already done and how little work they need to do—even if it means you doing their jobs for them, like filling out the city permit paperwork or whatever it is they normally do. If they ask something you don't know the answer to, tell them that's a great question and you'll need a little time to get back to them. Don't say 'I don't know' or that you hadn't thought of that."

The door to Christina's dorm opens, and her eyes flit to her roommate. "Hey, Vanessa!" Christina calls. "Want to meet my friend Vic—"

Vanessa, I presume, interrupts. "I've been up cramming in the library for a test in the morning. Can you keep it down over there? I gotta sleep."

Christina makes a face at me while Vanessa drops her bag to the floor by the sound of it, before quickly readjusting her features. "No problem, V. Heyyyyy, you both have V names. That's cool, right?"

I laugh and tell Christina goodnight. Last thing I want is for her pissing off her roommate because she's less inhibited at the moment.

––––––––––––

Saturday, after I've put in a few hours of homework and tidying up around the house, I call Kale.

"Hey, babe!" His voice is cheerful and bright when he answers. "I'm just running out of the house, on my way to meet the cross-country team for bowling and pizza."

My shoulders slump as I lean back on my bed. "Oh, okay. I guess I'll talk to you later then."

Kale hears my disappointment. "No, we can talk while I drive over. I'll put you on speaker."

Kale's quiet for a minute, and I hear the ignition to his dad's truck start. "Hold on," he says. "Hannah just texted me."

"Hannah?"

"The new girl on the team, the one from Carson I told you about," he says. "She wants to know if I can pick her up."

I swallow. Kale's mentioned Hannah before. He's mostly talked about how fast she is. But he's also mentioned how some of the guys on the team have a crush on her.

"Are you going to?"

"Yeah, she lives a couple of blocks away. Headed over now."

I don't say anything.

"So, what's up?" Kale asks. "How's your day going?"

Not as great as yours, I think bitterly. I pause, checking myself. There's no reason to be jealous of this Hannah girl. Kale is just being a nice guy. Friendly neighbor and teammate. His being so kind and welcoming is one of the reasons I fell for him in the first place.

I only wish his being the wonderful person he is didn't mean I would be alone at home, wishing I was talking to him on the phone, while he's out making sure the new girl in Silver Valley is having fun. Last year, I was that new girl.

"Fine." I sigh. "I mean, I don't have plans to do anything cool like bowling with friends or anything . . ."

"What about that Lana girl you mentioned? She seems cool." Kale talks loudly over the noise of the old truck. "Why don't you ask her if she wants to hang out?"

Great, now my boyfriend feels bad for me. His loser girlfriend with no friends.

"Maybe I will," I lie. "I hung out with my neighbor yesterday, the one I told you about, and he helped me practice my canvass spiel. So, I'm not completely friendless."

Kale remains quiet. "Are you okay, Victoria?" he finally asks. "Is something bothering you?"

Kale is having a blast without me. My aunt whom I only just learned of is now in my life suddenly, and I still haven't told him.

If he weren't on his way to go hang out with friends, maybe I'd tell Kale about Audrey.

But maybe I wouldn't.

"I just miss you is all." It's not a lie, just not the whole truth.

"I miss you, too, Victoria." I hear the truck screech to a halt. "I just got to Hannah's. Can I call you back later tonight?"

"I'll text you," I offer. "Tonight, it'll be like I'm there bowling with you."

Kale agrees. We say the usual I love yous and goodbyes. Suddenly he feels much farther away than just an hour and a half.

———————————

When our weekly family dinner time rolls around Sunday night, Tiffany shoots pointed glances at me while adding the last bit of chopped vegetables to the chili she's cooking. I sit at the table quietly, pretending like I don't notice, as I wait for Sarah to get out of the shower.

"How's everything going, Victoria? Anything new that

you'd like to share with Sarah?" Tiffany asks, faux innocently, as she stirs the chili. I head to the kitchen cabinets for bowls to set the table, rather than addressing what she's obviously getting at.

Tiffany sighs. She turns the faucet off and wipes her hands on the apron she's wearing. She stares at me. Awkward silence fills the kitchen, so I pretend nothing's out of the ordinary and get silverware.

Sarah bounds from her room, her outfit toned down from the big, bright prints and colors of last year. Today, she's wearing all black, from her shirt to her leggings. I smile when I see she's still got that Sarah splash of color in her red flats. She wraps me in a big hug.

Tiffany clears her throat and heaves a heavy sigh. I'm planning on telling Sarah and Tiffany that I met Audrey, so Tiffany doesn't have to be so annoying about it.

Sarah pulls away from me, blowing her blonde bangs out of her face. "Victoria! *Finally*, you're here. You know you could come more than once a week to see us." Sarah feigns indignation.

"I have something I want to tell you," I say. Tiffany smiles before busying herself with the chili. Or pretending to.

I take a deep breath. "Both of you."

Tiffany raises her light eyebrows and looks at us while continuing to work.

I put the last spoon on the table. Sink into my seat and try to think of how to begin.

Sarah sits slowly, her eyes darting from her mother to me. "Now you're making me nervous."

Tiffany brings the pot of chili to the table and sets it on a dish towel. "It's nothing to worry about, honey." Tiffany plants a kiss on her daughter's head before grabbing the corn bread from the stove. "Victoria?" She sits across from me.

"I have an aunt I never knew about." I fidget with my hands in my lap. "My dad has a sister, apparently."

I look at Tiffany, waiting for her go-ahead to continue.

Tiffany nods and speaks softly to Sarah, "I got an email from her Monday. She's in town visiting Jeffrey. She wanted to meet with me and Victoria. I didn't respond, but of course I let Victoria know." Tiffany puts her hand on Sarah's.

Sarah balls her fist under her mom's touch. "And you're just telling me this now?"

I open my mouth, but before I can say anything, Sarah seems to move on. Rapid firing questions at us.

"What does she want? Why is she writing you, Mom?"

I swallow. Sarah has every reason to be skeptical. She was abused by my dad too. And now this woman shows up, out of the blue, when he's in jail. It's definitely suspicious.

Tiffany leans toward her daughter. "We don't have to do anything. We never have to meet her or even talk to her, baby."

I bite my lip. "I already did."

Sarah gasps, and Tiffany's eyebrows shoot to the top of her pale forehead.

"Oh?" my stepmother says, as she slowly leans back in her seat. "And?"

I shrug. "It was . . . weird. I don't know what she wants." I hesitate. "I mean, she says she just wants to know me, but also for us to understand. I guess my dad and her were molested—"

Sarah's chair screeches away from the table as she pushes it back with her legs. She stands, glowering. "What does it matter?"

My shoulders slump. I'm curling in, as if to make myself smaller. I know Sarah's not mad at me, but her face is reddening, and her blue eyes narrow. Sarah's not one to get so angry usually, but I get it. This is how I reacted too.

"If something happened to him, that's all the more reason why he should have never laid a hand on us!" Sarah barks. "He would have known how awful it felt, he shouldn't have . . ." She trails off, and now the tears are spilling and she's shaking, falling apart faster than I've seen in a long time.

I've thought the exact same things Sarah is saying. Tiffany, I think, has too. Her thin lips are turned down in concern as she comforts her daughter. "Shhh, shhh. Baby, it's okay," she whispers.

I force myself up and step around the table to join their hug. Well, mostly to hug Sarah, while Tiffany just happens to be there.

"I don't care what she says, Sarah." I lean in, feeling her hair tickle my nose. "It doesn't make a difference to me. He hurt us. That's all that matters."

Dad groped Sarah, too, and kissed her. But before he got the chance to try anything else, she escaped his grasp, got to the remote, and turned her TV way up, waking her mother. Sarah was able to evade my father by locking her door and staying over at a friend's house, until Kale, Christina, and I showed up to help her.

Sarah sobs into my shoulder, and Tiffany releases her and pushes her seat back to give us room. She loves Sarah. She even loves me, I think. But she knows this is something only Sarah and I can understand about each other. And she gives us our space.

Sarah sniffs a few times and wipes her face on her shirt.

"I've been thinking, actually," she says, looking at her mom. "I know what I want to say for my victim impact statement. This just makes it all the more important that I make one after all. But . . ." Sarah closes her eyes. It's like my little stepsister has aged years in the span of just a few months. After all that happened to us, though, who could blame her?

"I've started writing one already, it's just . . . I don't think I can go in there and read it, in front of people. Mom?"

Tiffany's eyes glitter, and she nods her head vigorously. "I can read it for you, sweetheart. You don't even have to go. You're allowed to have a representative give your statement. You just leave it to me, baby." Tiffany looks at me. "And of course, I'm more than willing to do the same for you, Victoria."

I swallow, my mouth suddenly bone-dry. "I . . . I'll think about it. Thanks."

We sit to eat, not talking about Audrey or my father anymore. Pretending like everything's normal. Talking about my classes, Sarah's sophomore year, and the high school dance team. Tiffany's new job as an office assistant for an accounting firm. When I say goodbye for the night, I know one thing for sure: I am not going to see Audrey again. Not if it hurts Sarah this much. It's just not worth it. I'll just try to forget I ever met her and move on. For real, this time.

At home, I go over and over what Sarah said in my head. At dinner, I only felt pain that she was sad, and I wanted to comfort her. But alone, I imagine that night Dad attacked her. My fists curl. He had no right. She was so young, innocent. He's changed Sarah forever; why shouldn't his life change because of it? I pull out my victim impact statement and rip it up. Start writing a new one, on a blank page.

Victim Impact Statement

My father did what no man should do; he assaulted two young girls: his daughter and stepdaughter. We looked to him for love and protection, and he used that as a way to get us to question ourselves and let his inappropriate behavior go on for far too long. It wasn't until he forced himself on each of us, on separate occasions, that we realized how truly wrong what he was doing was.

By then, it was too late.

What my father did was terrible, and he deserves to be punished, no matter what his reasons were. The pain he caused my stepsister and me needs to be spoken for. It's not about revenge; it's about justice.

I stare at my statement for a long time after reading it, adrenaline pumping through my body. I think about texting a picture of it to Tiffany. My phone hovers over the paper.

If I send this now, there's no going back. Tiffany will have my words. She'll want me to send them to the DA. If I change my mind, she'll ask why. Sarah's balled fists and angry eyes flash in my mind. The way she looks when we talk about Dad.

I stare at the paper. I'm not going to change my mind, but . . .

I'm thinking of Dad as a small child, with his grandpa, the door closing behind them. Thinking about Dad again. Behind bars. He didn't get the help he needed. I didn't know he needed it until it was too late.

I set my phone down without taking a picture of the statement, without texting Tiffany.

Not yet.

I slide my notebook into my backpack.

Monday morning, I get a text from Trey. *There's an opening at one of the tables outside the Welcome Center. If you're around this afternoon, I think it'll be a perfect time for us to get some practice on other students before we go door-to-door.*

There's nothing I'd rather do less than tell other students why they should care about sexual harassment and assault when I haven't even succeeded on practice canvassing with Ray, the friendliest of friendly faces. I had meant to schedule a time to visit the shelter, or at least look up their website, but I got caught up thinking about my dad and Sarah, everything with my victim impact statement. But Trey's right. We could use the practice. And by we, I mean *me*.

When I arrive, Trey's got the table set up, covered with a blue tablecloth and flyers with sexual harassment and assault stats. Behind him, there's a SASAH poster on a stand. It all looks very official.

"I was thinking about what Jasmine told us the other day, and she's right," Trey tells me. "We need to talk more about the community and how assault and harassment affects people in general. We should definitely do that when we're canvassing around town. But here, at school, I think it'll be good to focus our message on issues that college kids face. That work for you? It'll still be good practice."

I nod and run my finger along one of the stat sheets, scan it for information for colleges. "Got it." I walk around the table to stand next to Trey. I won't make him do all the work, like I did in our practice session during the meeting. I'm going to talk this time. I can do this.

I can. If I tell myself it enough, maybe it will be true.

A group of three students, two guys and a girl, walk by our table. Trey calls out to them. "Hey, do you have a minute to talk to us about our club, SASAH?"

One of the guys, the short one with curly brown hair, keeps walking. "Sorry, gotta head to class!" He waves at the other two, a tall guy with red hair and a brunette with a pixie cut.

"I've got a minute," the girl says. Her friend joins her. "Okay, shoot."

Trey opens his mouth, but I cut in. "Did you know that, according to RAINN, over eleven percent of students everywhere are raped or sexually assaulted through physical force,"—I pause to look at the paper before continuing—"violence, or incapacitation?"

The guy's brown eyes widen. "That's a lot."

"That's for all graduate and undergraduate students," I quickly add, my voice rising and hands shaking. "And it's higher for just undergrads. Twenty-three percent of females and five percent of males. So, if it hasn't happened to you, it still could, or to one of your friends."

Pixie-cut girl grimaces. "Yeah, that sucks."

I stop to catch my breath. And then I stop, completely. Because I have no idea what I want to say next, I realize.

The pair watches me for what seems like a long time. Trey nods for me to go on.

"I . . ." I stammer. "That's terrible and . . . you should join our club so that you can help stop it from happening."

The girl nods. "We don't want that to happen, but, like, what does the club do about it?"

Redhead looks down at one of the sheets of paper between us. "How is this club supposed to stop a bunch of rapists?" He raises his eyebrows. "If you're going to rape someone, you're probably just going to do it, right? Even if there's a school club telling you not to."

He quickly adds, "Not me, of course. I just mean, like if some dude out there is messed up enough to do something like that, how is this club going to stop him?"

Suddenly I'm thinking of my dad, who was a lawyer. He knew the law. That didn't stop him from assaulting me.

My eyes start to well. Trey's eyes widen almost imperceptibly for a moment before he jumps in. "Great question. So what we do is—"

The girl looks down at her phone. "I'm sorry, I've got

to get to class. I'm going to be late." She smiles at me, with what might be understanding in her eyes, before she takes an information sheet. "Thanks for this. And good luck!"

She and her friend walk away, and it's all I can do to not break down in front of Trey, in the middle of campus. With so many people around.

Trey asks softly, "You okay?"

I nod quickly and sniff. "Ugh, yeah." I rub my nose. "My allergies are killing me lately."

Trey sighs. "You did great. It's a lot to try to talk to people on the spot about—"

"It's fine," I cut in. "I'm fine." I look ahead to some people walking by. "We better try again."

Trey nods slowly before calling out to the would-be passersby. "Hey, do you have a few minutes to talk . . ."

I tune out the rest of what he says. I don't say much to the people who stop, or to the next group, or the next, other than adding a statistic here and there to whatever point Trey makes at the time. When we say goodbye that night, Trey assures me that I did great. We both know he's lying.

CHAPTER
FIVE

The next morning, I wake up in a cold sweat. Another Dad nightmare, dreaming of the night he attacked me. I dream of that night often. I dream of him doing other things, if Tiffany hadn't walked in. I wipe the tears from my face and take a moment to focus on my breathing.

I jump out of bed. The longer I stay there, the longer the nightmare will stay with me. I have to do something else.

That's all I do now, really. Move from one thing to the next, as though I'm running. Running from Dad still. And I hate it.

But as much as I want to, I still can't hate him.

Tuesday's English class rolls around, and I ask Lana if the seat next to her is taken. She smiles and gestures for me to sit, and I do.

Trey appears in the doorway, hair ruffled, grinning. He holds his books and binders in his muscled arms, shown off by the rolled-up sleeves of the plaid shirt he's wearing.

"Victoria," he says as he approaches, the seats filling up all around us. He sits in the row behind Lana and me, not his usual seat up front. I stiffen, hoping he doesn't bring up my colossal failure yesterday. A few people we talked to said they'd consider stopping by for a meeting, but I'm pretty sure neither of us bought it.

"I just talked to Jasmine," Trey says. "She told me you

killed it with the written proposal you sent her for student government. When do you present?"

I exhale. He's talking about my proposal write-up, not canvassing. At least I did one thing right.

"Today, before the meeting." I look at Lana. "Rain check on coffee and studying? Jasmine texted me about it this morning, and I forgot we had plans."

Lana nods. "Of course, but I feel like I should warn you, before you present to the board—"

Tessa glides in, looking characteristically like the young professor type: hair pulled into a messy bun atop her head, loose jeans shoved into her boots, and books stacked in her arms. "Happy Tuesday, everyone! Let's get started, shall we?"

I can't help but smile as I watch Tessa teach. She seems so into the subject matter and invested in making sure that everyone in the class has an understanding of it. She's professional, yet comfortable enough to joke with her students.

I imagine what it would be like to be her, or to have her job. Not teaching this subject, but something I have a passion for. I remember how much I used to read for fun, not for school. History books. Nonfiction. I loved seeing the challenges people had overcome, even against what may have seemed like insurmountable odds.

Since I haven't chosen a major yet, this semester I took general ed requirements like regular math, science, and English, along with an information literacy course. Which is super boring, but I thought it would be easy and leave more mental space to focus on my other classes. But next semester, I think I should make more of an effort to get into some history courses. Because I'd like them, I'm sure. And maybe there can be a career there for me someday, in teaching.

I'll have to make an appointment with a college counselor to talk about what kind of classes I should take moving forward. But it's hard to focus on the future, even the near future, when so much is weighing on me *now*.

After class, Lana, Trey, and I walk out together. In the hallway, I ask Lana about what she said earlier. "You said you should warn me; what did you mean?"

At that moment, Jasmine walks through the double doors, her long braids swinging as she strides toward us. "I thought we could walk to the meeting together," she says to me. I look at Lana, who hangs back with Trey. Her eyes widen at me as if to tell me to not say anything. I nod. "See you two, later. Wish us luck."

Trey puts an arm around Lana, seemingly clued in on whatever is making her act weird. "You'll do great," he tells us. "Can't wait to hear all about it at the meeting tonight."

"Anything I should know before we go in there?" I ask Jasmine as she leads me outside and through the walkway between buildings. She opens the doors to the structure where the meeting will be, and I follow her in.

Jasmine's full lips are painted purple and she's wearing slacks and a nice blouse under a blazer. I, on the other hand, am in my typical jeans and T-shirt mode. *Oh, no.*

Jasmine seems to guess what I'm thinking. "I should have mentioned these meetings tend to be more formal."

She takes off her blazer and hands it to me. "Here, put this on. It'll help."

I slip her gray blazer on and automatically feel more like an adult. "Thanks."

Jasmine hands me a folder. "I made copies of the paperwork you filled out, so we can both have them on hand."

I follow her up the stairs.

"Okay, here we are." Jasmine stops us in a hallway outside a conference room with a sign reading *Student Government Association* out front. Folding chairs line the hallway, with a few people sitting in them. "Waiting for their turn to present too," Jasmine explains.

Before we get the chance to sit, the door opens and a few guys in suits walk out. I notice their jackets have pins on them with some kind of fraternity insignia.

A girl with long, shiny black hair appears in the doorway, wearing a skirt suit and a smile. She looks toward the hallway and calls out, "Next up, SASAH."

"That's us," Jasmine says, and I follow them into the conference room.

The room doesn't have a big table like the one the club meets in. Instead, four chairs are up front. Three of the chairs are occupied by guys wearing suits. In front of them, on a table, are name placards: *President Ross Simmons, Vice President Blake Rexby, Senator Thomas Ashton.* The girl in the skirt suit takes the empty fourth seat. *Senator Gabby Garcia.*

Jasmine and I take our seats, and I shake my leg until Jasmine shoots me a look.

Ross speaks first, looking at some notes in front of him.

"SASAH President Jasmine Price, welcome." He looks at me. "And you are?"

"Victoria Parker," I say evenly, trying to sound sure of myself. "I'm new to the club and trying to help organize our fundraiser."

"And we could use more support," Jasmine adds, "for feeding the people at the fundraiser and doing everything else needed to get it off the ground."

The guy with short brown hair and a strong chin, Blake, sighs, loud and heavy. "This club, Students Against Sexual Harassment and Assault, wants *more* funding? Didn't we give you the full amount at the start of the semester for pizza parties and whatever it is you normally do? Now you want more for"—he stops and looks over the pile of papers in front of him, our proposal probably—"a walk for a women's shelter. What does that have to do with TMCC?"

Jasmine sits up straight and smiles, making eye contact with each person on the board in front of us before continuing. "I think we got ahead of ourselves." Her smile seems forced. "I'd like to first thank the board for meeting with us and taking the time to go over our proposal for funding for a special event, which, as the student government by-laws state, is eligible for special event funding allowances." Jasmine looks at our proposal on the table in front of us. "The walk's purpose is to raise money for an invaluable women's and family shelter, which is in dire need of more beds and a new wing to be able to meet the needs of the Reno community."

My jaw clenches as I notice this Blake guy rolling his

eyes when Jasmine looks at one of the papers in front of her, before she looks straight at him. "You're right, Blake, it's not for TMCC, per se, but it's a huge part of our mission that we want to shape the culture around campus and in our community, and service projects are a fine way to do that. As you should know, given the service projects your fraternity is so involved in." Jasmine gives a sickly-sweet smile to Blake and then Ross, the student body president, sitting beside him.

Ross scratches his head full of brown curls. "Totally, and lots of clubs do community service projects, no problem."

Blake seems to tense beside him.

Ross continues, "But it's been brought to our attention recently that this particular club seems to have some controversy surrounding it, and we want to address that before stamping our seal of approval once again on club efforts. Care to talk about that?"

I look at Jasmine. Her lips purse. "I'm not sure what you mean."

Blake sits up in his seat as Ross continues. "Your club is rumored to have a 'whisper network'"—Blake uses his fingers to make air quotes—"where, through a group text message, they share claims about people on campus they supposedly deem to be unsafe. I believe it started with one of your club members, Lana Tyler?"

Jasmine sighs heavily. "*If* that's true, I don't see what the problem would—"

Blake pipes in. "The problem," he talks over Jasmine, "is

that people are accusing men of stuff they didn't do, and it could do a lot of damage."

At this, I decide to speak.

"Excuse me," I say, "I don't know about this whisper network or whatever you called it, but say it does exist." I pause to take a deep breath. Knowing this must have been what Lana was trying to warn me about, I look at the faces in front of me, pausing at Gabby's. She's biting her lip, looking at the table in front of her rather than at me. "The purpose of it would be to protect people," I continue, "and not harm others."

Blake's suit jacket crinkles as he crosses his arms. "You guys can't just go around ruining reputations without consequence—"

Thomas, one of the senators, sits up in his seat. "Let her finish, Blake."

Blake leans back, rolling his eyes. Gabby stops gnawing on her lip and looks at me.

I try another tactic. "Look, say this text message is out there, and it was started by a club member, which I won't even say that it was. I've never even heard of it. But anyway, say all those things are true. It doesn't mean the club sanctioned it." I look pointedly at Gabby. "With that reasoning, it would be like saying that if anyone from any group does anything, privately, then the whole group is responsible."

Gabby's eyes widen. I don't know what this whisper network is, but I can guess that Blake has an ax to grind against it for a reason. Does Gabby, or the rest of this board, want to be associated with whatever it is that he does?

Gabby clears her throat, her shiny black hair falling over her shoulder as she leans forward. "Fair point," she says. "If it's okay with the rest of the board, I'd like to hear the proposal. As Victoria said, the actions of one person affiliated with a group doesn't mean that the rest of the group is involved or supports it."

"I agree," Thomas says. "Ross, can we move on?"

Ross nods. He looks to Jasmine. "Let's hear it then."

After Jasmine reads my report and makes a few additional comments, Ross asks to have the room for them to vote. He says they will call us in when a decision has been reached.

Jasmine and I sit in the seats in the hallway. She checks her phone. "This has gone way longer than most meetings do. If they don't speed things up, we're going to be late for SASAH."

Just then, Gabby opens the door. Jasmine and I stand, but Gabby quickly shuts the door behind her. She walks to us and bows her head. My stomach clenches.

"I'm sorry, I really thought the vote would go the other way." She blinks. "You've been denied funding for the walk."

Jasmine's eyes widen. "You've got to be kidding me. Is this because—"

Gabby shoots a pointed look at the other people waiting in the hallway, and Jasmine lowers her voice. "It's the whisper network. Blake just couldn't get over it, and so what, he got his buddy Ross to side with him? What about Thomas? And you?"

Gabby blinks quickly. "Look, I'm not allowed to tell you

that." Her voice drops to a whisper. "I'm sorry." And then she speaks up again. "If you'd like to appeal, there's information on the student government website that instructs how to do so. But it could take a while, and in the meantime, your walk won't happen. I'd recommend looking into other fundraising options."

Gabby looks at me and then back to Jasmine, her pretty face puckering in disgust. "For both the walk and, to be safe, for club funding next year. In case next year's vote goes the same way."

Jasmine is a tornado of curses and fury as we rush to the SASAH meeting.

When we arrive, Trey's standing at the front of the room, chatting with Lana and Lance in their regular seats. "Great, now we can get started," he says when he spots us, before moving out from behind the podium so Jasmine can take her spot.

Jasmine takes a deep breath, before smoothing her blouse with her hands. I realize I'm still wearing her blazer. I take it off and set it on the table. Lana gestures for me to grab a piece of one of the party-size sandwiches they must have gotten for the meeting, but I shake my head. My stomach is in knots. We can't afford this food. We can't even afford to have the walk. There might not even be a club next year if Blake has his way.

Jasmine speaks loud enough so the group can hear her. "There's no point dancing around this, so I'm just going to outright say it. We were denied funding for the walk."

Sounds of anger and disbelief, scoffs and even growls

erupt around us, none so loud as from Candace, on the other side of Lance. "The fu . . ." she stammers. "Why?"

Jasmine continues once the noise dies down. "Blake Rexby was less than thrilled about a certain whisper network and my guess is he convinced his friends to vote against us." She looks at Lana, whose eyes narrow to slits at the mention of Blake's name. A few girls toward the back of the room, including Candace, groan.

Jasmine continues, "So not only do we not have money for the walk, but Gabby Garcia warned us that getting funding for the club at all next year might be a challenge."

Faux-Hawk Steve pipes in, shooting an annoyed look at Lana. "Maybe if we talked to whoever set up the whisper network about taking it down, he'd leave us alone."

My mouth falls open in shock, but before Lana or I get the chance to say anything, Candace levels Steve with a glare. "No fucking way. Us getting school funding isn't more important than warning people about predators on campus."

Tara and a few others nod and shoot Steve contemptuous looks. He shrugs and says, "It was just an idea."

Jasmine sighs in exasperation but doesn't address Steve's outburst more than that. "We have to come up with a contingency plan. So, what are your ideas?"

The room goes quiet. None of us were prepared for this.

Lance raises his hand before Candace puts it down for him. "No car washes," she says.

The faces all around me are somber. None more so than Lana's. I don't know what this whisper network is or why she started it, but I'm sure she has a good reason. And I'm sure that Blake guy is bad news.

Lana balls her fist. "This is what Blake wants," she says. "Only four to eleven percent of sexual assault accusations are later proven false, but Blake would have us think it's everyone crying wolf because he doesn't want anyone to know—" Lana stops herself. "So many more assaults go unreported because of fear of retribution and victim blaming, the kind of shit that people like—" Lana hits her fist on the table in front of her, and I flinch.

"Perpetrators and other defenders of toxic masculinity bullshit want us to think that rape is just something that people with ulterior motives claim," Lana continues, her voice cool and low now, "but did you tell them that studies show only about thirty-five percent of rapes are even reported to the police because victims know that if what they say becomes public, what they said or did, what they wore, everything will be scrutinized? They'll be shamed for their sexual history, and they'll be labeled with every terrible name you can think of."

Jasmine nods and dejectedly adds, "And even after all of that, many claims don't lead to prosecution." She looks around at all of us solemnly. "Even if a DA decides not to prosecute, that doesn't mean an assault didn't happen. The justice system is flawed; that's why we can't stop fighting."

Under her breath, Lana mutters, "And why the whisper network exists."

Jasmine and Lana share a look. Jasmine continues, "But

no, we didn't tell them that. It seemed Blake had already made up their minds."

The room goes quiet.

A thousand thoughts race through my head. I want to comfort Lana. I want to tell her I understand how important this is. I have to do something, *anything,* to help. I can't just sit by, powerless. I rack my brain.

The walk, that's our fundraiser, but we need money to have the food and permits in place to even have that. What do people do when they need money?

I massage my temple. Remember last year. I filled out scholarship after scholarship application to be able to go to college. That's what you do. You need money for something worthwhile, and you find a way to get it.

Lana is the first to speak. "What about a GoFundMe page?"

I nod vigorously. "Yes!"

Lana looks around the room. "We could all post about it on social media. We tell our friends and family about it, and I'm sure whoever can will kick in five, ten, maybe even twenty bucks. That'll be more than enough to get us the money for food and permits for the walk. The walk profits will go to the shelter, but if we have any leftover money from the GoFundMe, if what Gabby said is true, if student government denies us funding next year, we can use it for that."

Candace nods her head, a smile lighting up her round face. "I'm sure my parents and a couple aunts and uncles will help."

"Mine too," says Lance.

I look up at Jasmine, who is nodding. Trey's eyes are smiling as big as his mouth. "Great idea, Lana. Okay, so we need someone to write the copy, the ask, for the GoFundMe page."

"I'll do it," Lana says.

I pipe up. "I'll help you." My mind goes to Ray, the ad wiz, who gave the advice about making people care. And I'm thinking about how I've been putting off visiting the shelter. But maybe going is the perfect way to get our GoFundMe page off the ground.

Jasmine says, "I'll start the paperwork for the permit so that once we have the money we can submit. We'll have the GoFundMe page up by next meeting?" she asks Lana.

Lana nods.

Trey catches my eye from up front and grins, and I quickly look away.

Jasmine looks at Lana and me. "So, Lana, you're in charge of the GoFundMe page, and when we get the go-ahead, Victoria will take the lead with planning for the walk, since this fundraiser is her baby. Engagement club-wide is important, and it's fantastic our newest member is taking ownership on this. I encourage all of you to help as much as possible."

———

After the meeting, Lana is first to start for the door. I catch up to her. "Can we talk?"

Lana nods, and we head for the chairs in the hallway outside of the conference room.

I don't waste any time getting to the point once we're seated. "Tell me about the whisper network."

Lana's nostrils flare. But she says nothing.

"What's the deal with Blake?" I ask.

Lana looks away, staring at a few people leaving the SASAH meeting. Her eyes finally land back on me.

"He's a rapist."

I bite my tongue, shocked, and swallow saliva or blood or both. "What?"

Jasmine and Trey walk out of the conference room, hands full of trash from the sub sandwiches. Trey opens his mouth to say something but closes it quickly when he apparently thinks better of it. Jasmine speaks first. "You two all right out here?"

Lana nods. Jasmine looks at her, frowning for a moment, before her eyes land back on me. "Thanks again for today, both of you. I'm so glad you're hitting the ground running with this."

I nod. "See you later." I can tell Lana wants them gone. Trey waves, and Jasmine says goodbye. Lana is quiet for another moment, her expression deadly serious when she finally speaks.

"Look, it's not my story to tell. But I will say, she was a friend of mine. I tried to have her report him, but she didn't. She moved away; she couldn't face the chance of seeing Blake again if she went to college here. And I never hear from her anymore. It's like talking to me reminds her of . . ."

Lana blinks back a tear. "But I couldn't risk him doing that to someone else, or at least not try to warn people about him. So, I started this massive group text a while back, and then it turned into a blog I write. It's called the Patriarchy Pounder."

Lana's gaze seems far away as she remembers. "It happened at a party. My friend was tired. She went upstairs and blacked out in one of the guest rooms. When she woke up, Blake was on top of her. She screamed for him to get off, and someone heard and burst in. She got the hell out of there. She called me, crying, while she drove home."

Lana's shaking now, with anger. Hatred illuminates her face. I hold my breath.

"She had witnesses. Hell, it was even a girl who walked in, who saw Blake. She was one of our friends, Keira. But *our friend* told her it was probably a misunderstanding. That maybe Michelle, I mean my friend, told Blake it was okay, and she wanted it and just forgot."

Lana's fists are balled on the table between us. "Keira said there was no reason to ruin Blake's life over a misunderstanding."

The way Dad blamed me for what happened, how Tiffany wanted to believe there was something wrong with me, rather than him, flashes through my mind. And my throat closes. A tear runs down my cheek. I quickly wipe it away.

Lana's face is hard, her eyes blazing.

"I'm so sorry, Lana. I don't even know what to say. Just I'm sorry."

Lana shrugs, but her eyes are still angry. "I want to stop that kind of stuff from happening. I should have been there with her at that party. We always went to things like that together, but there was this guy I liked who asked me to watch a movie with him at his place instead. I should have been there. I want people to know how important the buddy system is, how they shouldn't ditch a friend for some guy, like I did."

I nod slowly. I want to tell Lana it wasn't her fault, but I don't. I know she wouldn't believe me. Just like I couldn't believe that it wasn't my fault what happened to Sarah. Like I still can't.

"And yeah, I started that whisper network," Lana says, a bite to her voice. "And I'm not sorry, not even a little bit. I don't care what assholes like Blake and his friends say. He just doesn't want any of this to come back on him when he runs for president next year, or for his rich daddy to get mad at him."

"You did the right thing." I put my hand on Lana's shoulder, before letting it fall into my lap. I'm ready to talk. I want her to know. "Something happened to me too. With my dad. He's in jail now. That's why I'm here. That's why I'm in the club."

Lana's mouth opens, but she snaps it back shut.

My chest tightens, and my heart races. That's more than I've said about what happened to almost anyone, without them practically forcing it out of me. Is it too much to tell a new friend? Even one who is so passionate about stopping that kind of thing from happening?

I look at Lana's stricken face, and I know that's not true. I can trust her, or at least I hope I can. Even still, that's all I can say for now.

I wipe my sweaty hands off on my jeans. I have to change

the subject. "So, Tessa, she's really something, right?" I offer. Lana holds my gaze for a moment, before blinking several times.

She inhales deeply before smirking. "I have a tally sheet in my notebook that I mark each time she says 'you know' per class. So far, we're at seventy-four as a class best. But I've got faith that she can make it to a hundred."

I crack a smile. Lana doesn't ask me anything about Dad, thankfully. After we head out the door, Lana pulls me into a hug. And it feels good, to be honest. To feel as though I'm understood and not alone. To have a friend.

CHAPTER
SIX

My mind reels after I tell Lana my secret, after I hear what happened to her friend. There is no way in hell we're letting Blake, *a rapist*, shut us down. No freaking way. We need to show people why they should care. I stop putting it off. I call the women's shelter to find out who's in charge and set a time to visit a couple days later.

And as I start to psych myself up for doing this scary thing, I realize there's something else I need to do—tell Kale about Audrey and how I'm struggling with what she told me about my dad.

On my couch, I could text Kale and ask if he's around. But that will just give me another chance to bail if he seems even the slightest bit busy. It's 4:50 on a school day, late enough that cross-country practice should be over, but too early for dinner. I take a deep breath. It's Kale; he loves me. *I love him.* I shouldn't be keeping secrets like I did last year.

I call Kale, rather than try to video chat him. Seeing his face while I talk about my dad might make it even harder than it's already going to be.

The phone rings three times before Kale answers. "Hey, good looking." I would smile, if my throat wasn't so dry. If my heart wasn't racing.

"Hey," I say shakily. "There's something I want to talk to you about. Is now . . . is now a good time?"

"What is it?" Kale's tone turns serious. "Victoria, are you okay?"

I nod, though he can't see me. "Yeah, uh, it's just . . . about my dad."

The line goes quiet. I hear Kale let loose a breath. "Okay," he finally says. "What is it?"

I stand, suddenly unable to sit still. Cross the living room to the kitchen and take a soda out of the fridge. The Coke pops open and fizzes. I guzzle some down, the bubbles burning my throat, before I answer.

"I should have told you before,"—I hesitate—"but I just didn't know . . . I wasn't ready to talk about . . ." I walk to the dining room table and plop down in a wooden chair. "I have an aunt. I didn't know about her, but she reached out to Tiffany a few weeks ago and said she came as soon as she heard from my dad about what happened."

I push the cold Coke against my forehead and relay to Kale the rest of the story. How she and my dad were estranged, and what she told me about what had happened with their grandpa when I went to see her.

"You went to her house?" Kale asks quietly, as though he's shocked. "And you didn't tell me?"

I close my eyes. I knew Kale would be upset that I kept this from him. "I'm sorry, Kale. I've been trying to wrap my head around it all. I just couldn't . . . I couldn't talk about it yet." I take a deep breath and try to slow my racing heart. "But I'm telling you now."

"Look, Victoria . . ." Kale trails off. "I . . . I want to be here for you. To be a part of your life, to know what's going on. *I love you.* I want to help, you know. This is big."

I exhale. "Yeah. Big. So, here's the thing." I run my thumb against the lip of the Coke can, focusing on the cold metal feeling, rather than the dread building in my chest. "I just . . . I wonder if . . . maybe, I should consider all that happened to my dad when he was a kid when I write my victim impact statement."

On the other end of the phone, I hear something smack the ground. Maybe Kale's desk chair, like the legs dropped suddenly or something. "What? Why would that . . . Victoria, how does what happened to him change at all how what he did *already* affected you? The whole point of that statement is to tell the judge how your dad hurt *you*. Knowing something that happened to him when he was a kid, no matter how messed up and fricking terrible it was, doesn't change anything."

I swallow, heat building in my chest. I knew Kale would say this, but hearing it still feels different. Like I'm being attacked.

"It changes a lot," I retort. "Or it could. You weren't there when Audrey was telling me what their grandpa did to them—"

"I don't care what his grandpa did to him!" Kale roars, and I move my ear away from the phone, shocked. Kale has never yelled at me before. "He should have never touched you or Sarah. What about Sarah? Don't you care—"

"Of course I care," I spit. Protective feelings for my father are being hijacked by the rage rushing through me at Kale insinuating I don't care that my dad hurt Sarah. "How could you even say that? After everything, after—" My voice breaks.

Kale knows how guilty I feel about what happened to Sarah. How I know it's my fault. If I had just spoken up sooner, maybe Dad would have never laid a hand on her.

Kale goes quiet on the other line. I hear him breathe, and then he speaks. Calm again. "Victoria, I'm sorry. I'm such an idiot. I'm sorry." He groans. "I shouldn't have yelled at you like that. It's him, it's *him* I'm mad at. Your dad. He's still hurting you, even from behind bars. It makes me so mad."

I blink several times. Kale might have apologized, but he still dared to throw Sarah's abuse in my face. He knows how guilty I feel about that. How it keeps me up at night.

And yet.

I hold the phone tight to my ear. "I just . . ." I trail off, because the words aren't coming.

Kale doesn't understand—he *can't* understand—what it feels like to know someone you love, even if it's someone you *shouldn't* love, is suffering. To know there's something you can do to help but to be unsure about whether or not you should do it.

Because I know it's not my job to protect my dad—that's what I keep telling myself over and over, but it's what I've done, what I've tried to do, ever since I was a kid. Since even before Mom died and he got so depressed. When Dad suffered, Mom and I both suffered. When he was angry, we walked on eggshells. When he was sad, we tried to make him happy.

That's just what we did.

Kale is quiet, and so am I. How can I explain to him how I'm warring with myself over this? To everyone but me, my dad is a predator I should hate.

Even having these thoughts and questions seems to be a betrayal to SASAH and everything we stand for.

What kind of advocate am I when I can't separate my feelings from my need to get justice? What kind of activist am I when I can't face these fears?

My jaw tenses, anger flaring up at myself and at Kale. I'm mad at him that he'll never understand me, even though I know it's not his fault. Mad at him for making me feel even guiltier than I already do. "This is exactly why I didn't tell you. Because you don't get it. And you never will."

Without thinking, I hang up the phone. There's nothing left to say.

My phone dings. A message from Kale.

Victoria? Please don't shut me out. I'm sorry.

I wipe my eyes.

Another text.

I know I don't understand how complicated things are with your dad. All I know is what he did was wrong. He hurt you. And no one is asking you to lie. Just tell the truth. Why are you mad at me for saying that?

I push my phone away as more angry tears roll down my cheeks. My shoulders shake as the room blurs around me. No one understands. No one.

My phone dings again.

I love you. I'm always going to love you, even if we don't agree. Even if you can't talk to me. I'll always wish you would.

Suddenly, I'm seized by fear. Kale says he'll always want me to talk to him, but will he really?

An image of him bowling, laughing with his friends, comes to mind. The new girl Hannah probably doesn't have a messed-up family like mine. She wouldn't hang up on Kale.

Maybe it's only a matter of time until he's with a girl like her. One who isn't as complicated. One who doesn't keep secrets. And where will that leave me? Alone again. Who would want to be with me, if not Kale? Who would want all this baggage and drama?

Sobbing racks my body now. I stare at the phone, willing Kale to text again. I can't bring myself to pick it up. What would I say? *Don't leave me.*

The phone lights up. Kale's calling. I answer quickly, unable to hide the fact that I'm crying.

"Kale." I shake as I hold the phone tight to my ear.

"Don't cry, please don't cry, Victoria," Kale says softly.

Instead, I cry harder.

"I'm so-sorry," I stammer through tears.

"You shouldn't be, you don't have to be," Kale says. "I . . . I might not understand or want you to feel bad for your father, but . . ." He exhales. "But it's your choice. I'm on your side, Victoria. I love you."

I let out a fresh wave of tears. "I love you, too, Kale. I . . . I don't know what I'd do without you."

Kale's quick with his reply. "Well, it's a good thing you don't ever have to worry about that."

After getting off the phone with Kale, I tear out my

victim impact statement but don't stop there. I tear it to shreds, into tiny pieces.

The next few days, I text Kale more often, tell him how much I love him. I can't fight with him, not now. Not when I need him more than ever. Kale stood by me all through last year, and he said he'll stand by me now.

I can't trust myself when it comes to this stupid statement. Knowing my dad's been hurt makes me want to protect him, to help him.

The thought pierces my heart.

To forgive him.

But he hurt me, and nothing about what happened or didn't happen to him in the past can take that back. Even the thought of this is causing problems in my life. It's making me fight with Kale.

It makes me want to scream. How can I feel all of this at once? How can I trust myself to do the right thing when I don't even know what that is?

But I can trust Kale. That's the one thing I know for certain. My steady source of love. He's been there for me through all of this, and I have to trust him, to hold on to him, now more than ever.

No matter what I do. I still have time to decide, and anyway, there are more important things to worry about—like my visit to the women's shelter. So, I spend my time thinking about and planning for that, looping Lana in. It seems like something the two of us should do together.

I stand outside of the shelter, waiting for Lana. We could have ridden together, but I wanted to take the bus and mentally prepare for what I might see at the shelter. Battered women. Or worse, children. People with stories like mine, even. Maybe.

I pull my skirt down, uneasy. No, that's not right. Uncomfortable—I'm more of a T-shirt and jeans kind of girl. But I wanted to look professional and show respect, so I'm wearing a pencil skirt Tiffany bought me and a white button-up. I take a few steadying breaths in front of the gray, nondescript building. There are no signs, likely to keep it secret that this is a shelter. A lot of the clients here are in danger and need to keep their whereabouts hidden from their abusers.

My phone buzzes, and I pick up. "Lana."

"I'm here. Just can't find the place."

I give her directions to the parking lot I walked through after coming from the bus stop. Once Lana is standing beside me, looking polished in a gray pantsuit, I push the call button near the building's front door.

A raspy voice answers. "Hello," a woman says through the speaker. "How may I help you?"

"My name is Victoria Parker." I lean closer to the speaker. "My classmate and I have an appointment to meet with the executive director, Karen Armstrong."

Buzz. The door opens, and Lana and I walk into the clean, spare waiting room. A gray couch with a wooden coffee table in front of it separates us from the woman at the front desk. She walks around the glass barrier between us and opens the door.

"Welcome," the woman says, smiling kindly. "Follow me, please."

The woman's heels clomp on the tile as she leads us down a hallway and uses a key card to access another room. My eyes widen at the difference.

"Wow," Lana breathes beside me.

We take in our surroundings. Warm, bright colors. Toy chests brimming with trucks and dolls and LEGOs. Kids chase each other, laughing, and a few women talk in a corner while a flat-screen TV mounted high on the wall plays the movie *Coco*. Another door opens ahead of us, and a blonde woman in her sixties, probably, wearing black slacks and a cream shirt, strides toward us.

She reaches a hand out and firmly shakes mine. "Victoria, so good to meet you. What a surprise it is to have a student reach out to us wanting to see what we're about here." She smiles warmly.

"This is Lana, the club secretary for Students Against Sexual Assault and Harassment," I say. "When I called, you said it was all right that she came too?"

"Yes, of course," Karen says, extending a hand to shake Lana's. "So glad you both could take time away from your studies to visit us."

She looks at the woman who escorted us in. "Thanks so much, Joy. I'll take it from here."

Joy smiles at me before walking back the way we came. I turn to Karen. "Thank you so much for having us."

Karen smiles. "Would you like to walk with me? There's someone I'd like you two to meet."

I nod, and Karen buzzes us in, leading our group through the door she came in. "As you can see, we take security very seriously here. We have to. The people we serve are often running for their lives from husbands, ex-boyfriends, or disgruntled coworkers who lost it when the woman turned them down for a date." Her mouth puckers in disgust. "You get the idea."

I grimace as Lana scowls, and Karen gives us a knowing, sad smile. "Yep. We've seen it all here." She opens the door to the outside. The afternoon sun shines bright on a jungle gym with tall, metal fences surrounding it. We follow Karen out.

A woman stands at the top of the slide and laughs, the sound musical and light, as she pushes a toddler down the slide. It's not until the wind blows her long black hair out of her face that I gasp.

The woman's face, her beautiful face. It's swollen. Her round eyes are brown, but one of them is red. So red. Like a blood vessel had popped in it. Dark bruises purple that eye all the way down her cheek and her collarbone.

Once her son reaches the end of the slide, calling to his mom that he wants to go again, tears fall down my cheek. Because his lip is busted. Cut up. Swollen.

I step back, clutching my side.

"Who did this to them?" I whisper.

Karen steps closer to me. "Do you still want to do what you said on the phone? Do you want to hear our clients' stories?"

I swallow and nod. "Yes. Yes, I do."

"Good. Because you'll find out why what we do here is so important, but you'll also meet some survivors. The strongest people I've ever met." She calls to the woman, who is pushing her son down the slide again. "Rosa, we're ready for you."

Rosa nods, before walking down the steps. "Diego," she calls, "honey, can you go inside with Miss Karen? Go find your brother. Ask him to read you a story."

Rosa stands in front as Diego waddles to her on his little toddler legs. He hugs her. "I love you, Mamá." She scoops him into the air, and he squeals before she sets him down. "I love you, too, mijo. More than you'll ever know."

"Rosa, this is Victoria and Lana. I told you about how the club they're working with at school is trying to raise money for us. Are you still willing to share your story?"

Rosa nods and smiles sadly at Lana and me.

"I'll leave you to it then," Karen says, before she and Diego disappear inside.

I take a small notebook with a tiny pen attached out of my pocket. "Can I take notes? Is that okay?"

Rosa nods. "Would you like to sit?"

"Whatever makes you comfortable," Lana says, and Rosa leads us to the bench facing the slide. Lana shakes her head when I offer the bench to her. She stands quietly, looking at the jungle gym rather than at me or at Rosa. Rosa and I sit next to each other.

Lana slowly turns away from the playground and faces

us. She looks at Rosa with more emotion in her eyes than I expected. "Would you tell us what happened?" she asks softly.

Rosa swallows, and she looks down at her red manicure. "I love doing nails. I love beauty. It feels good to make myself up, and I thought I could do that for others too. Make others feel beautiful. I thought I would like that. But my husband didn't."

I squeeze the notebook in my hands.

"He's gotten violent with me before," Rosa continues, "mostly when he's had too much to drink or when he's gambled away his whole paycheck. But he usually calms down. He usually doesn't take it out on our boys."

Rosa shakes her head. "But not this time, no. When I told him I wanted to go to school to become an aesthetician, he told me I didn't need to work. That was his job, and my job was to take care of the kids. I said I could do both, but he forbade me to look into schools."

My jaw clenches at the all-too-familiar story. A husband who doesn't want his wife to have anything but him, who tries to control her by not letting her work.

Rosa sighs. Looks back at the building. "You'd think Diego doesn't know all of what's happened, but I know he's always watching. And his big brother, Manuel, he's a junior in high school, and we're always telling him he needs to go to college. How would it be if I tell him to chase his dreams when I don't?"

I blink several times. Open the notebook.

"So, I didn't drop it. I kept pushing the topic of beauty school with my husband. And he beat me, he did, but nothing out of the usual. A bruise I could cover with makeup. Nothing major." She must see the look of horror on my face because she winces. "And yes, I know how that sounds."

I take down a few notes.

Lana sits on the arm of the bench, next to me. "You have every right to want an education, to go for it, not just for your family, but for yourself."

Rosa looks at Lana, nodding, but it's almost as though she's not convinced. I wait for her to continue.

"But when he found out I'd saved money secretly, that I'd scrounged every penny from walking my neighbors' dogs, babysitting, and even working as a substitute teacher at day cares that would allow me to bring my son, keeping this all a secret for months, and that I'd used the money as a down payment for school, he lost it. Beat me so bad. Did this." Rosa waves a hand in front of her face.

Lana's expression twists with anger.

"Poor Diego,"—a sob escapes from Rosa, low and guttural—"he tried to stop him, and he got punched in the face. He was crying, oh my poor baby. I ran to Diego. My oldest walked in at that moment, saw me and his baby brother cowering in front of their father, and got in between us. Told his father he was a coward for hitting a woman and a child."

The notebook is shaking in my hand. Rosa's whole face breaks, and her breaths are now quick and shallow.

"Conrad gave it to him then. He beat our son, he beat my baby Manuel, with a baseball bat. He was so angry, I honestly don't think he could have stopped himself, if not for me hitting him over the back of the head with a lamp, the first thing I saw that I could use as a weapon. We ran with nothing but the clothes on our backs. I'm afraid if we hadn't, he'd have killed us."

Rosa takes a tissue out of her pocket and wipes her face. "We slept on a park bench that night, until a jogger found us early the next morning and was kind enough to take us to the shelter. That jogger was Karen."

Rosa pauses as I continue to scratch notes down. Finally, I look at her, and without thinking, I open up.

"I know how you feel," I say stupidly.

Rosa's face shows confusion, not disdain, the way I would look if I'd just heard something so abrupt from a stranger, even if Rosa is the one who just spilled her heart to me.

"That's not what . . ." I stammer. "I mean, I'm not married. I wasn't abused by a partner . . . I . . ."

I stop myself because I can feel my throat closing up and my eyes starting to water. I don't normally talk about these things to people I know, never mind a stranger. But hearing Rosa tell us about what happened to her opened up something in me that I didn't know was there. Someone else, someone who needs to empathize. To share. Maybe so neither of us will feel alone.

I take a deep breath and look Rosa straight in the eye. "My dad sexually assaulted me. Last year. He's in jail now."

Lana inhales sharply but doesn't say anything. Rosa's lip quivers. "Oh, honey. I'm so sorry."

Part of me can't believe I just said that, told my deepest, darkest secret to someone I don't know, but the other part of me feels it is right. *She knows.* Maybe Rosa doesn't know exactly what it feels like. I'm guessing she wasn't assaulted by her father. But she knows what it's like to be betrayed, to be abused, by someone she loves.

"I-I'm sorry," I stutter. "I didn't mean to—"

Rosa tilts her head at me. "You have nothing to be sorry for. I understand. Sometimes we have to get these things out. And you see me, here,"—Rosa stops to wave her hand at the shelter behind us—"and well, you see my face. You know that I know what it feels like for someone to hurt me." She pauses and closes her eyes. Her voice shakes with emotion. "Someone I love."

It's like she read my mind.

We're quiet for what feels like a long time.

I set the notebook between us. I can't tear my eyes off Rosa, her big brown eyes, her strength to decide enough was enough. To stand up for herself and her family. "You're so brave," I say. "I want to help more people have the strength to get out like you did."

Rosa blinks several times. "Thank you." Rosa nods toward the door again. "Karen told me you think sharing our stories with people at your school will help them realize it's important. She says it will help the shelter."

"Yes," Lana answers. "We're organizing a fundraiser for the shelter, and to do that, we need to raise awareness."

Lana doesn't say we need to raise money for the fundraiser since our school vice president is a rapist and denied us funding, but I wouldn't have either.

She continues, "We're hoping letting our friends and

family know what the shelter does—how it saves lives—could help them give us what we need to get up and running."

I nod, before picking the notebook up again. I jot down a few things, before looking back to Rosa. "Tell me, what's life like for you and your boys at the shelter?"

Rosa tells us about the enrichment programs her sons are in, how the shelter is going to set her up with job training—they're going to help her get into beauty school—and how they're in family and individual counseling. Once we're done talking, she asks if she can hug me. I nod vigorously.

Rosa wraps me in her arms, and we both cry. "Thank you, thank you so much," I breathe. "Thank you for sharing your story with me."

Lana stands up straight. "You're a survivor," she says to Rosa. "You both are. Now let's keep fighting back."

A couple hours and a notebook full of stories from other shelter clients later, Lana drives me home. She takes poster boards and a package of markers from her car and we sit on my living room floor. Lana starts typing the draft for the GoFundMe page. I tell her to be sure to include bits of Rosa's story along with those of a few others, keeping them anonymous, of course.

"This brave woman is safe because of the shelter," I dictate to Lana, reminding her to omit Rosa's name, "and we want to help more people have her strength to leave their abusers, to support them as they do so."

I start a group text to Jasmine and Trey and tell them

about our visit to the shelter, along with what Lana and I plan for the poster boards.

That's a kick-ass idea! You should have told us, Trey writes. *We could have come with you!*

Sitting on my apartment floor, surrounded by markers and poster boards, I type back, *Sorry, but Lana came.*

I thought it was something she and I could do together, something to help us take back the power Blake took from us.

I text, *Do you want to come over and help us make these? That is, if you're down with the idea, Jasmine?*

About ten minutes later, Jasmine replies, *Sorry, busy working at the crisis call center. That's awesome that you guys did that, Victoria! I can't make it tonight, but you all have fun. Can't wait to see what you come up with!*

I'm about to respond when another text from Jasmine comes in.

P.S., I fronted the club the money for the permit application. We got our permits approved for the walk for next month! Great job, team!

I smile. We're not just going to take what Blake is trying to do. We're fighting back. All of us.

About twenty minutes later, Trey arrives. I open the door for him and jump back as I hear something screech from the ground. The stray cat leans its body against Trey's legs as he walks toward me.

"Friend of yours?" Trey asks.

I frown at the cat, and its piercing green eyes stare at me. "My neighbor and I keep seeing this little one lurking around. I was hoping it would have gone home by now."

Lana walks over to pet the cat, who backs away at first. She approaches slowly, and then the cat leans into her touch. "It doesn't have any tags or anything. By the state of how skinny it"—Lana pauses, looking underneath the stray—"*she* is, I'm thinking she doesn't have a home to go to."

The cat's still staring at me. I approach, slowly, and kneel in front of her.

She purrs loudly as she rubs herself all over me.

You don't have anyone who wants you, I think, staring at the cat. *I know how that feels.*

I think about what would happen if I said the words out loud. After what I did today, told Rosa what happened to me, in front of Lana, maybe I can open up more. Share more of who I am with my new friends. I swallow, because I know I won't tell Lana and Trey how lonely I am. How it feels to have no one understand me and what I'm going through—not even Sarah, not entirely, because she hates my dad. But after everything, I . . . I just can't.

So no, I'm not telling Lana and Trey any of that.

I tentatively try wrapping my hands around the cat's much-too-small belly. She lets me. "I guess that's settled, then. Come on."

We give the cat some water and decide to name her Sasha.

"It's a good idea, right?" Lana asks. "Because that sounds like our club name."

I laugh. Sasha, a name that reminds me of fighting back against rape culture and toxic masculinity, for the cat who is as alone in the world as I am. I like it.

Sasha settles in between Lana and me as we get to work on the poster boards. I show Trey and Lana the one I already made, the one with Rosa's story:

My husband beat me, and I put up with it, but when he turned that rage on my sons, I couldn't pretend things were fine anymore. The shelter has given my family safety and hope for a better future.

Trey reads the sign, his face puckering in disgust. "Got it," he manages.

Lana reads us her draft pitch for the fundraiser page. Trey and I offer a few small suggestions before we agree it's ready to send to Jasmine.

I hand Trey the notebook and pull out another poster board. "Okay, let's get back to work."

———————————

By the next club meeting, the GoFundMe page has already been approved and posted for a few days, and we've raised seven hundred dollars toward our two thousand–dollar goal.

"It's not the full amount yet," Jasmine says to the group, "but it's more than enough to pay for the permit and food for the walk." Jasmine doesn't mention that she already paid for the permit. I'm glad we'll be able to reimburse her.

"If we get any more money toward the goal, I think it should go to the shelter, not club funds," Jasmine says. "We'll find another way to raise money for keeping our club afloat next year, if it comes to that."

A few people nod around us as my stomach sinks. We're not nearly out of the woods yet.

Jasmine meets my eye and smiles knowingly. "One fire at a time."

As the meeting continues, everyone is thrilled to hear about the shelter visit and the signs Trey, Lana, and I made. We end the meeting early to put the signs up around campus.

Candace takes the sign that has the quote from Maxine, a teen mom I interviewed: *He raped me and told me no one would believe a skank like me.* Candace tapes the sign to the wall.

A few tears slide down her cheeks as she stares at the sign for a long time. Our eyes meet, and I nod at her. Saying nothing, but understanding.

As I walk away with my arms full of signs, heading to another building, I smile at how good this feels to actually do something. To fight back. To not give in to jerks like Blake, to use my power to make a difference.

My thoughts turn to Dad. To Audrey, who has texted me a few times, asking if I'm okay. I shake my head as if that will clear my thoughts. Like Jasmine said, one fire at a time.

CHAPTER
SEVEN

Sasha is skinny and probably hasn't been cared for in a while, so Ray and I decide to take her to the vet. Ray drives us in his white Toyota Camry after we're both out of class Monday, with Sasha clawing the daylights out of me the whole way.

Ray shoots a worried look at me as I pry Sasha's claws out of my lap. "Our girl's afraid of car rides, apparently. Good to know."

"She needs a travel crate," I mutter at my screaming legs. I should not have worn shorts today.

The vet inspects Sasha and is happy to report that she's healthy overall. "She needs a little more meat on her bones, so be sure to stick to that feeding schedule"—he points to the sheet of paper his assistant handed me—"and you should do just fine."

I pay the person up front the full bill. I have money in savings after scholarships and grants paid my tuition in full, but when I told Tiffany and Sarah I was taking a stray cat in, Tiffany insisted I accept some money from her, saying I'd need it to take Sasha to the vet and get some toys to make her feel at home. It was nice of Tiffany, and I'm grateful. But her giving me money still makes me a little uneasy.

"We're family," Tiffany told me, seeming to sense my discomfort. "Families help each other."

Ray stays in the car at the store and watches Sasha while I run inside to stock up on the cat food the vet recommended, a travel crate to save my poor legs, and a few toys. Ray drives us home and follows me up the stairs, lugging everything from the store, as I hold a fidgety Sasha in my arms.

Ray sets the grocery bag on the kitchen counter and joins me and Sasha in the living room. I sit on the floor, and she leans into my hand as I run it against her back. Ray hunches down to pet Sasha, but he came from behind her and she wasn't ready for him. She jumps back and hisses.

"Ouch," Ray says. "She is looking at me like Brian did after I told him we should see other people."

Ray hands Sasha a squeaking toy mouse to amuse her.

"You finally talked to Brian, then?" I think back to our conversation when Ray helped me practice canvassing. I assumed Ray was going to ghost the poor guy.

Ray gives me a look. "Mmmm-hmmmm."

I wait to hear the rest.

"Okay, so to me, he was just some guy I was dating . . . *casually*," Ray enunciates. "I didn't think I had to write a press release about it, but I told you Brian had other ideas. You remember, I just felt he was too clingy. He wanted to define the relationship, be exclusive, and we'd just hung out twice. It was too much."

I nod. Although part of me feels for the guy, Brian. Ray is great; it makes sense that someone would fall hard and fast for him.

Sasha purrs, and Ray smiles at her as she slides nearer his lap.

"But like, after you asked if I could work it out with him, I realized I could tell him how I felt and he'd probably back off, give me space, to salvage things. But I realized I didn't like him enough for all that effort. And just because I don't want to marry the guy, doesn't mean he doesn't deserve better, you know? So, I was honest and ended it with him. In person."

I raise my eyebrows. "That was mature."

Ray narrows his eyes at me and smirks. "Don't sound so surprised!" We both laugh, and after a moment, he sighs. "Oh, well. On to the next. How's it going with you and your man?"

My sigh matches Ray's. "It's good. But you know, the distance."

Ray nods, and we're quiet as we watch Sasha chew into the neck of her toy mouse.

"Thanks for taking me to the vet and to get all this stuff for her."

Ray shrugs, like it's nothing. "You're a better person than I am. I was going to call animal control."

I wince. Sasha at the pound, in a cage. Where no one would want her.

Ray looks at me. "I'm glad I didn't."

After Ray leaves, I make macaroni and cheese for dinner and pull my laptop out, rather than my phone. When Kale and I text, we don't bring up our argument. I just want to get along. I don't want to fight. It's the last thing I need right now. The last thing *we* need, with us being so far away. I want to see more of Kale's face. I wish he were here in person, especially after that fight we had. I want him tangible, next to me, where I can touch him and hold him. But Skype is the next best thing, I guess.

Kale answers, smiling. Behind Kale, I see his unmade bed, the blue, red, and white plaid comforter hanging off the edge.

In between bites of macaroni and cheese, I fill Kale in on what's new with the club, specifically about the money we raised from the GoFundMe since Lana and I had visited the shelter. "I'm really excited about it, except I have a feeling we haven't heard the last from Blake."

Behind his desk where he sits in his bedroom, there's a bang on the door, followed by a ridiculous amount of giggling.

Alicia, one of his younger sisters, calls out, "Why's the door locked, Kale? You don't want us to see you kissing your *girlfriend*?" Hysterical laughing and loud, sloppy kissing sounds follow, possibly made by one or both of his other two little sisters.

Kale's eyebrows furrow and his voice comes out annoyed, even though he's grinning. "And how could I do that, huh, when we're video chatting?"

"I'm sure you'd find a way!" Alicia shrieks. Uproarious laughter from the sisters rings out, before the sounds of their footsteps barrel away.

"Sorry about that." Kale shakes his head. "Where were we?"

I push my bowl away, even though I haven't finished eating yet. "Blake aside, I'm wondering if I'm the only one who thinks canvassing sounds terrifying. I completely botched it when I practiced in front of the club *and* when Trey and I tried at school. So how can it be any better with total strangers, when I'm showing up uninvited to their houses? Trying to get them to sign up to donate money or walk with us at the event." My stomach gurgles. "What if they all say no because I'm so bad at it? Or what if they ask me personal questions? I can't tell strangers my life story."

I told Rosa, but that was different.

I couldn't even tell you, I think, as a stare at my boyfriend's sympathetic face. Not at first, anyway. Kale and Christina had to practically pry it out of me before we went on our mission to save Sarah last school year. What happened with my dad. What he did to Sarah and to me. It was so hard to tell them.

Even though I know what my dad did wasn't my fault, I still don't want to talk about it with everyone, even if it is for a good cause.

Kale runs his hands through his light brown hair as if he's thinking. "Well, don't tell anyone, then."

I bite my lip, shaking my head. "I don't want to keep my past a secret from people close to me anymore, at least not how I did with you and Christina. I'm trying to be more honest with my new friends, or Lana, anyway, but strangers? That's a whole different story."

Kale sits up in his chair, his eyes widening as if he's got a brilliant idea. "You could have a code word, something random like *Frodo* or something, for when you need help from your canvassing partner —Trey was his name, right? Yeah, so if you need Trey to swoop in and redirect the conversation, you say *Frodo*. And you do the same thing for him, because you know, feminism."

He winks at me.

I laugh. "*Frodo?*"

Kale shrugs. "First word I thought of."

I sink back into my chair. "*Frodo.*" I chuckle again. "But I wish it were you coming with me instead of Trey."

Kale twists his desk lamp cord in between his fingers before looking back, his blue eyes piercing me with longing.

"So,"—I clear my throat, changing the subject obviously—"how's cross country going?"

Kale leans back in his seat. "Good. For the girls, especially. The girls' team is all stoked because they've been killing it at every meet."

"Sweet," I say. "And how's your run time? Have you—"

"Kale!" His mom's voice comes from behind his closed bedroom door. "Dinner's ready!"

My shoulders sag. It feels like we just started talking.

"Gotta go. Love you," Kale says.

My insides pinch. He says it so casually, effortlessly. Like those words come out as easy as breathing. For me, it's more than that. Or something else entirely. Like there's a gaping void inside me that Kale fills. When I say *I love you*, what I'm really saying is *I need you*. Because everything might be confusing or stressful or even falling apart around me, but not Kale. Kale, I can always count on. Kale is dependable. Loyal. Sturdy.

———————

Sitting on the bus, riding to campus where I'll meet Trey for our first time canvassing, my phone buzzes. It's Lana.

"You okay?" She's calling, not texting after all.

Lana starts in immediately. "Absolutely effing not, the nerve of that . . . I can't even believe. Not that I should be surprised."

"What happened?" I ask.

"Blake happened," Lana says. "He's pissed about our club getting money for the walk on our own so he's stirring up shit. He's been telling people I started the whisper network because I made a pass at him and he shot me down. I've heard it from three different girls now who he's warned not to trust me."

My mouth falls open. "That's . . . wow, Lana. That's messed up. I'm so sorry."

I hear Lana take a deep breath. "That's not all of it."

Something in Lana's voice makes me uneasy. She exhales on the line.

"Ugh, he's coming after you too. Saying that . . ." She hesitates.

I clutch the phone to my ear. "What's he saying, Lana?"

"He's telling people you're this crazy orphan and that you're mad at the world because . . . because of what your dad did."

It's as though the air has been sucked from my lungs. I sputter, shaking my head, "How . . . how does even know?"

Lana's voice comes out soft. "I guess he's friends with some kids you used to go to school with, and they said you disappeared in the middle of the school year. That your friend Jess searched for you and was like really freaked out not knowing why you disappeared but then it came out you were in foster care. And now your dad's in jail, and I bet that stuff is public—his arrest, that is. I guess he pieced it together somehow."

I think of the people I saw around campus whom I recognized from my old school. It could have been any of them.

I swallow the lump in my throat. "And he's telling people?"

Lana sighs. "I don't know what he's saying exactly, but I heard from a girl in world history that it's something in the vein of your dad abused you so now you hate all men."

We're both quiet for a moment. Blake, he's a monster. He will stop at nothing to beat us down.

Lana starts talking fast. "We need to make this walk amazing, Victoria. We need to show Blake he can't push us around. And anyone else who's watching. Just because he wants to be school president next year doesn't mean he can silence us. Just because his dad's on the school board, and—get this—his dad is running for mayor next year. Did you know that? Just another reason Blake wants to keep us quiet. He wants to get me to shut my blog down so no one calls him a rapist. He wants to get us to shut our club down, but we can't let him. We have to show him and anyone else who supports him."

Lana stops, as if catching her breath.

I nod, thinking of my dad trying to silence me last year. "We won't let him win, Lana."

———

"You ready?" Trey asks, knuckles extended and hovering a couple inches from the door in front of us. We're at our first house, canvassing. I clutch the paper with talking points to my chest. I think of my failed attempts and breathing becomes more difficult. Ray said I needed to make it more personal, so I remember Rosa's story and those of the other people we talked to at the shelter. Wanting to do this for them, for Lana's friend, for Sarah, and for me.

"I'll go first." Trey smiles reassuringly. "I'll do the talking until you get the hang of it, and you can jump in when you're ready. You'll be my closer."

I push out a laugh. "That's me, the closer." I nod for Trey to go ahead. The second he knocks, a dog starts barking wildly. A man opens the door and uses both hands to pull the German shepherd back. "Sorry about her," the man says, his voice deep. "Come on, now, Lucy." The man's scarf falls over his buttoned-up tweed jacket as he pulls Lucy inside.

"What can I help you with?" The man seems friendly enough, his rich, ochre cheeks wrinkling as he smiles.

And yet, the nerves still gurgle my insides. I stammer, "It looks like you're leaving, should we come back—"

Trey cuts in. "We only need a minute of your time to talk about raising awareness about sexual assault and what our club, Students Against Sexual Assault and Harassment, is doing on campus at TMCC, as well as in the community, to combat it. We can walk you to your car if you'd like."

The man chuckles. "No need." He nods to his sedan in the driveway. "It's right there. But I've got a minute. Hold on, and I'll get Lucy a treat so she calms down."

At the word *treat*, Lucy barks, wagging her tail. A moment later, the man returns to the front door, shutting it behind him.

Trey begins, citing stats from our paper by memory, "One out of every six American women has been a victim of rape or attempted rape in her lifetime. Colleges are rife with assault, with people of all genders falling prey to this epidemic. Part of what we do at SASAH is provide information and host events teaching college students what consent looks and feels like, safety tips for staying safe on campus and off, and ways to help make sure friends stay safe."

"That's great." The man scratches his bald head. "But what does that have to do with me? I mean no offense, it's good what you kids are doing, but y'all gotta let me know your ask." He looks at me. "Don't be shy."

This is exactly what Ray was talking about. The man looks from me to Trey and back. Trey waits a moment to see if I'm going to talk, but my mind goes blank.

"Fair enough." Trey smiles, taking command of the situation. "What we need is community support for the Women's and Children's Domestic Violence Shelter of Reno. As you may know, the city council hasn't increased funding this year, as was hoped, so we are going door-to-door asking for support by means of pledges." Trey pulls a form from the stack he holds. "Here's the information for the shelter, if you'd like to donate directly. But we're also having a walk to raise awareness that you can sponsor by . . ."

I stop listening to Trey. Instead, I watch the man's eyebrows furrow as he looks down at the paper.

"If the city council isn't raising funding that means they already fund them, right?"

"Well yes, but—"

"So what do they need more money for? I give to my community, to my church. I donate to several organizations and this one, too, is important. I can see that. But I'm wondering what's the extra need for cash. Why give here rather than somewhere else?"

Trey's smile falters. "The emergency shelter provides housing in a confidential location and is designed to protect individuals and families." His words start to come out rehearsed. They lack inflection, other than the slight tinge of panic or nervousness I hear as we lose this guy. "Residents can work toward self-sufficiency when they are safe. When they're able to focus on a future because they don't have the cloud over them caused by violent relationships." Trey's reading straight off the paper now.

The man shifts from foot to foot, looking at his car, keys jingling in his hand.

"They need more beds," I pipe in. "Ever since Hope House closed, the women and children's shelter has had more and more people coming who need help. The shelter is turning dozens of people, families with kids even, away every day since there isn't room for them." I look to Trey and then back to the man, his dark brown eyes focused on me.

"That leaves them with some impossible choices: go back home to be further abused and maybe even killed by an abuser, as happens all too often in these kinds of circumstances," I add quickly. "Or go out to the streets, where their odds of being assaulted go up too."

The talking points paper shakes in my hand. "Look, I could tell you that every seventy-three seconds, an American is sexually assaulted." My voice shakes, thinking of Dad. Thinking of me and Sarah and my nightmares. "Nine hundred and ninety-five perpetrators out of every one thousand rapists will walk free. Only five out of a thousand rapists will go to jail! But you know what, instead, I'm going to tell you about a Reno woman I met recently who is a *survivor*." I take extra care to enunciate the word. "She was beaten by her husband because she had the nerve to try to apply to school. And he didn't stop there. He beat their kids for it too. They barely escaped with their lives, with nowhere to go but a park bench—until they learned about the shelter. What kind of message are we sending to victims, to survivors, like her, *our neighbors*, if we don't try to help them?"

I blink back a few tears. Trey puts his hand on my forearm, steadying me. But he doesn't say anything. I take a deep breath and go on. "The shelter also offers support with transitional housing, temporary protection orders, and help with legal services to people who really need it. Supporting them financially is only the beginning. We also need you *to care*, to tell your friends why they *should care*. To get the city council members *to care*."

The man stops jingling his keys. "Well, damn." He looks from Trey to me. "Who do I make my check out to?"

———————

"That was awesome!" Trey whoops as we walk away, check in hand for one hundred dollars and a pledge promising further donations of five hundred dollars over the next fiscal year. "You killed it! My closer!"

I blush as we walk past the man's front yard, his car starting up behind us and driving away. I don't say anything self-deprecating. I don't act modest. Because *I did kill it.* We were losing that guy, I could see it, I could feel it, and I brought him back in. I made him see why the shelter matters. Why victims, I mean survivors, matter. Why what happened to me matters. *Why I matter.*

It might have taken me a while to get the hang of pitching, but I'm getting there. No, I *am* there. I'm good at this.

After canvassing for a couple of hours, and getting more donations that I honestly feel I can largely take credit for, my feet hurt from walking so much. Trey has a car, but I insisted we park it and do most of the work on foot. I'm not really sure why. "Before we call it a day," Trey says after we hit our last house, "want to grab something to eat? I feel like we've been all business and haven't really had the chance to talk."

I raise my eyebrows at him as the light turns for us to cross the street, heading back toward campus. "We've been doing nothing but talking."

"Not *talking* talking," Trey says. "You've been asking me about the club and sexual assault stats. That's why we're here and yeah, it's important. But it would be cool if we could get to know each other a little too."

An outdoor shopping center with several beige storefronts

is on my right. I scan the buildings—dry cleaners, hardware appliances, and a Subway. "Sandwiches work?"

Trey nods, and we head inside.

Once our food is ready, we sit across from each other at a table near the soda machine.

"You really have a knack for this stuff," Trey says in between bites of his meatball sub. "I thought I'd have to do all the talking, but you really showed up. We wouldn't have most of this"— Trey stops to nod toward our blue collection envelope—"if it weren't for you."

I set my chicken sandwich down, narrow my eyes at him. "You sound surprised."

Trey stares at me awkwardly for a second, and then I crack a smile. "Yeah, okay. After our previous attempts, I get it."

Trey laughs before taking another bite. He keeps his honey-brown eyes on me as he chews.

I pick my sandwich up, and my thoughts turn to Lana. I hesitate but push forward. "Lana told me Blake has been telling rumors about us . . . about me."

Trey's jaw clenches. "That guy needs a swift kick to the nuts. And that still wouldn't be enough."

We're both quiet for a moment. I figure Trey knows about Lana and Blake's history, but I'm not sure if he knows about me, what Blake has started saying specifically, or if Trey has heard about any of it.

Trey fills the silence. "Every time I see that guy, I want to do something, anything. But . . . you know, one of Michelle and Lana's friends, Jose, found out about what he did at that party and confronted him," Trey says, setting his sub down. Michelle, Lana's friend. Lana leaves her name out of most conversations, to respect her privacy, I bet. But she's let it slip a few times, and I guess a lot of people already have heard something happened, they just don't know who to believe.

He continues, "Well, anyway, Jose found out and punched Blake in the face. And Blake's dad sent a lawyer over to Jose's family's house so fast, threatening to sue. Jose's grandma lives with them, and she's undocumented. The family was so scared there would be blowback on her. I don't know what happened then, because Jose wouldn't say a thing about Blake after that. I think the lawyer had him sign something saying he'd be quiet."

My eyes widen. That poor family. And the girl Blake raped, she moved out of the state to get away from him. She must be in so much pain. All of it makes me sick. I push my sandwich away.

Trey takes a deep breath. "I'm not scared of Blake or his dad. I'm going to tell him to leave you and Lana alone." He looks at me. "I can't stand by and watch the people I care about get hurt."

I doubt Trey getting in Blake's face will help anything, but Trey's sincerity has pretty much sucked all the oxygen out of the room. Our eyes are locked in some weird staring contest until Trey nearly jumps out of his seat when the soda machine goes off behind him, a man filling his Coke.

We both start laughing now, and I'm horrified to realize mine sounds much more high-pitched than usual.

Trey's phone buzzes. "Speaking of Lana." He reads the text and chuckles.

"What is it?"

"Lana sent me a link to her most recent blog post." Trey scoots his chair closer to me and shows me his phone. The words *SASAH club meeting* stand out.

Another text from Lana comes in, and I can see the words since Trey and I are sitting so close. I scoot my chair back.

"Ah," Trey says, smirking. "Here's why. She's promoting her whisper network. Have you seen it? She's got this form where people can post names anonymously of people who are predatory at parties or behind closed doors. After the tip comes in, Lana lists the predator's name on the blog." He smirks at me. "She's challenging everyone who reads this to send it to at least five friends or to post about it on social media."

I nod, knowing this is Lana telling Blake she's not backing down. My phone dings with the blog post, and I forward it to ten contacts, not just five: girls I know from school in Reno before I moved away who might still live in town, a couple people I've met in class this year.

Trey's eyes dart back and forth over the screen, and the smile slips off his face.

"What is it?" I ask.

Trey shakes his head. "I know a few of these guys. Some of the new ones listed." His face puckers in disgust. "I had no idea they were such scumbags."

Trey pockets his phone and looks at the door. I put my

leftover sandwich in my backpack. We walk to school in comfortable silence.

"So, that was an awesome start to our canvassing efforts," Trey says as we stand in front of his old beat-up Honda in the school parking lot. He waves the arm holding the donation envelope. "I'll give this to Lana, and she'll get it in the club's bank account. See you Tuesday?"

"Tuesday," I confirm.

The leaves on the trees outside of my apartment are browning and beginning to fall, scattering piles around the trunks and the parking lot as the wind blows them. I stop and pull my keys out when I reach the mailboxes outside my small apartment building.

But before I open my box, I glance over at my door and see an envelope. Not where it should be, in the actual mailbox, but sticking out from under my door.

Cold dread fills my chest when I see the handwriting. I tear the envelope open, dropping my backpack to my feet, right there outside my apartment.

Dad. He wrote Audrey a letter. It's shaking in my hands. The world starts to spin around me, and I lean my head on the door, the wood cold against my forehead.

Audrey,

As you know I'm not supposed to write my daughter letters from jail, given the impending sentencing. An indignity, one of many, of being imprisoned is that other people have power over you like that. Something I hate giving away—that's one of the reasons I became an attorney.

You told me when you met my daughter that you let her know why I kept you a secret from her. I won't apologize for that. I was protecting her from my past. But I didn't protect her enough.

A tear falls on the paper, and I shake it off. This letter—if it's for Audrey, why has she given it to me?

Keys jingle behind me, and I jump. Ray stares at me, lifting his eyebrows. Probably wondering what I'm doing standing out here so deep in thought. His face falls when he registers my tears.

"Hey, are you okay?" He walks down the concrete stairs.

I hold the letter to my chest. "Just, um, not something I was expecting, I guess," I say. "A letter from my aunt, Audrey. Long story for another time. Um, I need to finish reading this."

Ray watches me with concerned eyes. I close the door behind me before he gets the chance to say something else. Ray has no idea, no clue. I've told him my dad's in jail and that he was abusive, but I didn't say anything about what he did to me.

He doesn't know I was sexually assaulted, that I'm reading a letter from my abuser. My own father. That this is the first communication, even if indirect, I've had from him since that day I confronted him at home with Sarah. When I tried to get Sarah away from him and Tiffany caught us. When I finally told the truth, when Sarah and I both did, and when Tiffany finally believed me, and we all filed a police report.

My knees wobble as I sink onto my couch and continue reading the letter.

I know I've hurt her. I have a lot of explaining to do and apologizing. Will you ask her to give me that chance? Will you beg her to come see me at the jail, to give her father a chance to say sorry?

Jeffrey

My phone buzzes. Ray is checking on me. I reply quickly that I'm fine and thank him for asking. No way I'm going to even try to explain the whirlwind that is my life right now.

My eyes land on the end of the letter where there's another paragraph, in different handwriting, from Audrey. It says she's sorry to have missed me, and that she'd like to have me over for dinner.

Dinner? With Audrey, after she left this letter from my dad on my doorstep? My head swims with Dad's words, too focused on those to try to decipher what Audrey was thinking when she left this here or to figure out how I feel about it.

I read the letter again. The part where Dad says he wants to apologize.

I wanted that, I wanted nothing more, after what happened. I needed that. Needed him.

But now?

The tears are rolling down my face quickly, so much so that I have to fold the letter and set it aside. I curl myself into a ball on the couch and hold my stomach tightly. What am I going to do?

What do I do?

I don't know what to do. I don't know I don't know I don't know.

I picture my dad's face as he wrote this letter. Were his eyebrows furrowed like when he was concentrating on work? Did his chin shake, his mouth quivering with tears? Tears like the ocean he cried for Mom after she died? Or was he angry, making excuses, lying, like he did when he threw me out? Is this a ploy, a way to trick me?

He says he wants to see me.

My breathing has become fast and short. And I'm wheezing.

Breathe.

Breathe.

Breathe.

I squeeze my eyes shut and hold myself and beg I don't know who or what to help me with this.

Breathe.

Breathe.

Breathe.

CHAPTER
EIGHT

I force myself to calm down, pick up my phone, and dial.

Kale doesn't answer. My mind goes to him laughing and being carefree with his teammates.

So, I call Christina.

"Hey, Vickster! I was just about to head out to meet some friends. Can I call you later?"

I open my mouth to reply but instead a sob splits my insides open. I hear Christina gasp. "Victoria, what's wrong?"

I finally filled her in about my aunt last week, so I jump right to the point. "My dad," I heave, sputtering, coughing up more tears, "he wrote my aunt a letter about wanting to apologize to me. She dropped it off at my doorstep when I wasn't home."

Christina swears. "That manipulative sack of shit. Both of them. I knew it. I knew she would be trouble. She has no right to bring him back into your life, Victoria, and you don't have to let her. You can tell her to shove it up her—"

Christina stops when she hears me beginning to hyperventilate. "Breathe, Victoria. Breathe!"

I take a deep, deep breath and let it out slowly. And then another. Christina reacted strongly when I first told her, too, which is why I'd held off for so long on telling both her and Kale. I knew they'd want to protect me, but how can I explain to them I'm still torn up about my dad? How I want to hate him, but I still worry about him? Feel bad for him.

Love him.

"I'm sorry," I finally manage. "You said you were going out; I can call you later."

Christina's voice comes out stern. "Don't. Apologize. And no way I'm going out. I'm here for you, even if it feels like I'm a million miles away." She pauses, and her voice comes out soft this time. "What did the letter say?"

I read it to her, stopping to cry and shake, but I get the words out.

A flurry of creative curses comes from the other line when I finish. "Please tell me you're not thinking of visiting that bastard."

I shake my head, though my best friend can't see me. Though she's so far away. And so is Kale. I've thought about calling Jess, to see if she wants to hang out. But she's been so involved in her new church group at school, and to be honest, it seems like since I left Reno for Silver Valley, we've grown apart. And I don't want to make us hanging out, if we ever do, about my problems. Jess probably wouldn't mind. But I would.

"I don't know." I pull my knees in close to me on the couch. My window blinds are open. Anyone walking by outside could see my breakdown. I stand to close the blinds but hesitate, my hand dropping to the cool surface of the window. The sky is starting to turn orange and purple over the mountains in the distance. My favorite time of day. Sunset. The lights go down, turning everything black. In the morning, when the sun rises, it'll be a new day, with new possibilities. But when the sun sets, the darkness envelops everything softly, slowly, ending a chapter. Good or bad. Giving a break from whatever happened during the day. It speaks to me.

Leaving the blinds open, I go back to where I was sitting, clutching my phone tighter. "Normally I'd say no, I really would." I sniff. "Without question. But after learning about what happened with his grandpa, even though that should make him not want to hurt others even more . . ." I trail off.

I've done some online research since meeting Audrey. Googled child sexual abuse and learned that often sexual abusers were abused as children. "It doesn't make it not his fault; tons of people who are abused don't go on to hurt other people, so it's no excuse. But it makes it more"—I pause, suck in a breath—"complicated."

Maybe whatever happened to my dad messed him up so bad that he couldn't help himself, I think. My eyes pop as the thought tears at my insides. No. That's not true. I can't think that. He had a choice. We all have choices. He made his.

Now I have to make mine.

Tell the truth, even though it will mean being the reason Dad might stay behind bars longer, because I'm supposed to stand for victims. For me, for Sarah. For people, everywhere, who are committed to stopping this kind of thing from happening. For everyone in SASAH. Everyone who has ever been abused.

Or downplay what happened, maybe giving my dad another chance to do better. Have compassion. Help him. Like I always have.

I hear Christina exhale heavily through the phone. "I can't tell you what to do. I want to, but I won't. All I can say is I love you. And if you need me, I can take a few days off and fly to Reno to be there for you."

"No," I blurt. "No, don't worry about me. I don't want you to miss school." Christina has done enough. She and Kale were with me, she's the one who drove me to get Sarah from my dad's, that day we all ended up coming face to face with him. "I just wanted to hear your voice."

"Have you told Kale?" Christina asks.

"Yes, and he, uh, well, he agrees with you. That my dad is a piece of garbage and I shouldn't give him the time of day. Surprise, surprise."

Christina goes quiet for a long moment. Finally, she says, "We're just trying to protect you, Victoria. We love you."

"I know." My shoulders slump. "I know."

After saying goodbye, assuring Christina that I'm fine or that I will be, I consider writing Jamie a letter. She's out of the treatment center and living in a group home in Carson. She hasn't "earned" phone privileges yet but they let us write each other letters. But I don't want to make everything about me again, like I did before my former foster sister drank that bleach. No, I want to write her my monthly letter when I'm calm, when I can tell her about school and be truthful about things and happy and better at being there for her. That's what she needs.

I could try calling Kale again. My fingers hover over his name in my favorites list but something stops me. Instead, I pull up Lana's name and text her.

What are you up to?

Immediately, the three little dots pop up on my screen. She's replying.

Hanging at home. But it's date night for my parents so I really want to get out of here before they come back, if you know what I mean. I've got some homework to do but could use company. Wanna hang?

Yes! Where?

After Lana texts me the address of a nearby coffee shop, I wipe off my face, throw on a jacket, and head out.

Fifteen minutes later, Lana and I sit, warming our hands on our drinks in front of a fireplace at the coffee shop she suggested. That's Reno weather for you—it could be hot, it could be cold, and you won't know until it hits you. "Hmm," I say, after taking a sip of my hot chocolate. I sink into my cushy chair, feeling much calmer than I have been for the last hour.

Lana reaches her index finger toward my face and wipes off the whipped cream mustache. We both laugh.

We pull our textbooks and notes out and do homework for about twenty minutes, stopping to joke about how many times our favorite teacher says "you know" or to compare some of our answers for the bio practice quiz.

"Thanks for inviting me out, Lana." I put my bio textbook back in my bag. "I really needed the distraction."

Lana sets her coffee down. "From what?"

The coffee shop is dim, the low light giving off a warm glow that matches the flickering fireplaces in each of the four walls. I look at my hands, now in my lap. I'm the one who said I needed the distraction. I invited the question. I want to be more open than last year. I don't want to be like how I was with Christina and Kale, before the truth about my dad practically ate me alive and I had no choice but to tell them.

Lana looks at me expectantly. I sigh. "It's about my dad. He . . . he wrote my aunt a letter, and she gave it to me. It said he wants me to visit him in jail."

Lana puts her hand on my shoulder, and I'm surprised by her sudden tenderness. "I'm so sorry, Victoria. That must have been hard for you to read."

A tear slips down my cheek and I nod, unable to say anything more. "Thank you, I . . . um, I'm not sure I want to talk about it right now, but I wanted to tell you. That's all."

My phone buzzes with a group text to members of the club, from Candace. My jaw clenches as I read the message. "You've got to be kidding me."

"What is it?" Lana asks, before pulling out her own buzzing phone.

Blake Rexby is starting a men's rights club at school, the text reads. I scan through the rest, my stomach feeling queasier by the moment.

Lana scoffs, her eyes blazing. "*TMCC Men Matter Too.*"

I put my head in my hands. Candace's message says that Blake has put flyers all over campus advertising the first meeting. They say that men's stories should be believed, not just women's without proof, and that they want to have an inclusive club that recognizes the way men are getting abused and bullied and how the lies of some women looking for attention can ruin lives in the era of #MeToo.

I look up to see Lana still reading the text. I'd only gotten about halfway through before giving up. She slams her phone on the table.

"And apparently, their meeting times are at the exact same time as ours, down the hallway."

Words fail me.

Lana's bottom lip starts to quiver. She mumbles, "This guy just won't quit."

Suddenly, my resolve strengthens. I want to crush Blake, make him wish he'd never even thought about coming after us.

I want to be strong, stronger than I am, for Lana. I reach for her and put my hand on her forearm. "Neither will we."

CHAPTER
NINE

Tuesday, I scowl as I take down a flyer from *our* meeting room door advertising the stupid men's rights club, TMMT, when I arrive early for the SASAH meeting. Even though I'm arriving early, through the windows in the room across the hall, I see several people, including Blake, setting up for their gathering. Rows and rows of chairs behind a podium for a speaker. A table full of appetizers, a cheese spread, sandwiches, and drinks. Looks like they didn't have a hard time getting funding from student government.

I turn to our meeting room, and then I change my mind. Enough is enough. I march straight into Blake's stupid meeting, ready to face him and whoever else is dumb enough to come to one of these ridiculous meetings.

"You lost?" Blake laughs at me. "Or did you finally realize what a joke your club is and decide to join ours instead?"

The crumpled flyer they had the nerve to put on our door is still clutched in my hand. I toss it in front of me and all eyes in the room watch as it lands at Blake's feet.

I look at a girl I've never seen before standing close to Ross. Based on their proximity, I'd guess she's his girlfriend. She watches me with hazel eyes that look nervous. "It's one thing to be in"—I wave my hand frantically at the group around me—"whatever you want to call this, but do you know why he's started this club? Do you know who you're associating with? Do either of you?"

I'm looking at Ross now, standing tall next to his buddy Blake. "This guy right here isn't just your friend from high school, some kid who thinks he's going to be class president next year. He's a rapist. He raped my friend's friend—"

Blake steps toward me. His voice comes out calm and cool, but his eyes blaze. "Really? Is that right? You were there, then? You saw it with your own eyes?"

"That's not . . . I know—"

"You know *what*? What your friend Lana told you? From what her friend told her? Let me tell you, Valerie, Michelle wanted me for years. She threw herself at me at that party, and when I told her I didn't want to be her boyfriend after, she lied about me. And now you're spreading that lie. You know how much trouble you could get into for that?"

I sputter. I don't care that he got my name wrong, but I do care that people are standing here doing nothing. Like they always do.

Ross's girlfriend is the one who answers. "Blake, come on. There's no reason to—"

Ross's arm seems to tighten around her. He says softly, with an awkward smile, "Melanie." She fidgets out from under Ross's arm, averting her eyes from me.

I wait to see if Melanie will say anything else, but she doesn't. Her strength seemed to diminish when Ross interrupted her. But mine won't.

"Sic your lawyer on me, then. But he can't do anything." I remember what my dad, a lawyer, said to me once about libel and slander and the like. "You can't get sued for slander if what you're saying is true. I'd love to give the girl you raped a chance to give a statement if she wants to. And anyone else who was there that night. I heard there were a few people who just didn't want to get involved. I have a feeling they could be persuaded otherwise, though."

I'm bluffing, really. All I know is what Trey told me about that guy Jose and that he's too scared to talk because Blake's lawyer threatened his undocumented relative. But then there was Keira, the girl who didn't believe Michelle. If even asking her to repeat what she *knows* happened could rock Blake's perfect little story, it would be worth it.

I turn on my heel, knowing there's nothing more I can say, when I feel someone behind me. My heart leaps in my throat; Blake's hand is on my shoulder, firm, hard, wheeling me back to face him.

"You don't want to do this," he says with a smile, all bravado.

Ross is shaking his head, laughing. But it doesn't reach his eyes. "Come on, man. Let it go. Enough drama for one day, am I right?"

"I heard Victoria has some experience with the law herself." Blake flashes a roguish grin at his friends, and my insides turn. "She likes pressing charges on people who've pissed her off."

Blake leans in close enough to whisper, and I freeze. "Don't think I didn't look into you when you started causing trouble for me with that little bitch Lana. I know all about you and your dad. And so will the rest of the school if you don't back off."

I wrench my arm away from Blake and rush out the door.

Completely unaware of what happened across the hall, Jasmine's bright smile awaits me in the conference room. She waves enthusiastically, her braids swinging down to her waist. I take a deep, steadying breath. "You're in a good mood, considering." I gesture to the garbage fire across the hall.

"Kill them with kindness," she says with a smile. "Or maybe just kill them, I haven't decided."

I laugh at this. It's either that or cry. But I won't give Blake the satisfaction of one single tear.

Melanie's hazel eyes widening when Blake went off on me, the way she moved away from Ross after he tried to keep her quiet, comes to my mind. I wanted to yell at her back there. To ask her what the hell she was doing with those assholes. But calling her out in front of everyone, in front of her friends, didn't seem the way to go. It doesn't work on most people, no matter how much they might deserve it.

Jasmine's been watching me while I ruminate. She sighs audibly. "You okay?"

I come back to the now.

"New color?" I nod toward the streaks of purple decorating Jasmine's hair.

"The red was getting tired." Jasmine smiles, her full lips painted a dark maroon today. She sits at the head of the conference table, and I join her at the edge. "I heard you rocked it canvassing. When Trey handed the checks and pledges to Lana and me, he swore you were the reason for most of them."

If I weren't so angry, I'd be happy to hear it.

At that moment, Lana and Trey storm in.

"Trey, give it up," Lana says. "Those guys are never going to listen to you."

Trey's eyes blaze fire. "That club is an abomination. If they think for a second that *they're* victims—"

Jasmine interrupts. "I see you've noticed TMCC's newest club. Don't let them get under your skin. That's exactly what they want."

Trey sits up front, and Lana seethes next to me. When the rest of the room has filled, Jasmine repeats what she just said to us. She doesn't want anyone to pay attention to the guys across the hall. If we let them get to us, they win.

Candace shakes her head. "Why can't they just leave us alone? They can't just—"

Jasmine cuts in. "Don't. Let. Them. Win."

Steve's faux hawk catches my eye. I watch him, the side of his face frowning, as he stares across the hallway. Tara whispers something to him, and he turns back around, still looking uneasy.

The next hour and a half goes by quickly. Jasmine compliments me again, this time in front of everyone, for my excellent canvassing skills and even adds an extra slide to the presentation about using emotion to compel people.

"That stupid microphone still not working?" Candace

asks after the meeting ends and most people have left. "We might need it to drown the noise out from those asshats across the hall."

Jasmine shrugs. "Didn't try it, since it wasn't working last time. We'll manage fine without it."

Candace huffs. "I emailed support services but haven't heard back."

Trey approaches the microphone, tries to turn it on and off, with no success. Lana inspects the cord.

"Would it kill them to give us some actual support?" Candace says, louder than I think any of us expected her to. "The least they could do is give us equipment that works!"

Jasmine strides toward the door. She looks back at us. "We've gotta learn to pick our battles, Candace."

Pick our battles. The words circle around my mind. Is it that we need to pick our battles or that we need to choose carefully how we fight them?

I pull out a notebook and pen.

"What are you doing?" Lana asks.

I shake my head. I don't want to tell her. Don't want to inadvertently sic Lana on Melanie. Not now, anyway.

Melanie, I write.

I imagine you have your reasons for being in the men's rights club. Maybe it's to support Ross or your friend Blake.

I pause. I don't know that Melanie would call Blake a friend, based on the look she was giving him, but maybe pointing out that supporting him in this way is the kind of thing a friend would do will show her what she's really doing. I put the pen back to paper.

I won't argue with your reasoning. But I will tell you why I think the work we're doing in SASAH is important. Did you know that only four to eleven percent of sexual assault accusations are later proven false?

I rack my brain for the other statistics Lana told me, my grip tightening on the pen as I remember what Jasmine said about how when a DA doesn't choose to prosecute, that doesn't mean the assault didn't happen. I keep writing.

After Candace, Lance, and the others leave, Lana, Trey, and I walk down the hallway, and Lana and I plop into our usual seats. "I'll grab the drinks," Trey says. After we tell him what we want and hand over some cash, Trey heads to the nearby coffee shop. The door to the classroom behind us opens, and new members of the men's rights club spill into the hallway.

Ross puts on a big politician's smile and strides over to us, his curly hair flopping with each step. A few guys I recognize from the confrontation earlier lurk behind him. Melanie isn't with them. I shove my hand in my pocket and clutch the letter I mean to give to her.

"Look, I know Blake's a little rough around the edges, but can you blame the guy?" Ross smiles at me like he's compelling me to be reasonable, to see his side. "With you and your friends accusing him of . . . well, I don't want to get in the middle of it. Hope there's no hard feelings."

I'm about to tell him absolutely there are hard feelings when he claps his hand on my back. I flinch away and scoot my chair out of his grasp. Ross tilts his head, as though he's puzzling over why I don't want him to touch me. "I figure there's enough room for all of us on campus, right?" Ross says.

His friends watch without comment. A few guys walk out of the classroom and stare at us as they do, Melanie trailing behind them with a full garbage bag. She stayed behind to clean up, while her boyfriend was out here. It makes me want to vomit. Ross smiles at Melanie as she tosses the trash in a big black bin in the hall.

Lana shoots daggers at him with her eyes. "I shouldn't be surprised you're a part of this shit show, Ross, what with the company you keep." She looks behind him as Blake approaches. "Speak of the *actual* devil."

Blake approaches. "Look who it is," he says, all bravado. "Our little miss whisper network creator herself. Didn't anyone ever teach you not to tell lies, Lana?"

Lana's chair screeches as she stands, knocking it behind her. Trey rushes over, our drinks in his hands, and ditches them on the table before he gets in Blake's face. "Back off," he says.

The two of them are nearly chest to chest, glaring at each other before Ross slaps his hands on each of their backs with a laugh. Like this is all no big deal. Melanie takes a step back. We lock eyes.

"Come on," Ross says, "the point of our club is that men matter too. It's a brotherhood, something positive, nothing for anyone to fight about."

Trey, Lana, and I all scoff in unison. Ross's smile fades.

Blake laughs, but there's no humor behind it. "Remember what I said, Valerie. You and Lana here aren't the only ones who can spread rumors."

"Her name's Victoria, dick," Lana growls.

"Yeah, okay." Blake gives us a smarmy smile. "I wouldn't want to give these two any new material. Since we know they like to exaggerate, we better get out of here."

My insides clench. He's gaslighting us. Lying about us. When he's the one who raped someone.

"You keep telling yourself that," I say, my hard voice surprising myself as much as anyone else. "I'm sure you have to, so you can sleep at night."

Blake spits at the ground near my feet. Like, actually spits, inside. At our school. Then he stalks off. Ross shrugs and then says to his friends, "Everyone's gotta be so melodramatic all the time." Then he and the rest of the guys walk out, thankfully. Melanie pauses over the spot Blake spit on and grimaces, averting her eyes from all of us as she turns to walk away. I grab the letter out of my pocket. As she passes me, I call out, "Wait, Melanie!"

I rush forward, and a lock of Melanie's curly blonde hair falls over her shoulder as she steps back in surprise. I hold the folded note out to her. "You dropped this," I say.

Her eyebrows furrow, likely because she doesn't recognize the note.

"Take it," I plead.

She hesitates, but then accepts it. "Thanks."

I nod, and she moves to catch up with her group.

Tears spill from Lana's light brown eyes the second Blake

is out of sight, her hands shaking even worse than before. Trey walks over and pulls a chair next to hers, gesturing for her to sit with him. She does.

"Those . . . I can't . . . Why do they have to . . ."

I put my hand next to Lana's. "It's awful. They're awful."

Trey nods and then looks at me. "What was he talking about? When he called you 'Valerie'?"

I take a deep breath, deciding how to talk about this with Trey. "He knows some stuff about my past, private stuff, that he threatened to tell everyone about if I don't stop"—I make air quotes with my fingers—"'harassing' him."

Lana scowls before grabbing her drink. Wanting to forget all that just happened, I unzip my backpack to take out some notes from class.

Dad's letter slips from my backpack. I watch it fall to the floor. Quickly, I reach for it, but then time slows as a few of Dad's words in the half-opened letter catch my eye.

Like *explaining*.

Apologizing.

And *sorry*.

Dad wrote about wanting to take responsibility, rather than lie and blame like he used to. Like Blake is doing.

He deserves for me to give him that chance. Or, even if he doesn't, I want to.

Trey clears his throat, and I'm reminded I've been sitting here lost in thought, letter clutched in hand, without explanation.

"You okay, Victoria?" he asks.

After everything that just happened, my emotions are

high. Like an unhinged person, I start to unravel, the panic in my eyes giving me away.

Trey leans toward me. "Victoria." His eyes are wide. "What is it?"

The words rush out of me like I'm a dam that's broken. "It's a letter from my dad. He's in jail. He's in jail for"—my chest heaves—"for touching me. Inappropriately." My voice breaks on the last word.

Trey pulls back from me, slumps down in his seat.

Lana sighs; she already knew of course. She leans toward me. "Victoria. I'm so sorry."

I shake my head back and forth quickly without knowing why. And I keep talking.

"He denied everything at first. When it happened, he said I was sick. That I had made a pass at him. And I went into foster care in Silver Valley and kept quiet about it, until I couldn't take worrying about my stepsister anymore. Her mom hadn't protected me, had refused to see the truth about what happened to me, and she didn't see it happening under her own nose with her daughter either." Lana hands me a tissue she got out of her backpack, and I take it, even though—for once—I'm not crying.

"By the time I was able to confront him, he'd hurt Sarah too," I say, shaking. "And that was it for me. I finally told the authorities, CPS and the cops, the truth. And now he's in jail."

A few bros I don't recognize walk by us, staring. Lana glares at them, and they speed up, rushing away. I tighten my fingers around the letter to keep it from shaking in my hands. "He wrote this letter and had my aunt give it to me. I didn't even know I had an aunt but now she's saying their grandfather molested her and my dad and that's why he is the way he is."

Trey's head is down, his lips puckered like he's going to be sick.

Lana stares at him for a second and something silent passes between them.

I swallow.

"He wants to see me, for me to come visit him in jail. So he can explain or something." I take a deep breath, bite my lip. "To apologize."

Lana's eyes flit back to Trey, her fists balling, before she turns her attention to me. "Don't go, Victoria. Why give that animal the time of day?" She shakes her head. "Why give him the chance to feel better about himself? That's his problem, his guilt, not yours."

I ignore Lana's comments, because she's saying what I guessed she would, and instead look to Trey. His eyes are focused on the floor.

Suddenly, I'm hot all over. Embarrassed. *Humiliated.* I can't believe I just vomited that all out.

Trey's face has paled, and he won't even look at me. He probably thinks I'm broken.

But I'm not. I'm doing things to help others. Being proactive. And yet, I feel hot shame wash over me. Because Trey can't meet my eye. He feels bad for me.

That's not what I wanted. Pity.

The word *victim* flashes through my mind.

I swallow, stammer out my next words. "And Blake knows. Somehow he found out about what happened with my dad and says he'll make sure the whole school finds out if I get in his way."

That gets Trey's attention. His eyes dart to me and to Lana and back. "We won't let him do that to you."

I look at Lana, who was just falling into herself, a mess over the trouble Blake's causing. And I see in her eyes what we both know. We can't stop Blake. Not from telling people about this. Not from doing everything he can to shut our club down. Maybe he's too powerful.

I stand. "I have to go." I'm already four paces away by the time I hear Lana call after me, but I don't turn. Instead, I run. Out the door, to the bus stop. As fast as I can. Away, I have to get away.

CHAPTER
TEN

The way Trey's body sank back in his chair, how his face lost its color, as I told him and Lana what my dad did to me, is all I can think about for the next few days. How telling people makes them see me differently. Like I'm someone to feel sorry for.

And I hate that my dad did that to me. I hate that my father made me into a victim.

Family dinner comes and goes with no mention of Audrey. I don't respond to her note.

My notebook I use for writing my victim impact statement is getting thinner from all the torn-out pages. I take it out and stare at a blank page for what feels like a long time.

Instead of empty space waiting to be written in, I see my dad's words in his letter.

Dad wrote to Audrey, *Will you beg her to come see me at the jail, to give her father a chance to say sorry?*

Nightmares.

That's where I see my dad. I dream of him as a little boy and his grandfather, a faceless old man, leading him by the hand to a bedroom, closing the door behind them. The dream boy morphs into a young man; I don't see his face, but by the back of his head—blond hair short on the sides, longer on the top—I know it's Trey. And he's running away from me.

I call his name. He doesn't turn back but instead disappears down a hallway. It goes dark. I can't see. "Trey!" I scream.

I'm alone.

Friday morning, I wake drenched in sweat and see that Christina texted me. She wants to come visit.

I would love nothing more, I reply. For an instant, relief floods through me. But then I remember my dream and the panic. The dread, thinking about the Men Matter Too assholes. The guys who want to keep us down, who want to keep us quiet. How Blake threatened to tell my secret to everyone he knows. Everything comes back to me at once, and it's crushing. I suck in a breath, and then another.

I can't stand feeling this way. Helpless. I need things to go back to normal. I squint toward the window. The sun shines through my half-open blinds—a new day. I text Trey.

When do you want to canvass again?

My heart pounds harder the longer I wait for a reply. He doesn't respond until I've settled down to a bowl of cereal at my tiny dining room table.

Monday work? We meet at the same time, same place?

I stare at the words for a while before answering. It's like nothing ever happened. Like I didn't tell him about my dad. Maybe it was weird when I told him, but how could it not be? Maybe I'm overreacting and things can go back to how they were before.

My mind flashes to Kale. Kale, who I haven't talked to in a few days. Saying how busy I am. But really, just feeling more distant from him than ever. My life is so different here, without him. And his life back home, without me. Kale's texted, told me about going to the movies with some of his cross-country friends, including that new girl Hannah. She seems to be in all his stories now. He says I'd like her, that I should come to Silver Valley and hang out with all of them sometime.

I bet I'd like Hannah more if my boyfriend would stop hanging out with her so much.

I miss you, I text Kale before responding to Trey, confirming the date and time for canvassing.

On Monday, I head to campus to meet Trey. I pull the hood to my jacket close to my face. It's October and unseasonably cold. The wind bites my nose and cheeks. Trey's car pulls into the parking lot on campus, and my muscles stiffen in anticipation. He walks toward me, and I squeeze my arms around myself.

"Cold?" Trey takes in my body language. "I thought you were from here. This is nothing. Wait until winter comes."

I exhale a strangled laugh. "I've lived here my whole life, except last year." I swallow, remembering how I mentioned Silver Valley and foster care in my whole monologue the other day. "I know how cold it gets. And this is Reno; it'll probably warm up within the hour."

After parking, we visit a few houses in the residential neighborhood before heading toward the sidewalk alongside the freeway, a WinCo and other stores in a shopping center ahead of us. By the time we reach the intersection where it's safest to cross, away from the stores and toward the houses on the other side of the busy street, the silence is really starting to get to me.

I open my mouth to say so, but Trey has chosen this moment to talk.

"Blake, don't . . . don't let him get to you," Trey says quietly. "I told him we'd make much more trouble than he can handle if he even thinks about threatening you again."

"Thanks," I mumble. But I know it won't matter. If I keep pissing off Blake, he'll come after me. I know it. Nothing Trey says or does will stop that from happening.

"It's been weird," I blurt. "Since I told you guys about my dad. I didn't mean to . . ." I trail off. Because really, I don't know what I did or didn't mean to do. I just had to get it out. I had to let go of the secret that was crushing me inside.

Trey blinks, his lips becoming a thin line. "There's a bench over here." He points to a sidewalk outside another shopping center before the road curves upward and leads to the houses we are planning to canvass. "Can we talk for a minute?"

I scrunch my hands in my jacket pockets and nod.

I follow Trey to the bench, and we sit there quietly for a moment. I stare at the snow-capped mountains beyond the houses.

"Sorry I've been"—Trey pauses and puts his own hands in his jacket pockets—"off."

I stare at the side of his face. Trey is looking away from me, and I have no idea how to make this less awkward. "I know it was a lot, what I told you," I begin. "I didn't mean to make you uncomfortable."

Trey's eyes blaze as he turns to look at me. His jaw is set. "We're in a club whose whole mission is to fight against sexual assault and to help survivors. Why would you ever apologize for being one? For telling me that you are one?"

He called me a survivor, not a victim.

I bite my lip. "It just seemed to bother you."

Trey laughs bitterly. "Well yeah, I would hope so. Who wouldn't be bothered by someone being abused by their father? Of all people. That vile—"

"I get it." My voice breaks. "It's disgusting."

Trey's eyes widen, and he turns completely toward me. "It is, what *he* did to you. Not you. It's not your fault." Trey's voice is fierce. So certain. Full of something I can't put my finger on.

"I know it's not my fault," I say quickly. "No offense, but how would you know?"

Trey's on his feet, almost instantly. "I know enough." He takes a few steps away from me. "We better get going, canvassing to do."

I stand, unable to catch Trey's eye as he starts walking uphill. My voice breaks. "Lead the way."

———————

We don't get half the donations or pledges we did last time. With Trey and I barely speaking to each other, the cold from outside has turned inward. I can't get away from him fast enough by the time it gets dark out and we have to call it a night.

"See you in class," I call to him as I'm walking away from

his car in the parking lot. He offered me a ride home. I said no. I can walk to the bus; hell, I can run.

Trey's disgusted by my dad. Of course he is. But he's got something else he's not telling me. And he's being weird about it. Distant and cold. And I can't deal with that on top of everything else I have going on in my life.

Can I?

———————————

Although he'd been sitting with us for the last couple of weeks, Trey doesn't take his spot next to Lana and me in English the next day. Lana turns and gives him a questioning look, but Trey shrugs like it's no big deal.

"You two get in a fight or something?" Lana asks me.

I huff. "No." I force myself not to look over at Trey. *At least I don't think we did.*

After class, I rush after Trey before he gets to the door. "Trey! Wait up!"

I catch his arm in the hallway, before quickly releasing it. "Sorry," I blurt. "But what's going on with you?"

A few feet behind us, leaving the classroom, Lana starts to approach. But after I give her a look, she thinks better of it. "See you later," she says, before slowing her pace.

Trey follows me outside. Between the buildings, there's a few benches facing the manicured lawn where a bunch of other people are playing Frisbee. Jess comes to mind. I realize I should text her. Ask how it's going at UNR.

Later. For now, it's time to figure out what Trey's problem is.

"Trey," I begin, twisting my fingers in my lap after we sit. The bench is cold. I can feel it even through my jeans. "Did I do something wrong? You've been, I don't know, different. And I just don't get it."

Trey frowns and drops his chin, as though he's thinking.

"I never told you why I joined SASAH." He looks away from me, watching the person with the Frisbee get tackled by a friend. Not following the rules of the game, a few others join in, falling in a heap on the grass. Trey doesn't smile. He looks back in my direction, but not at me; his eyes seem to be focusing just above my head.

I fidget in my seat. "I figured you just cared about victims. I mean, survivors. Wanted to make things better on campus and in town in general. You know, you're one of the good guys."

The statement comes out sounding more like a question, with my pitch rising at the end. Trey smiles sadly. "I am. You know, I try to be. But that's not how . . . or why . . ."

Instinctively, I grab his hand. Trey's eyes dart to mine.

"You can trust me." My voice is barely more than a whisper.

I feel his hand, warm in mine despite the cold, and let it go, quickly, heat rushing to my face.

Trey's shoulders sag. "My uncle was like your dad." Trey finally meets my eye. "He messed with me. When I was a kid. I was six years old."

Trey's eyes land on my hand and he stares at it, unblinking. "I told my dad right away. My parents had really drilled into me to always tell if something didn't feel or seem right."

Trey keeps his eyes cast down, not looking at me. "My dad confronted his brother, and it got ugly. Fast. They fought. Uncle Gabe took off. And he shot himself in the head with a shotgun that night."

I choke on a breath. "I'm . . . I'm so sorry, Trey." My eyes start to water, just seeing the pain on Trey's face. The way his nose and cheeks scrunch up. How hard he seems to try not to cry.

"Some people know. Jasmine knows. Lana knows." He shrugs. "It's not some big secret, but it's also not something I scream from the rooftops. I know it's not my fault, or it wasn't my fault. But it just doesn't feel like I need to tell everyone. It's my business."

"I get it." That's why Trey reacted so strongly when I told him about my dad. He knew how it felt.

And suddenly, I'm filled with rage. Trey, hurt by his uncle. Dad, hurt by his grandpa, yet he still came after me.

My fists curl. I want to scream. My father has the nerve to want to explain? He has the nerve to think I would give a crap about him or try to help him?

Audrey showing up—it didn't just hurt me. It hurt Sarah. She and my dad have no right. They need to get out of my life, both of them, and stay out.

My emotions are a roller coaster. One minute I want to hear Dad out, and the next, I'm filled with rage. I know that since I can't settle on one feeling it's been hard to write my victim impact statement. But right now, watching Trey suffer, it's hard to imagine feeling anything but anger toward my dad.

Trey's light brown eyes furrow. "What is it?" he asks.

My words come out sharp but controlled. "I do want to see my dad, I realize. I want to tell him to leave me alone. No more letters, no more aunt. I'm done, and I don't want him to keep pulling me back in. I want to be free."

Trey's inhales, his nose red. "Do you want me to come with you?"

I shake my head quickly.

We sit in silence for a few moments. Together—in a sea of students coming and going, living what I imagine, or hope at least, are less complicated lives—but alone too. I'm in this alone.

Once I'm back home, with Sasha in my lap purring as I stroke her fur, I text my aunt: *I want to see him. Will you get me added to the approved visitor list or whatever?*

She replies, *It might take a few days but consider it done.*

Days pass. I think of Dad, of coming face to face with him.

I go to class. Text Kale. Do homework. Call Kale. Panic when I get his voicemail. My life is unraveling all around me, and Kale was the one constant I could depend on. He's always been solid, a rock. And now he's too busy to pick up the phone?

———

Saturday, I sulk around my apartment because Kale is out of town at a cross-country meet, and I won't be able to talk to him all day. I wonder if he's thinking about me, missing me. I wonder who he's sitting with on that long bus ride.

It's better to focus on homework than on Audrey or my dad, or wondering when Kale is going to call. So I do, or try to.

Kale calls me Sunday morning.

"Hey, babe!" he says jubilantly, before explaining that he didn't call last night since they got back so late.

I let out a long exhale at the sound of Kale's voice. "How was the meet?"

"It was great," Kale exclaims. "I took second place. Not first, but I still made the top five!"

I lean back into the couch. "I wish I could have been there. Maybe I'll be able to get a car next year, but by then you'll be done with the team."

Kale laughs. "You say that like it's a bad thing. Then I'll be in Reno, and we can hang out all the time."

All the time.

I imagine Kale at my apartment every night, not just on a weekend here or there. Or maybe I could visit him at his dorm. We could annoy his roommate by making out all the time, or something like that. I imagine his phone buzzing with a text from Hannah or someone else from Silver Valley and Kale pushing it to the side. He'd only have eyes for me.

I smile. "You might change your mind when you see how permanently attached to you I'll be."

Kale laughs. "Maybe I can even join SASAH, if I end up going to TMCC, right?"

Oh.

I thought we'd put to bed the idea of him following me

to TMCC, especially because his parents can help pay for his tuition at UNR. "I thought you'd decided on UNR?"

Kale sighs. "Not this again. I told you: if I go to TMCC, it's because I want to, not because I'm settling or trying to follow you or something."

I blink. And my dreams of being with Kale all the time burst around me as I realize, with a pain in my chest, how things have changed from last year, when I did nothing but try to push Kale away.

I shouldn't have done that. I shouldn't have kept him at arm's length when part of me wanted to bring him in, but . . .

But.

Now it seems like I'm the polar opposite. Wanting to be around him all the time, wanting him to ignore his friends for me. Who am I becoming?

"I just don't want you giving up anything for me," I finally answer.

On the other line, I hear someone call Kale's name. His mom, by the sound of it. "I gotta go, Sunday breakfast with the family. Love you!"

"Really, Kale?" I snap. "We just got on the phone, and you're already rushing off?"

Kale's words come out slowly. "Sorry, Victoria, but my mom's calling me. We have breakfast out together every Sunday that my dad's in town. You know that." He waits a beat. "What's this about?"

I huff. Like it's ridiculous for me to be mad that Kale doesn't have time for me anymore. I open my mouth to say as much, before I hear Kale's mom say his name again.

"One second, Mom!" Kale calls back.

I grit my teeth and force myself to not sound psycho. "It's just—you didn't call last night."

"I got in really late, Victoria. You know that. I figured you would have been asleep."

"I would have happily woken up to talk to you," I lie. I stayed up waiting most of the night for his call.

Kale sighs. "Okay, I'll keep that in mind for next time, I guess."

Without meaning to, I scoff. "Next time?"

I hear banging on Kale's door. His sister Alicia calls his name now. "It's time to go!" she says.

Kale's tone is strained. "Sorry, Victoria. I really have to go. We can talk about this later." He pauses for a long second. Too long. "I love you."

I don't want him to hear the sob I'm trying to choke down, emotions whirling out of me, out of control all of a sudden. If Kale loves me, why is he blowing me off all the time now?

I'm pissed and I'm scared and I want to yell and cry all at once.

I hang up the phone.

I breathe quickly, in and out, panicking. Why did I do that? Hang up on Kale? He's busy, just like I've been busy. There are lots of times when I don't call him or text him, so why am I freaking out so much? I put my head in my hands. I don't recognize myself. I'm insecure, yeah, but still. This isn't me.

My phone vibrates with a message from Kale.

Victoria? What the hell?

My fingers can't type fast enough. *I'm so sorry. I shouldn't have done that. I'm being stupid and insecure, I know. I just miss you so much.*

I miss you, too, Victoria. But I don' t get it. Why would you say you're being insecure?

I pause. I'm not going to tell Kale I'm jealous of the time he's spending with Hannah. Because it's not just her. I'm jealous of the fun he's having with his friends, the times he's too busy to text or to call. It's like he's moving on with his life, without me. And I'm so far away. It feels like there's nothing I can do to stop it.

I'm worried you'll forget about me. That's what I finally type. And it's true.

It's a few minutes before I get a reply. Maybe Kale doesn't know what to say to me, his psycho-needy girlfriend. *Or maybe they just got to the restaurant and are sitting down*, I tell myself. He's with his parents and little sisters. He can't be glued to his phone the whole time. Well, he could, but that's not Kale. He's not inconsiderate like that.

I'm not forgetting about you, Victoria. I could never. I'll call you later, okay? I love you.

I love you, too, I reply.

And that's it. Now, Kale can see me for the needy and unhinged girlfriend I've become. Great.

With nothing else to do, I return to my homework. I guess I can always count on that. Work to be done to get my mind off my shitty life.

Sunday night, when I'm at family dinner, I get a text from Audrey.

Does Wednesday afternoon work for you? I can pick you up.

I look across the table. Sarah smiles at me. "Tell Kale I say hi."

My mouth parts, and I think about telling her how distant I feel Kale and I are growing from each other, no matter how tightly I try to hold on. "Will do," I lie.

My throat starts to close up. This isn't who I am, who I want to be. Lying all the time again. Lying to the people most important to me.

I look at Sarah. Her blonde bangs are growing longer, and she has them pushed to the side now. I want to reach for her hand, but I don't.

"There's something I have to tell you," I say. I look to the head of the table, at my stepmother. "Both of you."

Tiffany's hand wraps around her water glass. It's like she can feel my discomfort, like she knows something bad is coming.

I look back at Sarah. What I have to tell her is bigger than what's going on with Kale. "I want to see my dad; I want to hear what he has to say."

Sarah's big blue eyes widen. She's shaking her head. "Why . . . no. That's not . . . why?"

I stare at the untouched chicken breast on my plate, move the cooked carrots around with my fork.

"I don't want to run anymore." I drop the fork with a clang. I look back up at Sarah's eyes as they fill with angry tears. "I don't want to imagine what happened to him as a kid, to deal with that image breaking into my thoughts when I least expect it. I don't want to wonder what he wants to say to me. I'm tired. Tired of all of it. I just want to know, and I want to tell him to leave me alone. For good."

Tiffany puts a hand on Sarah's, but Sarah yanks hers away. Just like Sarah did last time we talked about Audrey, she pushes her chair back and jumps to her feet. I flinch as the chair crashes against the floor.

"He's just going to want you to help him. All he does is lie, Victoria! You can't go. You can't do this."

Tiffany looks from her daughter to me. "What is it that you're afraid of, Sarah? Tell Victoria. We talked about using our words in therapy."

Sarah scoffs. "I'm not a baby, Mom. Don't talk to me like one." Her arms are crossed, and she's standing over us, looming, and I hate that Dad did this to her, to sweet, trusting Sarah.

Sarah's eyes narrow at me. "He's going to want you to help him get a lesser sentence. I know it. That's all he cares about—himself."

I stand and walk to Sarah, slowly.

Even though I've fought with myself over this very thing constantly, I mean it when I tell Sarah, "I won't do that."

Seeing Sarah hurt this way guts me. Her breaths turn ragged as I come closer to her. If I can't tell the truth for myself, I will do it for her.

Sarah backs away from me, as if the thought of me touching her right now disgusts her. She stomps off to her room and slams the door shut.

Tiffany drains her water glass before finally speaking. "I understand where you're coming from, Victoria. I don't like that you want to see him, but I get it. Just . . ."—Tiffany hesitates—"we all know how convincing, how *deceptive*, your father can be. Be careful. Promise me."

I sigh. "I promise."

CHAPTER
ELEVEN

That night, after family dinner, Kale calls me.

"Hey."

"Hey."

I close my eyes and clutch my head with my free hand. I hate how awkward this is.

"I'm sorry about—" I begin, but Kale cuts me off.

"You said you think I'm forgetting about you, Victoria, but that doesn't really seem fair. You don't call me when you're busy with club or school stuff. I don't call you when you're at your family dinner. I have practice and school and a family too."

I swallow, my throat impossibly dry. "Of course, you're right."

Kale is quiet for a long time. I'm about to say something, but then he starts again. "I feel like there's something more than what you're saying. You're not being yourself."

I thought the same thing, that acting this way isn't like me, but hearing Kale say it makes me pause. Because I'm going through a lot, and he knows that. Can't he cut me some slack?

"Not all of us are perfect, Kale." My tone is flat. I won't yell at him again.

"I never said I was. Geez, Victoria. Can you give me a break?"

Can you give me one? I think bitterly.

"I should go," I finally say.

Kale exhales loudly. "Why won't you talk to me?"

I hold the phone tightly. When I'm not talking to or texting Kale, I miss him so much, but now that Kale's on the phone with me, I just want to get away. He doesn't get what I'm feeling, no matter how much I want him to. And that makes me feel even worse.

"I love you, Victoria. You know that, right?"

I hold my breath, not answering.

Kale lets out an exasperated sigh. "I can't keep up with these mood swings," Kale says quickly. "It's like I'm talking to—"

He stops talking abruptly.

"Talking to who?"

"Never mind," Kale answers. "I gotta go."

Kale hangs up the phone, and I'm left holding it up to my ear, in shock. I'm the one who said I had to go, so why do I feel so rejected?

I text him. *Talking to who?*

The three dots appear, then disappear, and appear again.

I'm about to call Kale and demand an answer when his message comes.

My dad.

I suck in a breath like I got punched in the gut. Kale just compared me to his alcoholic father. A man who he can't stand most of the time because he's always yelling at Kale's mom. Because he's on edge always, never happy unless there's a beer in his hand. And even then.

The three dots appear and disappear. Kale wants to say something but doesn't know how. I know the feeling.

I don't text him back. I don't call.

Later that night, as I lie awake in bed, mind still reeling from Kale's words, he calls me.

I answer on the first ring.

"I shouldn't have said that, Victoria. I'm so sorry," Kale says immediately. No hello, how are you? He just goes in for it.

I stare up at my cracked ceiling. "I get it . . ." I trail off. There's no excuse I can make. "I'll try to do better."

"Me too," Kale says. "I'll be better at texting, even if I can't call."

"Me too," I reply. "And I won't keep hanging up on you. I know that's not cool."

"Thanks."

We stay on the phone for a while, trying to get back to what used to feel normal. I tell Kale I love him before saying goodbye.

We each call and text each other more often over the next few days. We're holding on; I'm holding on. Because that's what you do when you love someone.

———

Audrey picks me up, as planned, Wednesday afternoon when I'm done with classes for the day. I slide onto the leather seat of her rental, some kind of fancy Lexus hybrid.

"You're brave for doing this, Victoria," Audrey tells me as she pulls the car out of the apartment complex parking lot. "I never faced my grandfather. I never told him how he hurt me. I never asked him why. And now that he's gone, I won't be able to." She sighs as we pass a row of much older cars parked on the residential street, some on the verge of breaking down by the looks of them. "I have so many questions that no one can answer."

I take Audrey's appearance in. Her manicured nails. Hair secured perfectly in a tight bun. Designer dress. She'd look like me, if I were older, plumper, and rich. She holds the steering wheel tight as we stop at the intersection nearest the jail. I know where it is. I looked it up, as soon as Dad was arrested. Just to see.

I never imagined visiting him here.

"So you know," Audrey begins, "in the future we can have you set up to visit him by video chat. You can do that on your phone."

Anger flashes through me. Audrey sinks into her seat, leaning away, like she can feel my rage and doesn't want to get burned. "I should have told you, but I thought maybe we could go in together this first time."

I inhale deeply. She *should have* told me, but thinking about sitting on my couch, seeing my dad's face pop up on my phone in a place that's supposed to feel safe to me, I don't like it. Visiting at jail is fine.

Audrey's beige skin pales as we turn onto the street where the jail's located. I clear my throat. "You've been here before. Why do you look so nervous?"

She chokes out a little laugh. "I'm just imagining how I would feel if I were you."

I wince.

She shakes her head quickly. "I meant to say, being here with you, thinking about what it must be like, it's bringing me back to what happened to me . . ." she trails off. "And though my brother hasn't admitted to anything, it makes things harder. Thinking of it that way. Wanting to love him, to help him, but also hating him a little."

I force a hand down to stop my leg from jiggling so much.

Audrey smiles weakly at me as she parks the car.

"I want to go in alone," I tell her. "I think that would be for the best."

Audrey hesitates. "I don't know if that's such a good idea."

I bark out a laugh, surprising both of us. "I wouldn't call any of this"—I wave my hand in front of me—"a *good* idea. But here we are."

Audrey smooths the cardigan over her dress. "I'll at least come help you check in."

"Fine," I mutter.

I follow Audrey into the nondescript building. Inside, she greets the officers stationed around the metal detector and puts her cell phone and purse on the conveyer built. I put my lip balm and phone next to hers in its own small plastic container and watch it roll away to be screened.

Audrey gives me a sad smile before she walks through the detector. The man on the other side nods at her—she didn't make the detector beep—and then he gestures for me to follow.

We don't get as much as a smile or a kind word as we

leave them behind, walking toward the front desk where we sign in. In Silver Valley, when I was arrested because my foster mom Connie called me in as a runaway for lying and going to a school dance, everything was different. Deputy Smith was kind to me. He told me I'd be all right and gave me advice. And Sheriff Scott made me promise to stay out of trouble. I seemed to matter to them, even if they didn't know me.

Here, it's like no one cares.

I hand my ID over to the woman behind the glass-protected counter before filling out the sign-in form she hands me.

Audrey swallows, her eyes darting between me and the door. "You're sure I can't come in with you, Victoria?"

"I need to do this alone."

The woman passes me a visitor's badge. She explains to me how I'll be led to a terminal with a computer screen, where I'll get a video feed of the inmate I want to visit, who's below us on the bottom floor in the jail, where the inmates have their visiting room.

"I'll wait right here in the lobby," Audrey tells me. "I'll be ready whenever you need me."

My eyes drift to the door, where a tall, burly guard waits for me. "Ready when you are," he says in his gravelly voice.

I'll never be ready.

But here I go.

I follow the man through a narrow hallway with faded walls. We reach a long, narrow room lined with people with telephones and computer screens in front of them.

My feet drag, heavy and slow. I hear each step pound in my ears. My heart thrashes in my chest.

The guard stops midway through the line of visitors, at two open chairs. "Here you go. Have fun."

He heads back toward where he came, to lead someone else in. Guards are stationed, one at each end of the room, watching. I look around and notice families, pausing to stare at a child crying on his mother's lap, saying he misses his daddy. I see all of this, but I don't see him yet. Because I won't look.

I sit, slowly, eyes cast down. Close my eyes as I reach for the phone.

"I'm so glad you came."

I hang up the phone quickly. Gasp air that refuses to fill my lungs. Open my eyes to see the face that has haunted my nightmares for months. Even if it's only on a computer screen, it's almost more than I can handle.

On the screen, my dad's green eyes turn down. They're faded now, somehow less bright than I remember. New wrinkles crease his forehead. Gray peppers his once dark wavy hair. And he's wearing inmate attire, a jumpsuit.

I swallow hard and grab the phone. Muster my courage. "Hey, Dad."

My father's bottom lip starts to shake.

"Don't," I force out. "Don't you dare cry. I'm done hearing you cry." *Being manipulated by his emotions.* Hearing him cry over Mom, seeing him be so broken after she died, it's what made me think I needed to take care of him, rather than the other way around. It's what kept me from telling the truth about the abuse, because *I felt bad for him.*

"You wanted me to come." I hold the phone near my face but leave a space between it and my ear. Who knows how often they clean these things? "I'm here. You want to talk? So talk."

I thought coming here would give me closure. I thought it would give Dad the chance to say what he wanted to say and let me move on. But I don't tell him I want him to leave me alone, like I had planned to. I'm here because I want to know who my father really is, what happened to him that made him this way. I want to hear him say that he's sorry. And that makes me mad at him and even more mad at myself.

I'm shaking as a solitary tear slides down my father's cheek. We stare at each other in silence for a moment.

"I'm sorry, Victoria," he cries. "I'm so, so sorry."

My chest feels as though it's about to squeeze the life out of me. Everything is tight. Tension behind my eyes, my teeth gritting. It hurts. I blink. Blink. Blink.

But the tears still come. Traitorous tears.

"I shouldn't have . . . I'm sick, not you," Dad finally says. "But you know that now. Audrey told you about my grandfather?"

I nod, wiping my soaked cheeks.

"How could you?" I croak. "After what he did to you, how could you do that to me?"

Dad won't meet my eyes now, shame withering his face. His jaw trembles.

"I can't explain it. I wish I could, but I can't." He looks

down at his hand, the one not holding his phone. His nails are bitten so short that he's got hangnails, red swelling around the cuticles.

"I told myself I'd never be like him, even when it started. When I started missing your mom the most, being lonely. When I started seeing you like her."

I hold still, so still. Terrified to hear him keep talking, but unable to walk away.

"Can you ever forgive me?"

I look to the family, the mom with the crying little boy, next to us. Talking to his dad on the video. What did the man do? Can his family forgive him?

"I want to," I whisper, telling him what I can only barely admit to myself. "But I don't know if I can."

Dad inhales deeply. He smiles at me sadly. "You've grown up so much, even in just a few months. You're in college now. I almost can't believe it."

My dad's eyes water, but not the pathetic, pleading kind of tears he sheds when he's trying to get me to do what he wants. These are different.

"Your mom would be so proud of you," Dad says.

I blink. Clutch the phone tighter. If she could see us now.

"I miss her all the time," I finally say. "I just . . . I don't talk about her, really, to anyone. It's like, her memory, how I feel about her, it's just for me. Mine only."

But that's not the whole truth. I also feel conflicted about my mom.

I think back to the ways Dad controlled and manipulated her too. The way she taught me it was my job to take care of him, to keep him from getting too mad or too sad, even before she got cancer. What kind of mom teaches her daughter to put her dad's needs over her own, no matter what?

Dad smiles at me. "You have done so much for yourself, so well, despite everything." His eyes stare at me and it's hard to keep eye contact. I look away.

"You graduated high school, in a town where you had no one. You're in college. I just . . . you've really come through all of this. I had no idea how strong you were before. Stronger than me."

We're both quiet. We can agree on that, at least.

"How's school?" Dad asks. "Do you like your classes?"

I'm here with my dad in jail because he hurt me. I haven't spoken to him in months. He attacked me, lied about it, and abandoned me. He sent me away. But right now, I hear the same voice that gently told me that I was brave enough to get back up and try again after I fell off the monkey bars and was scared in elementary school. Seeing the same face, although weathered, that has been around my entire life. So, I answer. Because he's my dad.

"School is good," I tell him. "I've got straight As. I have friends, and I joined a school club." I don't tell him *what club*.

Dad's eyes brighten. "That's great, Victoria. I'm so glad to hear that."

He reaches his hand out to the screen in front of him. I see it on my screen, think for an instant about doing the same. Our hands meeting, even just on the computer screen.

But I don't.

Dad drops his hand. He sits straighter, resolve coming

into his voice. "I'll never forget what I've done to you. My life will never be the same. And I don't deserve to forget. I know that, but I wonder if you could help me with something."

Instinctively, I back away in my chair. As if I'm trying to make space between us. Heat floods my chest, and my muscles flex as if I'm readying to run.

"My lawyer thinks you can help me, with your victim impact statement. He said if you tell them about the stress I was under, how things were good before they got bad . . . maybe even explain that all I ever did was kiss you that one ti—"

I slam the phone down on the receiver.

A guard approaches, and the little boy at the station nearby stares at me with eyes as round as saucers. On the video, I see my dad's mouth moving quickly. Even without the phone to my ear, I can hear him plead. "Please, Victoria. What could happen to me in prison, it could be worse than death. You have no idea."

This is exactly what everyone told me he would do. Exactly what I was afraid of.

I'm running to the door before I'm yanked by the back of my sweater by a guard.

"What the hell do you think you're—?" He sees my face and lets me go.

I sob, heavy and loud and ugly and broken, running past Audrey in the lobby. Out the door, run run run. Don't stop. Can't.

I'm halfway through the parking lot when I hear Audrey

screech, "Victoria! I have your keys in my car. You need them to get home!"

Like a wounded animal, I turn, look around for an escape, seeing the cars around me in the parking lot but not really seeing. I stop at a car, probably not Audrey's. I don't see the color, the make, or the model, as I collapse against it and slide down to the concrete. Crumple myself in a heap and wish I could disappear. Be swallowed whole. Be nothing.

I am nothing.

Audrey takes my shoulders gently and lifts me. I let her. Too shattered to fight. She brushes a soaking wet clump of hair off my snotty nose. "Shhh, shhh," she says softly. "Let's get you home."

The car ride is silent as she drives me back to my apartment.

When Audrey parks, she opens her mouth like she's going to say something but then closes it. I take my keys and phone out of her center console and get out of the car. Walk away, to my apartment, without a word.

CHAPTER
TWELVE

Victim Impact Statement
My dad is a liar. He only cares about himself.

I push the pencil so hard against the paper that it snaps in two. I scream and throw it against the wall. Frantic, I paw through my backpack until I find a pen. Start writing again, but this time it's not to the judge. It's to *him*. My own personal monster.

You are not a father. You are the most selfish, twisted person I've ever met. You want me to help you? Were you even sorry, or did you just write that so I would come? Did you just say that to me to try to get me to do what you want?

Do you even care about what you've done to me? Do you ever think about how you shattered my entire world that night? You're my FATHER! How could you? If you were really sorry, you wouldn't ask me to help you. You only care about yourself.

I hate you.

I hate you.

I HATE YOU!

And then I throw the notebook too.

Minutes or hours pass. The sun sets outside, except I don't feel grateful for the time of day. No new possibilities will come tomorrow. Just another twenty-four hours of the same wheel turning and turning. Me inside, running like a hamster. Running to and from my dad but getting nowhere.

I'm alone in my room, unless you count Sasha sleeping in the cat bed I bought her. Lights off, blinds drawn, me tucked under my covers. Although I don't miss the strict rules at Connie's, having all that structure and her breathing down my neck had its benefits. I couldn't sit around and stew about how crappy my life was. I had to act. Write essays for financial aid. Study. Clean, even.

But at home, with no one telling me what to do, I can lie around and ruminate. Hate Dad. Wonder if he ever loved me.

I could call Connie. Tell her what's been going on. We text sometimes. I tell her about school, and she tells me about her daughter, Annie. Connie tells me she's been taking more foster care training to brush up on her parenting skills so she can be a better foster parent.

For the same reason I didn't tell Kale and Christina right away, I haven't told Connie about Audrey. Telling Connie, someone who was sexually abused as a kid by her stepdad, would have made everything too real. It would have made me have to face my conflicted feelings. Talk about them. Figure out what to do about that stupid victim impact statement. So, I've kept her at a distance by pretending I've just been busy with school.

But I miss Connie, unimaginable as that once would have been. She'd get it, I think. How I feel now. But something about that—imagining Connie's thin brows furrowing with understanding. Hearing the softness of her voice. Knowing how much this hurts. *Knowing me.* It just seems like too much right now.

My dusty blinds could be cleaned. My backpack, lying on the floor by the door, has homework in it I could do. I stare at the wall in front of me for a minute or an hour. And then I stare some more.

I squeeze my eyes shut. *Enough.* I jump out of bed. My fingers hover over Kale's number on speed dial.

Things have been strained with us. I hate that I've made them that way. That my loving, goofy boyfriend felt reminded of his emotionally abusive father by how I've been treating him.

That our conversations are less him joking about something silly and more him going out of his way to see how I'm feeling. Like he's walking on eggshells.

Like I used to with my volatile father.

I sigh. I'm not calling Kale. Instead, I text Trey. Ask if he wants to hang out. Tell him I saw my dad at jail and don't want to talk about it but could use a distraction.

About a half hour later, I'm locking the door behind me. Trey's car is running; he's waiting for me in the parking lot.

"Victoria! Long time no see!" Ray calls as his feet thud on the stairs above me. He hops off the last couple, two at a time.

"How's my girl Sasha?" he asks.

"She's fine," I tell him. "She's been sleeping all day. That cat has less of a life than I do."

Ray nods toward Trey. "Looks like that might be changing?"

"A friend from school. He's taking me to the batting cages."

Ray pulls his scarf closer, gives Trey an appraising look. He lifts an eyebrow at me. "I thought you had a man back home?"

I whip my head to Trey, in his car still. The windows are up. He probably can't hear us. "It's not like that, Ray."

Ray grins at me. "Well, not that you asked, but *I* have a date tonight. How do I look? Gotta step up my game for this one."

I give Ray a quick once-over. "You look great." I put a finger up in the air, catching Trey's eye to let him know I'll be there in a minute. "What's his name?"

"Jake. Another white boy. My mom wants me to bring a nice Chinese boy home to meet her, but you know, she married a Mexican against her parents' wishes so I don't plan on listening. You love who you love, am I right?" Ray gives Trey a pointed look and then wiggles his eyebrows at me.

I roll my eyes. "Bye, Ray." I can hear chuckling behind me as I stomp away.

As I shut the car door, a smile on my face, Trey asks, "What's so funny?"

"Nothing," I rush out. "So, batting cages, huh? I haven't swung a bat in ages. Or, come to think of it, like ever."

Trey pulls us out of the parking lot. "I'll teach you. That's half the fun of this, actually. I think I might like showing people how to play more than playing myself. It's why I want to be a teacher, mostly. So I can coach." Trey grins, and sitting so close to him, I see the small gap in between his front teeth. I like his smile.

I look at Trey, one hand on the wheel, baseball hat covering his blond hair. "I want to be a teacher too, at least I think I might. I really like history and, as weird as it sounds, just learning in general." I haven't told anyone I've been thinking about teaching one day, but telling Trey now feels easy. It feels right.

Trey nods. "It's not like it's gonna make me rich, but I can't think of anything I'd rather do. Stuff was bad at home after what happened with my uncle. My parents were always so wrapped up in feeling guilty for not protecting me, it was hard to be around them for a while. I pushed them away, and they let me. They gave me all the space they thought I needed, when I really needed them." Trey scratches his head through his hat, eyes still on the road as we drive through an intersection.

I suck in a breath as Trey talks about his past, listening eagerly.

"Sorry." Trey chuckles awkwardly. "Didn't mean to go there."

I shake my head quickly. "No, no. I . . . want to know. It helps, knowing I'm not alone."

I force myself to look up from my lap. Trey's watching me, but his eyes quickly return to the road.

"Okay," he exhales. "I started acting out, talking back to teachers, skipping school. If it weren't for my little league coach taking an interest in me—like just hanging out with me and listening and taking me to batting practice when I was so mad I could barely speak—I don't know that things would have gotten better. I like to think being on a team and having a goal saved me, but really it was him. Coach Martin."

We're quiet for a moment as I turn that over in my head. It's amazing how just one person caring can make all the difference.

"We're still in touch," Trey says. "He came to most of my games all the way through high school. I want to be like that, you know? I think it would be awesome to be the kind of coach or teacher who helps a kid who's struggling."

My eyes are glistening. I blink several times, thinking about the people in Silver Valley who helped me, who believed in me. Principal Nelson helping to make sure I got to graduate even when all my credits didn't transfer from my old school. Ms. Claire helping me fill out scholarship applications, saying she believed in me. My old teacher Santa's teasing, making me laugh when that was the last thing I wanted to do.

I clear my throat. "So, we both want to teach," I say lamely. "I didn't know that we had that in common."

The right side of Trey's mouth lifts into a half smile as he glances at me. "Now you do. I bet there's a lot we don't know about each other."

I look back at the road as Trey pulls into the lot. A big sign out front shows two bats, crossed over each other, with a mitt and ball next to them.

"I bet you're right."

"Hold the bat like this, with your legs bent one foot in front of the other," Trey says as he stands behind me, arms around each side, his hands sliding mine to the correct position gripping the bat. I'm holding the bat he brought. He put tokens in the machine for the balls, but we haven't gotten to that part yet.

"Good, now let's practice swinging." Trey lets me go and steps in front of me to demonstrate. He takes the bat. "Hold it this way, and then use your lower body to power the bat forward, elbows coming first. Like this." He shows me slo-mo how his legs and torso twist, with first his elbows, then his forearms and wrists, then the bat following.

"Got it." I mime what he does, as though I'm holding a bat.

"I'll show you a few times. But you have to step out of the cage. These balls fly pretty fast, and you don't want to take a knock in the face." Trey grins at me. "I'll lower the speed when it's your turn."

I head to the other side of the net, and Trey pushes the button for the first round to fly. *Swoosh.* A ball soars toward him, and I hold my breath. He'll never be able to hit a ball flying that fast at him.

Crack.

The bat smacks the ball, and it soars into the farthest edge of the top end of the net, dropping on the blue mat with a thud.

Trey keeps smacking each ball away from him as it comes. I watch him in awe. He's wearing black athletic sweats, ones he got from the student store with the TMCC logo, and a plain gray T-shirt. His legs twist and his arms punch through, striking ball after ball.

After the last one, Trey takes his helmet off and turns to me, grinning. "Your turn," he calls.

I take the helmet from him, along with his gloves. Although Trey adjusts the setting so the balls come at me much slower, I still miss more than half of them. But when I do connect, when I use my whole body to smack that ball away and it flies, I feel a little better. I think of Dad, his selfishness. *Smack.* Audrey coming here out of nowhere and expecting me to see him. *Smack.* Things changing with me and Kale since I moved away. *Whoosh.*

I almost fall over as I miss that last one, the green ball whirling by me as I lunge for it.

Trey opens the door to join me in the cage. "You okay?"

Inhaling deeply, I take the helmet off and shake my hair out. Like that will help my whirling thoughts. Shake the image of my boyfriend's face from my mind. "I might need a little more practice."

Trey chuckles. "Win, win." He takes the helmet from me. "You get your anger out, and I get to work on my coaching skills."

I hand Trey his gloves back. "How'd you know I was mad?"

He shrugs, looking at the ground in between us. "Because I would be."

Once we reach my apartment, Trey rushes to my side of the car before I get the chance to say a word. He opens the door for me.

Heat rushes to my face. Instinctively, I look up at Ray's window. The lights are off, so I'm guessing he's not home. *Good.* His date must be going well.

I step out as I send Ray a quick text saying I hope he's having a blast and I want all the details later.

When I look up, I realize I'm standing only a couple inches away from Trey. Our faces are so close I can feel his minty breath. Without thinking, I reach up and adjust his hat so it's not skewed slightly to the left anymore.

Trey's smile slides off his face. His eyes smolder. They flick to my lips and back up.

I clear my throat and step around him.

"Thanks for the ride!"

Breathing hard, right before I open my door, I turn back. Trey's feet are firmly planted on the ground where I left him, his body angled toward me.

"And thanks," I begin, "for everything. I, uh, I needed this."

Trey's gaze is soft, the heat from a moment before, gone. "See you at school, then." His inflection rises as if he's asking a question.

"At school. Goodnight, Trey."

Once the door is closed behind me, I lean up against it. Catch my breath.

I felt . . . *something* right now with Trey. But . . .

It's not like he likes me, I think, remembering the way his eyes lingered on mine. He just wants me to know I'm not alone, that he's been through what I have.

He's just being a good friend.

I squeeze my eyes closed tightly. Because I'm being an idiot. *I have a boyfriend.*

Sasha meows and pads over to me. She leans into my legs. Slowly, I slide to the floor and sit, petting her for a few minutes. My breathing slows. After I feed Sasha dinner, I call Kale. He answers on the second ring.

"Victoria!" Kale chirps. "Was starting to think you forgot my number." His words come out cheerful, but my stomach sinks nonetheless.

Kale and I went from calling and texting each other nonstop for a few days to us both checking in less frequently in hardly no time at all.

"Sorry," I breathe. But then I stop myself, because he doesn't answer my texts half the time either. "School's been keeping us both busy. And cross country for you, club stuff for me."

"Is that what you were doing now? Club stuff?"

I walk to the couch, slump down on it.

"Not exactly." I kick my shoes off and pull my legs toward my chest on the couch. "I went to the batting cages with Trey. He wants to be a coach someday, so I thought I'd let him teach me how it's done."

Silence on the other line. I bite my lip.

I hear Kale exhale. His words come out slow, measured. "You seem to be hanging out with this Trey guy a lot." Kale pauses for a second, and I consider defending myself. I could tell Kale how Trey and I are just partners for canvassing, and I'm allowed to have friends. And when did he become the jealous type anyway? But before I can, Kale continues, his voice returning to upbeat. "He sounds like a cool guy. Maybe I can meet him, when I come visit. Which reminds me, if it's okay, I want to come next weekend. My dad's out of town for a long drive so I can borrow his car again. I could come see your new college life in action!"

Dread fills my stomach and I'm not quite sure why. I shake off the feeling, though, because that reminds me. "Actually, Christina's coming next week. She's taking a few days off since her professors don't actually take attendance, and she's on top of all her school stuff. Hey, wouldn't that be nice if SVHS was like Georgetown like that?"

I chuckle awkwardly when Kale doesn't say anything. I keep talking, my words coming out fast and nervous. "Anyway, the trip is for visiting her parents, but she's coming here first, Monday night. She wants to check out a club meeting. It's too bad you'll miss each other. You sure you want to come the weekend before and not just skip school when she's here?"

I laugh, because of course I'm joking. Kale can't miss school just to visit me. Although it would be nice if he could.

"That's cool that she's going to a meeting. I wish I could stay the weekend *and* a few extra days and miss school to hang out longer." Kale pauses. "I'd like to meet some of your friends, though."

"I'm sure we could work something out." I squeeze my legs closer to my chest and try to ignore the returning dread. "It'll be great."

———————————

Christina and I are texting when I hear Kale's dad's truck pull into the parking lot. I tell her I have to go because he's here. Christina sends an eggplant emoji and I laugh. My doorbell rings.

Kale drops his bag and envelops me in his arms the second I open the door. I breathe deeply into him. My head fits perfectly into the space between his chest and neck. I smell his soap, his deodorant. *Kale.* And I want to cry because I've missed him so much. Why is it that I seem to forget how it feels to be with him when he's not around? How easy it can be when he makes me feel so safe, so loved.

My hands reach up to his neck and I kiss him, soft and slow. Unbidden, I think of Trey. Guilt claws at the pit of my stomach. It feels like I'm doing something wrong, holding Kale so close. But I'm not. Kale's my boyfriend.

I pull away and take Kale's hand, bringing him to sit with me on the couch. My phone buzzes. Trey's name pops up. Kale and I look at each other, my face warming and my hand immediately starting to sweat in Kale's. The guilt in my stomach flares up to my chest. I toss my phone to the other end of the couch. "Club stuff, probably. I'll deal with it later."

I force a smile, and Kale watches me quietly for a moment before standing. "I'm starving," he says. And then he rummages through my kitchen, finding ingredients to cook us dinner.

———————————

That night in bed, Kale holds me in his arms and fiddles

with a wisp of my hair. "So, do I get to meet your friends? This Trey and Lana I hear so much about?"

I lean into him, snuggling. "You don't want to stay here all weekend?"

Kale laughs. He doesn't push me, and that makes me feel terrible.

I sit up. "Texting them now."

Sasha climbs the cat stairs I ordered online and set up next to my bed. She sniffs Kale's feet, and he giggles.

Like, actually giggles. Then he reaches over and attempts to tickle Sasha under her chin, before she swats at him with a paw. Kale makes a face at her, blowing his cheeks out and widening his eyes, before he pretends like he's a cat, too, and paws back at her.

And that makes me smile. My silly boyfriend.

A few minutes later, I tell Kale the plan. "We're going to get pizza at this place near school tomorrow for dinner. That work for you?"

Kale grins as Sasha climbs up his body and plops herself on his chest, right under his chin. He blows a fur ball away from his mouth. "You know I never turn down pizza."

My phone buzzes. A message from Ray. *It's about time.* I've been waiting to hear back from him.

VICTORIA!!!! That was the best date of my life! it says. I smile and keep reading, swatting Kale away like Sasha did when he asks what's up. "It's Ray," I say quickly. "Telling me about his date. Let me read!"

Kale chuckles and I glue myself back to my phone.

Jake is the funniest, cutest, most thoughtful guy I've ever met.

He's ambitious, and he wants to be a lawyer—can you believe that? My parents are going to love him! He's kind and amazing and omg, I CAN'T WAIT TO SEE HIM AGAIN!

I'm smiling big as I relay to Kale the gist of what Ray texted.

"Sounds like how I feel about you." Kale wiggles his eyebrows before looking at me with love in his pale blue eyes.

I blink, suddenly at a loss for words as my chest tightens slightly.

I remember Kale being as excited about me when we first got together as Ray is about Jake. But I'd been hesitant. It was hard to throw myself into a relationship, to trust someone, after everything that happened with my family.

But Ray's over the moon, and even though it's so soon with Jake, I trust his judgment. This might be the beginnings of them falling in love.

I force a smile at Kale. Who I do love. Who loves me and feels all those strong feelings, all that passion, for me.

I lean over to kiss Kale before he reads too deeply into my sudden confusion and discomfort. Before *I* read into it too much.

So what if I never felt those feelings for Kale? What we have is strong. It's real.

The next day, Lana and Trey are already seated at the pizza joint when Kale and I arrive. Lana hands me and Kale our drink cups, greeting him. Trey nods at Kale and they introduce themselves, not unkindly, but is it just me or does it lack something?

I look at my boyfriend, whose regular smile returns, thankfully, when Lana tells us she's already ordered.

"Victoria tells me you'll eat just about anything," she says to Kale, "but we got an extra-large meat lover's. That work?"

Kale grins and sits. "A woman after my own heart."

Kale asks about the club and the walk. We talk about the posters we set up and how the joke of a men's rights club already took the ones off the wall near their door, plus a few others in the hallway.

Kale sips his drink. "What losers."

Trey nods. "Unfortunately, some of those losers are in student government and like to throw their power around."

I look at Kale. "I told you about the meeting where they made us defend why we'd want money for the walk, only to deny us. It was so stupid."

Trey twists his straw in his hand. "Actually, there's more."

Lana whips her head to face Trey beside her. "What?"

Trey runs a hand through his blond hair. "Jasmine and I were going to wait until the next meeting to tell everyone but, since we're talking about it now . . ." He hesitates, as though he feels the heat emanating off Lana. "Ross denied the club funding for next year. Apparently, Blake and their *club* can't merely satisfy themselves with complaining about the unfair treatment of men and handing out pamphlets about it; they've been getting people to sign this petition that SASAH is a hate group and—"

Lana spits, flecks of soda splashing Trey in the face.

His eyes widen, and Lana quickly grabs a napkin from the dispenser in between us and hands it to him. "Sorry!" Her words are loud and shaky. "But what the hell are you talking about?"

Trey wipes his face off. "Blake and Ross are saying that our club hates him and men in general and that we tell lies to ruin reputations. It's complete bullshit, but somehow they got Thomas to agree. From what I gather, Gabby was the only dissenting vote, but I guess they recently changed the rules that votes don't have to be unanimous anymore. Probably how they denied us funding for the walk too. Anyway, it all went down last week. So now Jasmine and I are filing a complaint with the school."

"Lana!" the guy up front behind the counter calls. "Order up for an extra-large meat lover's!"

Kale stands, looking at each of our stricken faces. "I'll get it."

By the time Kale gets back with plates and the pizza, Lana has already muttered probably every swear word I've ever heard and some I haven't. As Kale slides me a slice of pizza, my stomach gurgles. Why would Thomas and Ross listen to Blake? Why is the default always to believe the accused and not the victim?

Kale brushes a piece of hair out of my face gently. His pale blue eyes stare at me with affection, but also worry. Because he knows how much the club means to me. I give him a small smile and lean into his touch.

But when I feel Trey's eyes on us, I instinctively move away. Hurt registers on Kale's face as he looks at me for a second, as though no one else is there. I force myself to not glance at Trey to see if he's noticed. But then Lana rails on about Blake, and I take Kale's hand and let the moment pass.

An hour later, we've only talked about the terrible excuse for a human Blake is as well as anyone who associates with him. I guess that would include Melanie, too, since I haven't heard from her. I gave her my number and email address in the note, saying she could reach out if she ever wanted to talk. Promising secrecy, even from my friends.

I guess it didn't work, though.

Trey brings up the appeal he and Jasmine have been working on and says they have it under control, but Lana and I so badly want to do something, anything to help.

"Please," Trey says, pushing his empty plate away. "Let us handle this, Lana especially." He looks at his friend, his voice softening. "If you get involved, that will just add more fire under Blake. This is personal, I know, but don't let him drag you down to the gutter with him. Let me and Jasmine take care of this."

Lana crushes a napkin in her hand but doesn't say anything. Kale has been quiet just about the whole time. I reach my hand out and put it on top of his between us on the table. "I'm sorry. I know this isn't what we had in mind when we planned on you meeting my friends."

Trey's eyes linger on my hand on top of Kale's but when I look at him, he quickly looks away. Kale doesn't seem to notice, thankfully. He squeezes my hand and then lifts it to his lips. "Don't apologize, Victoria. It's messed up, and you guys are mad. You should be."

As we're saying goodbye for the night, I wrap Lana in a hug. "We're going to get through this, Lana," I tell her. "Blake won't win. We won't let him win."

Trey's eyes hold mine as I wave to him before following Kale out. Kale and I hold hands the whole ride home, but I feel uneasy.

I'm quiet that night, as Kale spoons me in bed.

"Victoria," he whispers in my ear, "your club will get funding. I'm sure you'll work it out."

I pull the blanket close to my chin.

"I love you," Kale murmurs, and my stomach clenches.

My back is turned, I can't see his face, and I tell him I love him, too, but it feels flat. My mind is racing with thoughts of my dad and Blake, trying their best to get away with the sick things they do. Not caring about how they hurt people.

"Talk to me, Victoria. What are you thinking right now?"

I breathe shakily. I don't want this to turn into another fight. Not like last time.

I close my eyes for a second, gathering my thoughts, grasping for what to say. I told Kale I visited my dad and I told him the gist of what happened. But I also said I didn't want to talk about it, not yet, anyway. I don't want to talk to Kale about what happened and how I feel about it. I don't want to tell Christina or Lana. I don't want any of them to have the satisfaction of being right, even if I know they would never rub it in. I just want someone to listen. Without judgment. And to maybe understand.

I want to tell Trey.

I turn to face my boyfriend. "I've got a lot on my mind is all. You know, the stuff with my dad. And even besides the drama with Blake, we're still short for sign-ups for the walk."

Kale takes my hand in his and runs a thumb over my palm softly. "I'm walking, and I can see if I can get some kids from school to sign up. Hannah mentioned that she wants to—"

I snatch my hand back. "You seem to be hanging out with Hannah a lot."

Kale blinks. I hold his stare. I'm tired of hearing about this girl. So what that she's new in school and great at cross county? What's so exciting about that?

Kale's light brown eyebrows furrow. "We're just friends, Victoria. Kind of like you and Trey."

"I hang out with Trey for club stuff. And I wouldn't compare Trey with some sophomore. You wouldn't understand."

Kale's jaw clenches as he recoils. "What wouldn't I understand?"

I swallow. "We've been through . . ." I trail off; Trey's story isn't mine to tell. "He just gets what I've been through is all. And we care about the same things: activism, survivors. We're in some classes together."

Kale stares at me for a moment, hurt and anger flashing through his eyes. Kale can never understand me the way Trey does but I can't tell him that because it would out Trey's abuse without his consent. And it would put another barrier in between Kale and me when it seems like we're each surrounded by walls already. I look away from my boyfriend because I can't take it.

"Trey," I begin, but then I stop myself because I don't know what I was going to say. But his name lingers on my lips. My cheeks flame.

Recognition dawns on Kale's face, and part of me hates myself for making Kale feel like this, but another part of me wants to keep going. Wants to light the match and watch everything burn. Because why are Kale and I even doing this if we can't be honest with each other? If I can't tell him how I really feel about stuff, no matter how hard I try? My heart thumps in my chest wildly. Anticipation creeps through me, and I'm not making things better, I know it, but I can't bring myself to utter an apology or say anything to reel this conversation in.

Sasha climbs up her cat stairs and onto the bed. She paws at Kale, playfully, like she did before. But instead of making faces at her or pawing back, or even meowing at her like he's done before, Kale turns away from her.

It's like the breath has been knocked out of me. Kale and I are here again, his formerly ever-present smile nowhere to be seen, because of me.

"I'm tired," I lie. "Maybe we should just go to sleep." Kale's eyes harden and he blinks, his long eyelashes fluttering. I lift my hand to cup his cheek softly. At first, Kale bristles, and I'm terrified he's going to tell me I'm acting like his dad again, but then he leans into my touch.

We sleep. Or I try to at least. But I spend a lot of time

staring at the ceiling. Thinking about my dad. Thinking about Blake. Thinking about Kale and how we're growing apart.

And thinking about Trey.

CHAPTER
THIRTEEN

The next day, I wake with a start. I dreamt Kale was hanging out with a bunch of people I didn't know. Somehow, the floor underneath me started pulling me away from him. When I called Kale's name, he looked at me. I was certain he was going to turn away, back to his friends, but I woke up before finding out.

I turn to face Kale and lean into his chest. He stirs and smiles a little when he notices what I'm doing. "Hey," he mumbles, still half asleep. "Good morning."

I cuddle into him more. Holding tight. "I love you," I say leaning into his chest, inhaling his scent. Trying to take him all in, keep him close. "I'm sorry about last night. I shouldn't have gotten so defensive."

Kale blinks, his light blue eyes focusing in on me under those long eyelashes. "I get it," he says. "It's hard for me too."

Despite the fact that neither of us have brushed our teeth yet, I kiss him. First softly, and then not so soft. With need. I don't know what I was thinking before. He might not understand me like Trey can, but Trey's just a friend.

Trey might listen well when I talk about hard stuff but that's just because he's a survivor. It's not like he likes me or anything. Not like that. And he certainly doesn't love me.

Kale does.

As our kisses get deeper and our hands start to roam, I'm not thinking about Trey anymore.

After, Kale and I make pancakes and eat together, the last moments before he has to leave rushing by too quickly. I bury my face into Kale's neck as I hug him goodbye. "Let's not let the distance become a problem for us, Kale. We can get through this. We just need to keep talking. I'll try to do better," I say again, like I did after our last fight.

Kale hesitates and I hold my breath, but then he runs a hand through my hair. "Don't be so hard on yourself, Victoria. We're okay. It's all going to be okay."

I close my eyes as he kisses the top of my forehead. When he drives away, I stand outside in the parking lot, watching the spot where his car pulled out for a long time after he's gone.

———

Monday night, I take a bus to meet Christina at the airport. She walks out of the sliding glass doors, a rolling suitcase in hand, smiling big.

I slam into her, hugging my best friend fiercely. She laughs, and pushes a piece of her long, black, perfectly curled hair out of my face.

"Good to see you, too, Vickster."

I grab her suitcase and walk in the direction of the ride-shares. "Special occasion," I say, showing her my phone. "I called an Uber."

"Fancy," Christina says. "How was your visit with Kale?"

I take what Christina deems as too long to answer, I think.

Christina arches an eyebrow at me.

I sigh. "It was . . . good."

"Not buying it."

Figures Christina would see right through me from the moment she gets here. A black sedan with an Uber sticker on its windshield pulls up. "Here we are." We greet the driver as she puts Christina's luggage in the trunk. "Thanks."

Christina leans her head into my shoulder once we're both situated in the back seat. "I'll see Kale when I see my parents, you know. If I can't get it out of you, you know he's the weaker one and will fold under pressure." She grins at me.

I don't smile back. "Kale and I argued because I got jealous. We're fine now, but I feel . . . I don't know, uneasy still."

Christina's easy smile falters. "You can tell me," she says, giving me an appraising look. "If something is going on with you and Kale, I can be neutral. You don't have to worry about me taking sides."

I lean my head against hers. "I know, and that's good to hear. Things are fine, they're just not *great.* It's hard to explain. If I could even understand it myself, it would be easier, but I just feel like it's been really hard lately."

Christina gives me a sympathetic look as the car pulls up to my place. Ray's outside getting his mail. "The famous Christina Martinez," he beams as we step out. "I've heard all about you!"

Christina raises both eyebrows at him. "Hey . . ."

The driver takes the suitcase out of the back and hands

it to Christina. As she drives away, I pull my keys out. "This is Ray. I told you about him."

"I know who he is," Christina says, rolling her eyes. "I just didn't expect such a warm welcome."

I stop, turning slowly toward Ray. "You do seem like you're in a really good mood. Are you going to keep me on pins and needles waiting to hear the latest on Prince Charming Jake?"

Ray flashes us pretty much the biggest smile I've ever seen. "I'll be seeing Jake again this weekend. I'm making him dinner at my place."

"Dinner, wow. You cook?"

I walk past him and unlock my door. Turning back, I see Ray's indignation.

Laughing, I say, "Yes, I'm aware that you are a big fan of instant noodles and mac 'n' cheese. Which dish will you be preparing for Jake?"

"My papa is calling me tonight to tell me how to make enchiladas, I'll have you know. Gotta step up my game for this fine man if I want to keep him."

Ray laughs as Sasha meows and makes a run for him. He scoops her up and says in a sweet voice. "Sasha, you're going to love Jake so much. As will your mother, when she meets him."

I raise my eyebrows. "You're already introducing him to your friends? I thought that was a problem with you and Brian, you not wanting to get serious so fast."

Ray hands me Sasha. She rubs against me and purrs.

"That was Brian," Ray tells me. "This is Jake. I like him a

lot and want him to be a part of my life. I want him to meet my friends and my family, too, when they're in town next."

Ray looks at me like this is common sense and I'm obtuse for not getting it. "Yeah, we're new, but he's important to me, and I want him to know that. Plus, he's so great—why wouldn't I want to show him off to all of you?"

The tight feeling in my chest is full force. Because I don't really integrate Kale into my life here. I didn't really want to bring him to meet Trey and Lana.

Mail in hand, Ray heads for the stairs. "I'll leave you two to it, then. Let me know if you want to hang out later. I'll have enchiladas."

I shake off the weird feeling Ray's happiness gives me and wave goodbye to him as I lead Christina inside. After giving her the tour—the very short tour since my apartment is tiny—we flop on the couch. "You hungry?" I ask.

Christina looks to the door. "I want those enchiladas when they're ready."

I laugh. "That can be arranged." In the meantime, I grab two pieces of string cheese from the fridge and toss one at her. Sasha leaps onto the couch and steals it from her lap, and Christina and I bust up laughing as the two of us chase my silly cat down and take the cheese back.

"So, you want to tell me more about Kale?" she asks once we have the cheese and are back on the couch.

I stop mid-bite, thinking.

Finally, I swallow. "When he's not here, sometimes I miss him so much. But sometimes, even if we're together, it feels like we're a million miles away . . ."

I twist a piece of string cheese around my finger. "Our lives are just so different now."

"Our lives are different now too. Do you feel distant from me?"

I shake my head quickly. "Of course not! I'm so proud of you for chasing your dreams to DC."

Christina finishes her cheese and crunches the wrapper. "What is it, then?"

"If I knew that, I don't think I'd be having this problem."

I think Christina senses that I'm in need of a lighter subject, so we go back to talking about school. We have dinner at Ray's that night—and I'm not just eating enchiladas, but also my words since Ray, it turns out, is an excellent cook.

Monday, Christina sends me off to class with a hug and a promise to check in with me after she has lunch with her parents, who are driving here from Silver Valley to meet her. That night, we watch movies and eat ice cream and we don't talk about Kale or my dad or my aunt. It's the best night I've had in a long time.

Tuesday after English, Christina meets me on campus, and we walk with Lana to get coffee and study while we wait around for the SASAH meeting.

Lana hands Christina and me our coffees and sits across from us in our usual chairs in the hallway outside the SASAH meeting room.

"Thanks," Christina says. "So, Victoria told me about her awesome idea about the signs. But I don't see any. Where are they?"

I frown. "We put a few up in this hallway, but it looks like someone took them down."

Lana scoffs. "*Someone*, as if we don't know who that asshole is."

Christina fiddles with the lid of her drink. "Can you report this Blake jerk?"

Lana shakes her head. "We don't have proof that he's taking our signs down." She grimaces into her coffee. "We don't have proof of anything."

I know she's not just talking about the signs. My shoulders slump.

At that moment, Thomas, the student government senator, strolls by us. He's got a baseball cap on low over his eyes, but I still see the surprise register when he sees us.

"Hey," he says to me. "Um, how's it going?"

My eyebrows furrow. He seems uncomfortable. He's not in the men's rights club with Ross and Blake, and he's not behind that petition. Not that I know of, at least. But he did vote to deny us funding. "Fine, aside from a stupid petition circulating about our club slandering the *good name* of certain individuals." I glower at the words *good name*. "You wouldn't know anything about that, would you?"

Thomas purses his lips before looking at Lana and then Christina. "I didn't sign that, but you should know that Blake—"

At that moment, Blake appears behind Thomas and claps his back. "Hey, buddy. What are you up to?"

Thomas's mouth snaps shut when he sees Blake. "I gotta go, actually. Good seeing you all." He scurries away.

Maybe Thomas was feeling guilty. *But if he was, why sign off on denying us funding?*

"Haven't seen you around." Blake looks at Christina like he's undressing her with his smarmy eyes. "I'm Blake." He reaches out to shake her hand.

Christina grimaces at Blake's hand and makes no move to touch it. "I know who you are," she says. "And I couldn't be less interested. *Bye.*"

Christina would skip small talk with Blake. Lana and I both laugh at Blake as he mutters something about Christina being a bitch—*real original*—and stalks off.

Following Lana and Christina to the meeting room, my breath catches as I feel someone behind us. I turn to see curly hair and wide hazel eyes. "Melanie."

Christina turns to see what the holdup is.

"Go ahead," I tell her. "Sit with Lana. I'll meet you in there."

Christina spares an inquisitive glance at Melanie before shutting the door behind her.

Melanie swallows. "I read your note."

We stare at each other in silence. She read the letter, but she's in the hall outside of the men's rights club.

She seems to read my thoughts. "I talked to Ross about what you said." She blanches at the look I give her. "I didn't tell him about the note, just the statistics. He didn't . . ."

Melanie takes a deep breath. "It's only fair for this club to exist, too, for equal representation. Don't you think?"

I shake my head. "I don't," I say. "And I don't think you do either."

I look behind her as Ross opens the door to his meeting from inside. "You coming, babe?" he asks her.

Melanie looks at me.

I lower my voice to a whisper. "I don't think you believe this club is doing good, or that it's even necessary for *equal representation*, otherwise you wouldn't be trying to convince me, or yourself."

Ross opens the door wider. "Melanie!" he calls.

She turns from me and walks away.

———————————

Inside the conference room, waiting for the meeting to start, I can't help but look around and notice a few empty seats. "There are usually more people," I tell Christina, after introducing her to Jasmine and Trey. There's one faux hawk missing. "Where's Steve?"

Tara shakes her head. "Don't know." She looks at the room behind us, apprehension lining her face.

Jasmine overhears from up front. "Look, it's nothing to worry about—"

Trey, who is sitting between Lana and me today, cuts in. "Blake and Ross have been harassing people with that stupid petition, and Blake has been ranting on Twitter about us being a man-hating, lying . . . well, you get the idea." Trey hands me his phone. I focus in on Blake's latest tweet.

SASAH aren't the only ones who can start rumors. The difference is what they say isn't true, and I can prove what I know about one of them. So maybe they should think about that next time they spread lies.

I swallow. He's talking about me and my dad. Blake's account has thousands of followers. "What does that have to do with . . ." My mouth falls open. "You mean club members aren't coming because of what Blake's doing?"

Lana's voice is icy. "We can't let him get away with this."

Lance and Candace slide into their seats near us.

Jasmine sighs. "I think that's all we're going to get today," she says, addressing the eleven or so people who are here, rather than the usual fifteen. "So, I think I should start by saying we have a problem. We all know about Blake and what he's been up to with that stupid club out there,"—she gestures to the hallway—"but he's gotten some traction with that petition. Three hundred signatures."

My stomach drops. Christina's manicured nails tap the table angrily beside me.

Jasmine continues, "Student government leadership has voted to not fund our club next year."

Gasps erupt from around the room. "They said that the club is a hate group. That it's"—she pauses, and her next words are venomous—"*anti-men.*"

Protest breaks out all around.

Jasmine shakes her head, her eyes hard as she looks toward the door and continues, "They say the school shouldn't give us funds for our 'radical agenda.'" Jasmine makes air quotes around the words.

"They can't do this," I exclaim. "It's not true. Blake just doesn't want the truth out about—"

"I know," Jasmine interrupts. "And I'm going to appeal to the school president—not the student body president, but the actual person who runs the board. But I expect we might have an uphill battle. Blake's dad is on the board too."

Lance slams the table and Christina and I flinch. He immediately apologizes, deflating as he lets loose a breath. "This isn't right," he says. "What else can we do?'

Jasmine inhales deeply. "Each of you write a statement about what the club is and what it means to you. Hand them in to me as soon as you can, and I'll present them to the president along with our case. In the meantime, don't give anyone any reason to think what Blake is saying is true. Don't engage with him or Ross or anyone else who might try to get a rise out of you to prove their case. Got it?"

We all agree. Jasmine smooths her blouse and lifts her chin. "Now, to the good stuff. Why we do this in the first place. Our fundraising walk for the shelter is coming up soon. So, this is the last week of canvassing, and we really need to bring our A games."

Trey leans toward me and whispers, "You want to canvass Thursday night? That way we can be done with it and focus our attention on the walk?" He's sitting beside me, rather than up front with Jasmine. Christina leans closer but without looking at us. As though it's not obvious she's eavesdropping.

I nod, suddenly aware of how close Trey's hand lingers next to mine on the table.

Lana smiles smugly from Trey's other side. And I'm smiling too. Until I feel Christina staring at me. Her thick, black eyebrows are so high they've practically disappeared into her hairline.

"Care to tell me what that was about?" Christina asks as we're walking away from the conference room.

My face warms. "The meeting? I already told you about how Blake is trying to sabotage the club."

Christina shakes her head. "You know that's not what I meant."

I sigh as we arrive at the bus stop. I lean against the tall advertisement for a realtor attached to the bench. "I don't know," I admit. "It's . . . confusing."

Christina tilts her head at me and sighs. "Just be careful."

Christina and I knock on Ray's door rather than going to my place when we're back at the apartment complex. His company seems like a nice distraction from the tightness forming in my gut from my conversation with Christina about Trey.

Ray opens the door, grinning at us. "You two are going to eat me out of house and home," he says. "I'm assuming you're here for leftovers. I'm going to cook a fresh batch for the date tomorrow anyway."

I nod appreciatively.

He opens the door and gestures for us to sit at the kitchen table. His living room is the same layout as mine, with a small couch in the same spot.

After Christina and I inhale two enchiladas each, Ray takes our plates and gestures toward the living room. "Go sit. I'll get you two a drink."

Ray doesn't ask us what we want but returns with each hand holding a cocktail of some kind with an olive in it.

"What's—?"

Ray shakes his head, cutting me off. "Try it."

Christina looks at Ray knowingly before taking a very small sip.

I take a long pull and start coughing, sputtering the strong, bitter drink. Christina laughs, before taking another measured sip.

Ray takes mine from me and tastes it. "Martinis not your style? I'm practicing for when Jake comes over."

Christina sips her drink again. "Martinis with enchiladas?" She raises an eyebrow at him. "Not exactly the first thing I'd think of. What about margs?"

Ray rolls his eyes at her before taking another drink of the martini he confiscated from me. "Basic. Margaritas would be too obvious. And I'm nothing if not original."

Christina nods appreciatively. "Well, I think this is great, then. As good of a martini as I've ever had."

I scoff. "What? You knew what these tasted like and didn't warn me?"

Christina laughs. "What would be the fun in that?"

Ray sets the martini on the wooden coffee table in front of us. "Something bothering you, Victoria?" He waves a hand in front of my face. "You've got the whole sad puppy thing going on."

Christina and Ray both watch me. Finally, Christina supplies, "Boyfriend trouble."

Ray nods knowingly and waits for me to say something.

I sigh. "It just feels like, I don't know, like we're distant. Like no matter how much I want to open up to him about how I'm feeling, I just can't. I don't know why."

Ray's phone buzzes and he grins wildly when he looks at it so I know it must be Jake. I can't help but roll my eyes at him, but then immediately I feel guilty. Ray's my friend. I should be happy for him.

Ray sits on the floor across from us. "Have you tried?"

I scoff, my guilt forgotten. "Of course I tried! I just clam up every time. Or worse, freak out and yell at him."

I watch Ray as he leans back on his hands. "Look, I'm not perfect, you saw how I avoided talking about feelings with Brian until I broke up with him. But you know, it was actually what you said—when you asked if I could work it out—that made me realize, yeah, I could. I just didn't want to. And that meant it wasn't good for me, the relationship. I wasn't feeling it enough, and that wasn't good for Brian either."

I swallow. Ray better not be getting at what I think he's getting at.

At my glare, Ray raises his hands in defeat. "Whoa, there." He gives Christina a quick look and laughs. "Not telling you to break up with Kale. Just saying that we all deserve to know what's up in our relationships. Communication is key, right?"

He gives Christina another look and I grit my teeth.

"You tell Christina stuff, yeah?" Ray continues. "You talk to your homegirl Lana, I'm guessing, and that Trey guy.

Why not Kale? As your boyfriend, he deserves that as much as anyone else. Maybe even more."

As if it's that easy. Like I can just force myself to spit out the tangled messy feelings I have whenever I have them. Like I can talk about something I can't even put into words for myself.

Christina pats my leg. She raises her glass to Ray. "Cheers to me not being the only friend you have who tells you how it is."

Ray laughs and for a second the tension leaves the room. Still, I can't help but feel defeated. My shoulders sag. "I'm trying. I'll keep at it though, I guess."

Ray smiles down at his phone as he reads another text from Jake, before taking another sip of martini. "All I'm saying is, you seem to be piling up secrets and that is making you cranky."

He looks up from his phone as though he's remembering something. "You still haven't told me what's up with that aunt of yours. Audrey, right? That's who has been leaving you letters under your door? What, like she's never heard of sending a text?"

I sit up, ramrod straight. "Letters? As in plural?"

Christina sits up straighter too. We both stare at Ray, waiting.

"She was here earlier. Or some lady who I assumed was her because she looked kind of like you. I saw her from my window slipping a note under your door. I just remembered."

I stand, and Ray does the same. "I guess I better go check that out," I say.

Ray opens the door for us. Christina follows me over the threshold.

"Good luck," Ray says. "And thanks for being my taste testers." He takes Christina's half-empty martini glass from the table beside the couch. I rush down the stairs, Christina at my heels.

Inside, I hold the letter and stare at it for a moment before turning toward Christina. Suddenly, I don't want to open it. I don't want to know what she wants, not yet.

"Can we not do this now? I want to enjoy your last hour or so before we go to the airport. Without this, whatever she wants, hanging over me."

Christina hesitates. "Are you sure? After what we just talked about with Ray? I'm here for you, Victoria, I want to help."

I nod. "I'm sure. But I will fill you in later, *I promise*."

I walk to the kitchen and set the letter on the table. "I want to be here with you, talking about Georgetown or something fun. And deal with this later."

Christina nods and sinks into the couch. "Well, the signs that you made gave me a good idea for my campaign for freshman president actually. I was wondering if you could give me some advice."

We spend the next hour talking about campaign strategies, Christina doing her best to distract me from the dread I'm feeling, I would guess. I hug Christina at the airport, her hand resting on the handle of her suitcase. "I needed this," I say. "Thank you for coming to visit me."

Christina wraps me in her arms. "I love you, Victoria. I'll always be here for you."

As I watch my best friend walk away, my thoughts go immediately to that letter at home.

Waiting for me.

CHAPTER
FOURTEEN

Once inside, I feed Sasha. Then I do the dishes. I'm procrastinating reading Audrey's words and I know it. Finally, envelope in hand, I sit on the couch and read the letter. There's not much to it. Audrey came to see me to apologize for my dad in person, but I wasn't home. She said she should have warned me he might ask me to vouch for him in my victim impact statement. She wants to talk.

I'm so tired of talking. What could she say to me that would fix our wrecked family?

Dad wants me to lie for him. To help him get a lesser sentence. What about me? What about his daughter who wants to move on? I want to be a normal college student and not have to worry about my twisted father.

I wanted him to tell me the truth about what happened with his family when he was young. I wanted to really know why he did what he did. I wanted to hear him say sorry and mean it.

For him to change.

I crumple Audrey's letter and toss it into the trash across the living room, behind the TV that I never watch. Because who has time for TV when they're too busy dealing with their long-lost aunt and jailed father?

Outside the window, the sun is setting, purple streaks

hovering over orange clouds just over the mountains. It's beautiful. Serene.

It makes me miss Silver Valley. Even though Christina was just here and I didn't want to talk to her about this, there's someone from home that I do think could help.

How's Silver Valley? I text Connie. Pitiful, but I don't know what else to say.

Not the same without you, she replies. The knot in my chest loosens, if only a little. I remind her about the walk and tell her I hope to see her there.

I'm sorry, Victoria, she replies. *I can't make it. We just got a new girl last night. She's only here for a few weeks for a temporary placement before she's moved out of state with her grandparents for kinship care. Lilly, the little girl—she's real upset missing her mama. I don't think she'd take well to staying with my mama and Annie or coming to the event with me. I know you'll do wonderful at this walk, and I'm so proud of you. I can't wait to hear all about it.*

My shoulders sag. No Connie at the walk.

Kale texted me earlier this week, asking how the visit with Christina was. He told me he wanted to come support me at the fundraiser. I haven't texted him back yet. And he didn't follow up to ask why I didn't.

My eyes linger on the crumpled letter in the garbage. There's another letter I need to send, to Jamie.

I settle in to write to my former foster sister, since she doesn't have access to a phone or an email account. Now that she's out of the treatment center, I ask her about her new group home and about school. She's got several new friends and seems to be thriving there. I write about the club and my new friends, too, but I don't tell her about the hard stuff I'm going through. I don't want to burden her. She's got enough on her mind.

After I seal the envelope, Audrey's crumpled letter catches my eye again.

I text her the details of the fundraising walk. Maybe Audrey could actually learn something. *Meet me there, do some good. We can talk after.*

The next day, Ray invites me to his place after he and Jake have had dinner. It's time to meet this amazing guy Ray can't stop talking about.

Ray's dimple appears with his huge smile as he opens the door to let me in. Behind him, a tall, thin blond with light eyebrows and brown eyes stands and smiles at me. "Jake," he says, as he reaches out to shake my hand. "I've heard a lot about you, Victoria. Glad we finally get to meet."

My apprehension melts away at the warmth of his greeting. I follow Jake and Ray, who sit side by side on Ray's couch. I take the chair across from them.

Ray raises an eyebrow at me. "Can I get you a drink? Not a martini though, right?"

He and Jake both laugh. Ray must have told him about my practically spitting out the last drink he gave me. I roll my eyes and shake my head. "I'm good, thanks."

Jake leans forward, resting his elbows on his knees. "Ray

tells me you're working on a big fundraiser to raise money for that shelter across town. That's really awesome."

I nod. "Thanks. Ray's helped me practice my pitch. Asking for money from strangers wasn't the easiest thing in the world. Who knew?"

We all laugh. "I'd totally come," Jake says, "but Ray told me the day of the walk is the same day my parents are going to be in town to visit."

I nod. "No worries. Where are they coming in from?"

"Monterey. So not too far from here, but I still don't get to see them as much as I'd like because they're both so busy with work."

Ray puts his arm around Jake, their interaction with each other already seeming so effortless. "They're both surgeons." He smiles at Jake. "No wonder this one's such a smarty-pants."

I stifle a laugh. *Smarty-pants?* Wow. Ray's being such a dork. He's got it bad.

"This one's going to be a big-time lawyer after he goes to law school," Ray says proudly. "And get this, you know how I wanted to apply to some advertising internships in Los Angeles? Well, guess who just so happens to be applying to a few law schools in the area? USC, UCLA, and even Pepperdine in Malibu."

Jake smiles at Ray. "I could get used to seeing you at the beach."

I swallow. Ray's told me he wants to get out of Reno after graduation and leave for a big city, LA being the closest and most attractive option in his mind. And he doesn't seem to care that Jake might want to be in the same area as him, even if it's for his own career. In fact, judging by the goofy grins they're both wearing, they're thrilled about it.

Exactly the opposite of how I was when Kale told me last year he might want to go to TMCC instead of UNR.

My eyebrows furrow. I remember what Ray told me about his parents and how they used to want him to be a doctor or a lawyer. He said that isn't who he is. But dating one is?

Ray narrows his eyes at me and wrinkles his nose. "I know what you're thinking."

"Do you?"

Jake answers, "Why does he want to date a guy who wants to be a lawyer if that career was too boring for him?"

Ray's eyes widen and my mouth falls open. Jake starts laughing so hard that he snorts, and then Ray laughs at that too.

"The thought crossed my mind," I finally manage.

Ray puts his hand on Jake's knee and squeezes it. "This guy is so smart and creative that he could talk about paint drying and I'd find it interesting."

I let loose a breath. These two are too cute to not be happy for, even if the rest of us aren't so lucky.

Ray takes Jake's hand in his and squeezes it. "Actually, I, um, wanted to ask you, Victoria, if it's okay if I miss the walk too." He looks at Jake, and they hold each other's stare for a beat. "Jake's parents invited me to dinner with them at around the same time and—"

I raise a hand. "Say no more. Who am I to get in the way of new love?"

The second I say the words I regret them. *Love,* way too soon for that. I freaked out when Kale even alluded to his growing feelings for me. My stomach sinks as I look to Ray, expecting a glare for my mistake.

Instead he's all eyes for Jake, who's blushing.

Dear lord.

I start to laugh, like, hard. And so do they. The rest of the visit goes by quickly, Jake talking about what studying for the LSAT has been like and the law school application process. Ray asks questions and brags about Jake to me, simultaneously. When I walk downstairs to my apartment, my fingers go for my phone automatically.

But something makes me pause before I call Kale, a feeling of unease. Instead, I text him that I'm sorry for not responding earlier this week. *I'm too tired to talk tonight,* I type. *Sorry things have been like this. Just know that I love you.*

He replies that he loves me too. And he misses me.

I text back. *I love you so much, Kale.*

Because I do love him.

I do.

I love Kale.

That night, after I hear Jake's car start and drive out of the parking lot, I text Ray.

Thanks for having me over tonight. It was really great meeting Jake. I can see why you like him so much.

Ray replies quickly. *He's the best, isn't he?*

I take a long time typing and deleting and then retyping

what I want to say. Then I just don't send anything back. A few minutes later, Ray replies.

You know I can see those three little dots when you're typing, right? Is something wrong?

The tightness in my gut tells me there is something wrong. Ray lights up when Jake texts him. I don't do that with Kale.

How do you know when something's right? With the person you're seeing, that is. You seem so happy, and I just want to know.

A minute later, there's a knock at my door. *Great.*

"I didn't mean to freak you out when I texted, I—"

Ray breezes by me and plops on my couch before I've invited him in.

"Might as well come in," I grumble.

Ray laughs as he crosses his legs. "What's up, Victoria? You having doubts about Kale?"

I sigh and sit next to him. "Things just seem so easy with you and Jake, so right. And that makes me see how things haven't been with me and Kale."

Ray tilts his head at me. "Don't get it twisted; just because I'm happy doesn't mean things are perfect. Relationships take work. I'm putting that work in."

"How do you mean?"

Ray uncrosses his legs. "Well, for starters, communication. I didn't have that with Brian and it ended up hurting him. I like Jake and I'm not here for games. I'm not going to mess things up with him that way."

Like I've been messing things up with Kale. I swallow. "What kind of communication?"

Ray jiggles his foot over his knee. "Well, I was scared to tell Jake that I wanted to intern in LA after he told me he applied to schools there. I didn't want him to think I was clingy. But also, that's stupid, right? I applied to intern before I even met him, and anyway, even if I hadn't, I want Jake to know and love the real me, not some perfect version I concoct to get him to like me."

I bite my lip. "But you'd already applied so . . ." I trail off. The risk wasn't that high. Ray is following his dreams and so is Jake.

"Okay, well, I've never been in a serious relationship before and part of me was a little nervous. I know it probably looks like I've jumped in headfirst, but I was afraid of how much I liked Jake so quickly. What if he didn't feel the same? I didn't want to get hurt."

I shake my head. "I had no idea. You both seemed so sure of each other from the beginning."

Ray laughs at that. "That's because Jake called me on my shit. He could tell I was holding back from him and asked me what was up. So, I made myself be brave and I told him." Ray's eyes twinkle as he smiles at me, his dimple creasing on his cheek. "Jake told me he was glad I opened up to him because then he could tell me I shouldn't worry. He was falling hard for me too. And we promised each other from then on that we wouldn't keep secrets. If one of us wanted to know where the other stood or had something on his mind that was bothering him, we promised to share. Because our relationship is important to us and we want to keep it strong. Protect it."

My eyes start to glisten and Ray looks at me sadly. "You're going to be okay, Victoria. Just talk to Kale."

I swallow. I wish it were that easy to tell Kale how I feel. But how can I, when if I do, I know it will only hurt us both?

Trey picks me up at my place, rather than at school, for our last time canvassing. He opens the car door for me.

"Oh, um. You didn't have to do that." I twist my hands in my lap as I sit. Trey grins at me from the driver's seat and my palms sweat.

My phone buzzes, another text from Kale.

You around for FaceTime?

I hate that I'm doing to him what I got so mad at him for doing to me before, even if avoiding talking to Kale lately seems easier than the alternative because I don't want to fight. But right now, I don't have a choice.

Sorry, about to canvass.

Tonight then?

Trey looks at me and I set my phone down. I'm unsure why, but I don't want to text Kale when I'm with Trey. I grimace as the knot in my stomach tightens.

"You okay?" Trey glances at the road and then back at me.

I nod. I can't tell him I'm avoiding my boyfriend and feel bad about it, but not bad enough to stop doing it.

Trey takes us to our last neighborhood. Our last shot to bring more excitement to people outside of school about the walk. We pull out all the stops—our facts and compelling stories about the people I met at the shelter. We get a handful of walk sign-ups and a few donations. It's still early, but I'm spent, and I tell Trey as much. The tension of everything going on in my life creeps up on me. On the drive home, he takes a different street. Trey keeps his eyes on the road as he asks me, "Can we talk?"

That sounds serious. My heart is in my throat, but I nod. Trey pulls into the parking lot of a small park. The wind blows blades of grass in the empty lawn in front. The slide gleams at us, shimmering in the late afternoon sunlight. No one else is here.

We're quiet for a moment, both staring at the monkey bars ahead, before Trey kills the engine and turns to me completely.

I'm looking at him. His brown eyes, the curve of his lips. I want to see him smile, see that small gap in his teeth I've grown to like so much.

"So." That's it. That's all I've got.

"So," Trey repeats.

His eyes soften, and he reaches for my face, slowly. I hold my breath as he touches a finger to my cheek, just under my right eye.

"You had an eyelash." He drops his hand to his side. Trey parts his lips. I hold my breath, watching him watch me. I'm leaning forward, my heart hammering in my chest, and we're so close.

So close.

Suddenly Trey pulls back from me.

I wish he wouldn't.

Trey looks down at his lap. "You have a boyfriend."

I blink several times. My thoughts race. What am I thinking?

Kale's face comes to mind, but I shove the thought away. Not with Trey sitting right here. Not with what just almost happened. Something almost happened, right?

Have I gone completely delusional or does it seem like ...?

I don't know what it seems like to him.

Trey seems to be waiting for a response to his boyfriend statement. "It's complicated." I grimace at the clichéd way I've chosen to describe my relationship with Kale. It's true, but I don't want to give Trey the wrong idea. Whatever that might be.

Trey's lips pull into a smile. I wish he had an eyelash on his cheek so I had an excuse to touch him right now. Trey's looking at me again, serious and wanting at once—if I'm not imagining it—and my heart turns to putty under his stare.

"Complicated," he says. "Well, then."

Well. Then.

I swallow, waiting. An eternity passes, or a moment.

"That's why I wanted to talk." He's looking at me, his eyes probing, and it's making it hard to breathe.

"It feels like there's something here, between us." Trey says.

My heart thumps in my chest wildly. I *haven't* been imagining things with Trey.

He starts the car up again and I exhale, disappointed.

Trey pulls the car out of the parking lot. "Let me know

if your situation uncomplicates. We're going to have to do this right."

A piece of Trey's hair flops into his face as he laughs at my confused expression.

"A real date," he explains.

"Oh." That's all I can say.

Oh.

Trey actually *likes* me. Like, for real.

My chest warms because I like Trey too. I think I have for a while; I just wouldn't admit it to myself.

But the warm tingly feeling is quickly replaced by nausea. Because *Kale*.

These feelings. They make me a terrible girlfriend. A terrible person.

We stop at a light and I look out the window as the sun sets. I don't marvel at the beautiful colors of a Nevada sunset like I usually do. Kale might be looking at the sun setting in Silver Valley, waiting for me to text him back. Not knowing what I'm doing, what I'm thinking about doing. I curl my fists, angry that I'm so selfish.

My dad is most certainly not enjoying a Nevada sunset, locked behind bars. *Good.*

I feel Trey's eyes on me, so I turn to him. I'm forcing an all-too-familiar smile. And it's like I'm back to last year, hiding the truth from everyone. Like I've learned nothing.

———————

At home, I want to see Trey again. Like, a lot. But I can't

shake the feeling that I'm betraying Kale. Who I still haven't texted back yet because I just . . . can't.

Trey's my friend, and I like being around him. Things have gotten so heavy lately, with the club drama and the disaster that is my father. Lana and I are just trying to keep our heads above water with all the Blake stuff.

Lana. Lana's my friend, too, and I have a feeling she could use a break just as much as I can.

I grab my phone. Hoping this doesn't seem desperate since Trey and I just spent the afternoon together. He's barely dropped me off at home and I am trying to hang out with him again. I send a group message to Trey and Lana. *I need something to get my mind off everything. Can we do something? Batting cages? Bowling? Anything? Only rule is no club talk. Or Blake talk. You in?*

Lana pulls up in her car about a half hour later, with Trey in the front seat. I slide into the back, thanking them for meeting me.

"Any excuse to get out of my parents' house," Lana says. "They were watching a marathon of *The Golden Girls.*"

Trey laughs. "You don't like *The Golden Girls*? I think you're the weird one here, Lana," he says.

The tension building in my chest loosens, even as Trey meets my eye in the center mirror. I smile back at him.

Once inside, we walk to the other end of the batting cages, near a set-aside area for exercise equipment. Apparently, this place doubles as a gym. Trey doesn't bother showing Lana the dos and don'ts like he did for me.

"I know what I'm doing." Lana answers my question

before I ask it. She takes the metal bat from Trey's hand and, without wearing gloves, readies herself in the batting position. Trey and I watch from outside the net.

The first ball zooms and Lana smacks it away, like the pro she apparently is.

"I taught her everything she knows," Trey tells me.

Somehow, even with a ball flying at her face, Lana hears that. After she thwacks it hard, she balks. "*Please*. I miss fewer of these than he does. My dad taught me how when I was eight."

Trey shrugs as I laugh at him.

When Lana's run out of balls, she bounces out to meet us. "See that guy over there?" She nods toward the small weight area behind a few ellipticals, treadmills, and an indoor bicycle. I notice a guy who could be around our age lifting weights by himself.

"I'm going to say hi," Lana says, before walking away without another word.

I stand there watching her for a while. First as Lana smiles at the guy, who looks pleased to have her company as she shakes his hand, apparently introducing herself. And then even as she joins him lifting, using one of the bicep machines.

Trey walks under the net to stand next to me. "Watching her work is amazing."

I turn to look at Trey, a question in my eyes.

"She's got game is all I can say," Trey continues, nodding at them. The guy is laughing at something Lana just said.

He lifts one of his arms and scratches his head, but it's clear he's trying to show off his muscles under that T-shirt.

"I guess Lana and I have never talked about her love life," I realize. We only talk about club stuff or even Kale sometimes. My heart sinks. I don't want to be that kind of friend.

"Oh, Lana's not the talking type, not about that kind of stuff. And I wouldn't call it a love life, anyway. She's not the *relationship type*, if you know what I mean."

I stare at him before he adds, "She just likes to have fun, nothing serious with anyone."

"Oh."

Trey and I are both quiet as we creepily continue to watch Lana flirt. She sees us staring and gives us a look so hard we both quickly turn away, laughing.

"Whoops," Trey says. He hands me the bat. "Your turn."

I twist the metal in my hands. "You said Lana's not the relationship type." I stare at the bat. "What about you? You're not seeing anyone, are you?"

The second I ask, I feel like an idiot. Trey said he'd take me on a date, if and when things uncomplicate with Kale. And then there's Kale. *My boyfriend.* I have no right to ask Trey this at all.

Trey answers despite the inappropriateness of the question. "Nope. I was, but you know. It didn't work out."

I look up at Trey. He blinks.

"Why not?"

Trey shrugs. "We dated since sophomore year in high school. I wanted to stay together even though she was going to go to Northwestern for college. But I could feel her pulling away in the summer when it got closer to her leaving for Chicago. Finally, I ended it."

I lift my eyebrows at Trey and he actually smiles.

"What? Yeah, I loved her and everything, but I didn't want her to stay with me if she wasn't into it. I didn't want to keep her from whatever life she thought she would have there, without me, if that's what she really wanted." Trey shakes his head and then takes off his batting gloves, twirling them in his fingers. "I didn't want her to resent me."

We're quiet for a moment before Trey hands me the gloves. "And I'm no one's second choice."

I squeeze the gloves in my hands. Walk slowly to the cage, wondering if Trey's watching me. Wondering if I want him to. And I think of Kale. Does he think I resent him? Is he my second choice?

———————

Kale calls late that night. He texted a few times when I was out, but I didn't respond. Finally, after having a night off from my problems, I feel like I can breathe again. I call Kale.

"Hey."

"How was canvassing?" he asks.

"It was fine." I don't elaborate.

"Fine? That's it?"

"Yeah, fine."

I know I'm being weird and distant but I can't bring myself to stop.

I change the subject. "How was your night?"

Kale starts talking about playing Candy Land with his

sisters. My thoughts turn to Trey. The way I feel seen when his honey-brown eyes look at me, without having to try so hard to explain what's on my mind.

"Victoria?"

How Trey looks in a baseball hat and athletic pants. The way his body moves when he hits a baseball.

"Are you there? Are you even listening to me?"

Kale's voice breaks through, loud and frustrated.

"Sorry, sorry," I sputter, heat rising in my chest. "It's been a long day. I'm tired, I think. Can we say goodnight now?'

Kale goes quiet for a long moment. "Sure," he finally says.

We tell each other I love you, our routine send-off, and say goodbye.

A few moments later, Kale texts me.

What's going on with you, Victoria? You hardly answer my texts. And now on the phone, it seemed like you weren't even listening to me.

I swallow. I told Ray I'd talk to Kale, like *really* talk to Kale, and try to get him to see how I'm feeling. But I'm so confused, now more than ever, and telling him that wouldn't help him feel any better. And I don't want to lie to him.

I just need some space to figure things out, I type.

The three dots appear and then disappear. Appear again, disappear. Finally, Kale's reply comes in.

Okay.

That's it.

My Kale nightmare returns that night, but the image of Kale walking away from me turns into my dad, behind bars. Reaching for me.

I run but feel a hand grab my shoulder. I turn to see who it is but wake with a start. Tears stream down my cheeks.

A week passes with no word from Kale. But I guess I haven't texted or called him, either, so I can't really blame him. Christina has texted, checking up on me, and I've given her short responses.

I'm fine.

Don't worry about me.

And then when she asks me what's going on with me and Kale, since clearly he's told her we're not talking at the moment, she asks why I'm ignoring him.

People change. Maybe we've grown apart. I don't know, I need to figure it out.

I need to focus on school, on club stuff.

There's one message I type and delete, over and over, without ever sending. *How's Kale?*

I delete it, one more time. Tonight, I need to focus on the walk, seeing Audrey. Figuring out what to do about her and my dad. Then I can deal with the rest of the garbage fire that is my life.

I text Sarah and Tiffany to let them know I invited Audrey to the walk. She wanted to see me, and I thought it would be a good place to show her why we should support victims.

Tiffany replies, *I understand why you did that, Victoria, but I hope you understand why Sarah and I will no longer be attending.*

My breath catches, panic barging in. Quickly, I type a reply. *I'm sorry, I didn't even think about that. I will uninvite her. I'd much rather have you two there.*

I hold my breath as I read Tiffany's response. She says she and Sarah aren't willing to risk it, since Audrey might still show up. *We love and support you*, Tiffany writes, *but we have to protect our own emotional health as well.*

Sarah doesn't reply at all.

I slam my phone down on the coffee table next to me.

I hate feeling helpless. Hate it. It feels like the world is spinning out of my control and I'm desperately trying to hold on. But I'm not helpless, or I don't want to be. I want to be strong. For Sarah, for women like Rosa at the shelter, for me.

I open my computer and type out what the club means to me so Jasmine can show it to the school president. We aren't a *man-hating* club. We have guys in the club, but that's not the point. The point is to be a safe place to support survivors and to educate our community about rape culture and what each of us can do to stop it. We can stop it.

We have to.

CHAPTER
FIFTEEN

The day of the walk, Trey and Lana pick me up, and we head to the park together about an hour before everything is set to start. Trey pops his trunk open, and Lana and I help him unload the hamburger patties and buns, along with all the other food he got from Costco for the barbecue we're having when walkers finish.

Jasmine's at a table, the sun glistening on her bare arms as she shows off one of the custom SASAH shirts she ordered for walkers. She moves a pile of shirts out of the way for us to drop off the food and then flips around so we can see the back of her light blue shirt. *Walk now for a safer future.*

Virginia Lake glitters behind her, a few ducks paddling on the water. Lana and I will lead club members and other walkers around the one-mile loop, while Jasmine and Trey cook the food. It'll be ready when we get back.

Jasmine grabs a shirt and looks at its tag. "Size small should work for you, right?" She tosses me the shirt. I quickly take my sweater off and put the shirt on over my tank top.

Lana flips through the shirts and then grabs one in her size, putting it on over her long-sleeve black T-shirt.

Trey grabs one for himself and does the same. "Club members should get here in about twenty. Then, say, fifteen after one, you give your speech, right, Jasmine?"

Jasmine stands up straighter and then begins, "It's not

244

enough to not sexually harass and assault people. We have to help those who are abused, unless we want to be complicit." Our club president puts on faux bravado, lifting her chin and reaching her arms out. "And don't forget to use the hashtag when you show all your followers how much of an activist you are, because if no one sees it online, are you really helping at all?"

Lana grimaces. After losing a few club members, we've really amped up SASAH's social media presence to try to recruit members. It's clear by some of the responses that some people are only in it for the hashtag.

"Oh, what it would be like if only more than half the people show up because they actually give a shit." Lana hangs her head, looking defeated. A little piece of my heart breaks. I'd rather see her angry than sad.

Trey puts a hand on Lana's shoulder. "Money is money. If it means more beds for the shelter, who cares if people are here to show off? More families will have a safe place to sleep at the end of the day. That's what we're here for."

Lana and I both sigh as a couple cars pull into the parking lot.

"That'll be Candace, Tara, and Lance with the signs," Jasmine says. "It's showtime."

We set up big bright SASAH signs at the front of the park and at different places letting people know where to leave their cars, as well as where the walk starts and ends. Trey and Lance blow up balloons to tie to the signs, while Lana, Candace, and I take the extra poster boards and write stats about sexual violence on them. We add them to the signs we collected from school, the ones with the stories of some of the women from the shelter—except for those we suspect Blake took down and probably tossed in the dumpster.

Jasmine's got the credit card reader up and running on an iPad for people who want to make donations and pledges today. Tara hands out SASAH shirts to people as they approach. Before we know it, we've got a crowd of more than one hundred people gathered, including a couple workers from the shelter.

I look around; there are so many more people here than I expected. "Wow," I breathe, "nice turnout."

Lana grins. "Well, not to brag, but I blogged about it. I've gotten a ton more interest online lately, people following me as I write about the Blake saga."

"Hashtag humble brag," Trey chuckles.

I laugh, but it quickly turns into a grimace. "Shoot, we didn't bring a microphone, did we?" I ask Lana.

"That shitty thing that never works during club meetings?" Candace mutters. "No, we'd rather skip the embarrassment. And now that we've been denied club funding for next year, I doubt we'll be able to get another one."

Trey puts an arm around me and Candace. "Jasmine is going to meet with the president next week, with all the good work we'll do today to talk about. Don't count us out yet."

Jasmine looks around and sighs. "I sent an email to the president inviting him to attend today. I thought maybe if he saw for himself the important work we do . . ." she trails off. "But I don't see him."

As more people gather, Jasmine steps on top of the picnic

bench to address the crowd. She thanks everyone for coming, including members of the community and SASAH activists and our families, and says we are lucky enough to have the executive director of the shelter join us, along with a woman who has been helped by its services. Karen and Rosa, I see, are striding in our direction.

Karen, dressed in a tailored suit, walks past the crowd. She doesn't join Jasmine atop the bench but stands in front of it.

"Thank you all for coming," she begins, reaching a hand for Rosa to join her. Rosa smiles at me, her lips shaded bright red and the rest of her makeup on point, and I wave before Karen continues. "We can't tell you enough how much we appreciate the time and money given to support our shelter. Instead of listing all the stats about why it's needed in our community, I think it would be more powerful for you to hear it from the source, one of our clients." She puts an arm around Rosa. Everyone here might see a slight woman with long, shiny black hair, her brown eyes wide, but I know better. I see a warrior. I see a survivor.

"This is my friend who we will call Martina." Karen nods to Rosa, who understandably is choosing to keep her identity private. "She's been staying with us for several weeks. After overcoming what seemed like insurmountable obstacles, Martina and her children are thriving. She has found a job as a receptionist at a beauty salon while she's in school learning how to become an aesthetician."

Rosa lifts her head and tells the group her story. We listen to her talk about the beatings and how she thought she had no options but to stay since she didn't have a job or a way to support her children. I listen to the familiar story. A tear slips down my cheek as Rosa explains to the crowd the final assault she and her children suffered and how they slept on a park bench, huddled together with nothing but jackets for warmth, the first night they escaped their abuser. That is, until a jogger found them early the next morning and told them about the shelter. I smile, knowing that jogger was Karen.

Rosa's eyes gleam, shiny with unshed tears. "Not only did the shelter help me press charges and get a protective order against my abuser, they also set me up with job training and helped me get a job. They gave us a recommendation and the money to pay first and last month's rent on our own apartment. We move in next week!"

Cheers resound all around us. I look behind me, at the large crowd wearing the blue SASAH shirts we passed out, and my eyes land on Audrey. She's sticking out amid the sea of blue, wearing jeans and a gray sweatshirt, with a SASAH shirt on top, far less dressed up than I've seen her before. She smiles at my half-hearted wave.

After Rosa's story, Jasmine thanks everyone again, and tells them to follow Lana and me. We wave from the front, and the walk starts. Lana and I snap pictures of the people strolling behind us and upload them to Instagram and Twitter as we go. Lance, Candace, and Tara join us up front and the rest of the walk goes by quickly, us chatting and laughing with friends.

"We're back!" Lana plops herself on the picnic bench

where Trey has organized the condiments and plastic utensils. Jasmine uses her forearm to wipe the sweat off her brow before stacking more burgers on a plate.

People start piling in behind us. I spot a few other SASAH kids, their friends, and some of their family members. Audrey, at the back of the group, makes eye contact with me. I haven't talked to her since she got here, but I guess now is as good a time as any.

"I'll be right back."

Lana gives me a look before I go. I pointed out Audrey to her during the walk. She sets a hand on my forearm, and I mouth *thanks.*

Audrey's smiling at me, several feet away from some TMCC students I don't know who are standing in a group, chatting.

"What a great turnout!" Audrey says. "This is really something."

I thank her and wait.

Audrey shifts, seemingly uncomfortable. She gestures to the glistening lake behind us. "My goodness, you couldn't have picked a more beautiful day. If you don't mind, I'm going to take this off."

I nod, and Audrey takes her SASAH shirt off, followed by her gray sweatshirt, revealing a tailored salmon-colored blouse.

"Much better." She looks around. "Can we go somewhere to talk? Alone?"

I lead Audrey a few hundred feet, back on the walking

path around the lake, until we get to an empty bench. We sit next to a tree whose purple leaves are falling off.

"I love autumn." Audrey picks up a leaf that recently fell near her foot. "It's my favorite season. What's yours?"

I think about that. It used to be summer, when Dad and Tiffany would take Sarah and me to Lake Tahoe and we'd play beach volleyball. Volleyball was my mom's favorite sport; she taught me how to play.

"Spring, I guess," I say, without thinking about it much. "When things are new, and there are more possibilities."

Audrey smiles but it doesn't reach her eyes. "I know your father put you in an uncomfortable position by asking you what he did. And I'm afraid I'm here to do the same thing."

Audrey's mouth puckers and I know whatever's coming isn't going to be good. I hold my breath.

"This isn't how I expected our relationship to go. I wanted to get to know you, not to make this about Jeffrey. I didn't want to make any of the mistakes my parents made." Her voice breaks. "I just don't know what to do."

A shrieking laugh makes me flinch. I turn to see a girl from the walk running from a boy. Flirting. Trey catches my eye and takes a cautious step toward us. I shake my head no.

When I turn back to Audrey, she's crying, tears slipping down her flushed cheeks.

"What is it?" I ask, my words clipped. "Please, just get it over with."

"Your father," she croaks, "he isn't doing well in county. Someone somehow found out what he's accused of, and well . . . child abusers, specifically those who're like your father, aren't treated well by other inmates."

Audrey's sobbing now. She pulls a handkerchief out of her purse and wipes her eyes. "I'm so sorry. This isn't your fault. But he's getting beaten every day. When I saw him last, his face was purple, swollen. And it's only going to get worse after his sentencing, if . . . if . . ." Audrey sniffs. "What he did, it was terrible, unforgivable. But"—Audrey chokes on a sob—"*he's still my brother.*"

"Victoria!" Lana's voice calls behind me. I'm frozen to my seat.

"Please," Audrey begs, her eyes frantic as she looks at Lana and then back at me. "Consider saying that he didn't kiss you in the impact statement. You could say he tried and that you got away or Tiffany walked in just before. I hate myself for asking, but if they give him more leniency in his charges, maybe he won't have to suffer like we have while he's in prison."

"Come on over here!" Lana calls, waving at me. "Trey's giving a speech!"

I look back at my aunt, this broken woman, and I see my face in her watery eyes. Stricken. Afraid.

I have to focus on my breath for a second. Of all places, Audrey's here, at a walk to raise awareness about sexual assault and harassment. A walk I worked so hard to make happen. My friends are waiting behind me, waiting to celebrate with me. Yet here is my aunt, asking me to help my abuser. She's completely missed the point. Or is ignoring it.

I'm leaning toward the edge of the bench, wanting to get away from Audrey, to be with my friends. But can I really blame her for what she's asking me? She's motivated by wanting to protect someone she loves, someone she feels at least partially responsible for.

Audrey's scared for my dad. And now I'm imagining every violent scene from prison movies and what I learned from the documentaries I watched about being locked up after Dad went to jail. I'm squeezing my eyes shut to keep tears from coming.

"I have to go." I stand. "I'll think about it."

Audrey nods, her face relaxing, clearly relieved.

I blink several times, looking around at all these kids from school who are here. Waiting on me. I jog to the picnic table. Once I'm there, Trey stands on it.

"Now that we're all here, I want to thank everyone for coming and supporting our walk for raising awareness about sexual harassment and assault and raising money for the family shelter." Trey starts clapping. "Give yourselves a hand."

After the applause dies down, Trey continues. "I want to thank Jasmine Price for all of her hard work. This club wouldn't be what it is without our fearless leader. So, let's hear it for Jasmine!" Trey starts clapping again, and we all follow suit. "Thank you also to my favorite pain in the—well, you know where—our club secretary, Lana." He grins at Lana and she gives him an exaggerated eye roll back.

"She keeps us all focused, which is a big part of why this day has been such a success," Trey continues.

The group claps again, and Lana calls out, "So far, we've raised six grand from donations and pledges from canvassing and from this walk! So, give *yourselves* a round of applause," Lana tells the crowd. "It's because of you that our support isn't just in the form of words but is actually meaningful. It's going to change the lives of people in need. Woo!"

My eyes widen at Lana—I hadn't heard the final count of donations yet—and she nods in confirmation. Six thousand dollars. Wow. The crowd goes wild, clapping, shouting. Audrey's in the back, I notice, and she's clapping too. Once I make eye contact with her, she turns for the parking lot. Her car beeps as it unlocks.

Trey, still standing above me on the bench, shouts over the crowd. "There's one special person who has really invigorated our efforts with her arrival." Trey reaches a hand toward me, like he wants me to stand up there with him. My face flushes, and I shake my head no.

Trey chuckles. "Our newest member, Victoria, joined the club this semester and hit the ground running. She's visited the women's and family shelter and heard the stories of those it helps, and she's made sure others know about them too. She's canvassed and really gotten the people she's spoken with to care about our cause, raising a hell of a lot of donations. She's reminded me why I do what I do. That this is important work and that it's an honor to do it. So, thank you to our newest member, Victoria Parker."

I smile and study my hands as the crowd claps for me. For what I've done. I put my time toward something positive, helping others through this walk and through SASAH. What happened to me didn't crush me.

I'm not a victim.

I look back at the parking lot, but Audrey's gone.

CHAPTER
SIXTEEN

I wake up with sweat sticking my hair to my neck, sheets tangled around my legs, and tears in my eyes. I dreamed of Dad, in prison, circled by angry men. Ready to make him pay for what he did to me.

The blue light of my phone hurts my eyes as I text Audrey, not caring that it's two a.m. I tell her I'll write in my victim impact statement that Dad did attack me that night; I won't lie about that. I'll say he tried to kiss me but nothing more. I'll say I forgive him and want them to be lenient in sentencing. That I don't think he's a danger to anyone else.

The next morning, I check my messages. Audrey has thanked me. She's told me how grateful she is. Bile rises in my throat. After everything I went through last year, everything I learned, it feels like I'm back where I started: protecting Dad.

But this isn't the same. He won't ever be allowed to see Sarah again, and I don't want to see him either. I just don't want him hurt. Not after he suffered so much when he was a kid. This is compassion. Not covering for him.

It's not the same thing.

Is it?

But when I take out my notebook and stare at a blank page, I can't bring myself to write my statement. I hold the pen and stare at blue-lined paper for a long time, before I shove it away.

I get a text from Jess later, asking how I'm doing. I tell her everything is great. Our walk was a success. I wish she could have come, I write, and I suggest we get coffee some-time soon. I don't mean it, and I know it, just as much as I know she doesn't mean it when she says she'd love to meet up after mid-terms when things are less stressful.

My childhood best friend and I have moved on. We're different people now. I am, at least, since I moved away from my past life living with Dad, with Jess as my best and only friend at my old school in Reno. Since I went into foster care in Silver Valley. I don't even care that much about my upcoming tests, not like Jess says she does. I love school and learning, like I told Trey. I study and do my homework, but I'm not going to stress about it any more than that. There's not enough space in my head with everything else going on.

How much things have changed for me when school was my lifeline. The thing that kept me going. Now, it's the club.

Lana is in a mood Tuesday evening at the SASAH meet-ing. She attacks the broken microphone behind Jasmine's po-dium with a fervor Candace couldn't come close to. Banging it on the podium, shaking it, yanking the plug in and out of the socket.

"What's with her?" I nudge Trey with my elbow. He's sitting next to me again, rather than up front with Jasmine.

"Just more Blake shit," Lana answers my question for him. "He had a lawyer send me a threatening note to take my blog down."

I gasp. Lana shakes her head. "I'm not going to do it. I'll get a lawyer, too, if I have to. My parents said they'd help me."

My stomach sinks. If he's going after Lana's blog, he might start telling people the truth about me and my dad. He said if I didn't back down, he would out my secret. I don't blame myself for what Dad did to me anymore, but that doesn't mean I want everyone at school to know. That doesn't mean it's not humiliating.

But I can't think about that. Because what can I do? Stop trying to help the club fight back against people like Blake and those who support them? There's no way.

Jasmine congratulates us all for raising record-breaking funds during the walk. She's still waiting for an update from the shelter, but it's safe to say the money we raised will go a long way toward funding the extra wing to house additional families.

"Equally as important," Jasmine says, her big brown eyes gleaming, "is that we raised awareness about sexual assault in the community and the need for us to do something about it." She pulls a newspaper from her backpack. "The *Reno Times* wrote a news story about our walk, and online they set up a link to a donation page for the shelter!" Jasmine's smiling big now as she claps her hands together. "Give yourselves a hand, everyone. *We did that!*"

After the meeting, as Lance, Candace, and the others clear out, Jasmine makes eye contact with me. "Can you three hang back a minute?" She looks at Lana and then Trey. "There's something we should talk about."

"Of course," Trey says.

Jasmine walks to the door and closes it before turning back to us. "I didn't say anything during the meeting because I didn't want to bring everyone down. What we did with canvassing and the walk is incredible, and I'm proud of us for that."

Lana's eyes narrow at Jasmine. "You're starting to scare me."

Jasmine swallows. "The school president and I met yesterday afternoon. He said he won't intervene. Ross's stupid order to not fund us next year stands."

"What?" Trey and I say in unison. And then I blurt, "That's not fair."

Jasmine shakes her head, words seeming to fail her.

Lana's jaw works furiously, her fists balled. But she says nothing. That worries me more than anything.

Jasmine paces the room. "I looked up the president online. Travis Johnson. And well, I found out he was in the same fraternity as Blake's dad at UNR when they were in school." She stops in front of us. "I found pictures of their families vacationing together on his Instagram."

Jasmine sinks into an open chair on the other side of me. "How could I have been so stupid?"

I put a hand on Jasmine's shoulder. "It's not your fault."

Trey agrees. "Them being family friends . . . it shouldn't matter. The school president shouldn't let it matter."

Lana scoffs. "It shouldn't, but it does."

"What do we do?" I ask.

Jasmine takes a long while before answering. "I don't think there's anything we can do, except raise the money ourselves. Or charge club members dues."

Lana groans. "We're losing support as it is with Blake and his stupid antics. And people shouldn't have to pay money to be in a club like ours. It's not right!"

Jasmine's eyes turn down. "You're right. I just don't know what choice we have."

Lana is about to reply when I cut in.

"Let's all just think about this, brainstorm solutions, and get together when we have a few that we can present to the club." I look at each of them. "Lana's right, we have lost members. We want to make sure we don't lose more."

Jasmine's shoulders slump, like she's defeated already.

"It'll be all right," Trey tells her.

The four of us walk out together, and Jasmine waves half-heartedly as she heads for the parking lot.

Angry tears fill Lana's eyes.

I move forward, slowly, as if to hug her, and she lets me.

Lana sighs heavily before pulling away. "Coffee?"

Trey, Lana, and I sit in our usual chairs in the hallway once we get our drinks. Lana rails about Blake for a while but then looks at me abruptly and says, "Wait, I completely forgot. How did it go with your aunt-lady? I never got the chance to talk to you after the walk, but you seemed pretty upset when you two were talking at the barbecue."

Trey's eyes meet mine. I haven't told him what happened either.

I run my thumb against the lid of my coffee cup. "She told me my dad's been getting beat up in jail." I keep my eyes on my cup. "She said someone found out about what he's accused of, and he's been getting attacked for it. Mostly just punches so far, but she thinks it might eventually turn into . . ." I cough, squeeze my eyes shut. "Well, you know."

Silence. I open my eyes, and Lana and Trey are both staring at me.

Lana reaches a hand out to mine, pulling it away from my cup and squeezing it. "It's not your fault, Victoria. And anyway, karma's a bitch."

I know I told Audrey I'd write a plea for my dad in my statement, but I realize now I was tired, upset from my nightmare. I want to talk to someone from the DA's office first. I would have asked Tiffany to ask a few questions for me, if they wouldn't give away what I *might be* planning to do. But I've been avoiding Tiffany and Sarah. I didn't go to family dinner the day after they didn't show at the walk, or the time before that. The distance between Sarah and me when I told her I saw Audrey has only grown.

I chew on my lip. "I'm going to talk to the DA, ask about what effect my victim impact statement might have," I say. "I'm not going to lie. I'm just thinking about asking for leniency. After what he's done to me, I won't be around him, and neither will my stepsister. So, he isn't a threat to us."

Lana's eyebrows shoot to the top of her forehead. "You can't be serious." She looks at me, her eyes hard, but when I don't respond she glances at Trey. "She's joking, right?"

Candace and Lance enter the hallway. Lance heads toward the meeting room. "Forgot my backpack," he says.

"Hey, why weren't we invited to this party?" Candace smiles, sliding into Lana's chair, scooching herself on and Lana half off, oblivious to our conversation.

Lana snaps, "Victoria, why don't you tell Candace, another member of a club against sexual assault and harassment, what you're planning to do? Tell her how you're going to speak on your child-molesting dad's behalf to the DA."

I blink. Lana is just going to throw my secret out there—something I've trusted her with—to Candace without a thought?

Trey's eyes pop, and Candace almost falls out of Lana's seat. Lance walks out at that moment, heading in our direction. He looks at Lana and then me, before taking a half step back. "Uh, did I miss something?"

Trey sucks in a breath, ignoring Lance's question. "Lana, don't." Trey's words come out slowly, as he looks back at me. "It's not anyone else's business."

Lana hits her hands on the table. "Un. Fucking. Believable."

I blink several times. Take a breath to try to calm down, so I can get Lana to see reason. "I get it, I get why you're mad—"

"Why are you even in this club, then? Do you even mean half the shit that comes out of your mouth?"

Candace slides off the seat, standing, looking stricken. "Your dad is a child molester and you're going to stick up for him?"

Lance's mouth purses, staring between Candace and me.

Something about Candace's posture, how her shoulders slump almost to make herself seem smaller, makes me want to reach out for her. But I don't.

"My dad hurt me," I say, measured, mad that I have to defend myself. "And I told the police, and he's in jail now. But he's being . . . he's in danger there. I'm not going to lie. I'm just going to . . ." I trail off. "Maybe if I say I forgive him, that it wasn't that bad—"

"That's bullshit," Candace says. "People do fucked up stuff all the time and *they get away with it.* Like my ex who date-raped me when I was too drunk to say no. But I didn't have proof, so he's walking free. Your dad's in jail, great! You can actually get justice. Not all of us are so lucky!" She grabs Lance's arm and yanks him with her. "You're my ride and there's no way I'm staying for a minute more of this."

Lance looks at me uncomfortably. "I'm sorr—"

"Don't apologize to her," Candace spits. "She's the one who's a traitor. She's the one who should be sorry."

My heart breaks as Candace rushes away, with Lance behind her. Lana turns her angry stare back to me. "Let's just let our abusers off. Let's just all do that, shall we?" she snaps. She pushes her chair back, and it topples over as she stands. "Do whatever the hell you want, Victoria; I can't stop you. Just don't expect me or Trey or anyone else to support you. We're in a freaking club to stop sexual harassment and assault for fuck's sake."

Lana stomps away before I get the chance to reply.

I watch her leave, my chest crunching in, before someone coughs, announcing himself, behind me. I turn and gasp as

I see the two worst possible people to have overhead this conversation. Blake and Ross. No Melanie. I rack my brain. I haven't seen her hanging around the men's rights club in a while, I realize.

"Trouble in paradise?" Blake smirks.

Trey stands. "Not the time, Blake. Not that it ever is with you."

Blake laughs and turns to Ross.

Ross's characteristic ease isn't with him. He grimaces. "We should go," Ross says.

Rather than stop to think about what Ross and Blake did or didn't overhear, I go on the offense. "Where's Melanie?" I look directly at Ross. "I haven't seen her around in a while."

Ross blinks but doesn't say anything.

"That's why she dropped our club?" Blake scowls at me. "You man-hating bitches talk her into it?"

Not even Blake's insults can keep me from smiling, really smiling. "She quit? Good. That means she sees what you really are, what all of you are, for supporting such a"—I glare at Blake—"*disgusting* cause."

Blake lifts his chin, staring down at me. "Don't change the subject. We heard what you guys were talking about before. Sounds like you don't put your money where your mouth is, Valerie."

"It's Victo—" Trey starts, but I silence him with a look.

I've faced much worse than Blake, and I won't let him intimidate me. "If you think you can scare me into dropping out of the club, you're wrong."

"We'll see," Blake says.

I let out a breath as they leave. *What did they hear?* Not that it matters. Blake says he already knows enough about me that I wouldn't want him to. Maybe it was someone from my old school; maybe his dad knows a blabby cop. It doesn't matter how he knows, just that he does. And that he'd use my past to hurt me.

Trey returns to his seat. He leans toward me, speaking softly so if anyone else is around, they hopefully won't be able to hear. "Look, Victoria, I meant what I said. This is your business, but do you think you might want to reconsider?"

I open my mouth to argue but Trey continues, reaching his hand on the table closer to mine. "I get it, I really do. Intergenerational abuse—it's real. Your dad was abused. You feel bad for him, but that doesn't make it right to pretend like nothing happened."

"I'm not," I cut him off, my blood pressure rising. "I'm just, I don't know. You wouldn't understand."

Trey scoffs, sitting up in his seat. "I would, actually. You know that."

I open my mouth to apologize, because of course he's right.

Trey rises slowly, slinging his bag over his back. "It's your call, obviously. Lana should get that, but maybe she'll need some time." His voice softens. "Either way, you don't have to decide right now."

I called the DA's office this morning to set up an appointment. But I'm not telling Trey that. "I guess I'll see you around."

Trey sighs. "Want a ride home?"

"No, thanks." I blink back a few tears. "I'll take the bus. I want to be alone."

I might as well get used to it.

And I do. Get used to the silence, that is. No word from Kale; he's giving me the space I asked for. Part of me thought maybe he'd come to the walk to support me anyway, but I guess I can't blame him for not doing so. No texts or calls from Sarah or Tiffany. Nothing from Lana. Trey checks in on me, but I don't really know what to say to him.

A couple of days after my blowup with Lana, I'm sitting across from a woman in a conference room at the district attorney's office. There's a pitcher of water between us. Her name is Kelly, she told me as she invited me to sit across from her. She looks like she might be in her thirties, and she's well put together. Not a hair out of place; nails perfectly painted. Kelly pulls her pencil skirt down. A legal notepad is on her knees, the yellow of the paper contrasting with the black of her nylons. The folder with my dad's information in it lies open on the table, but I can't read it upside down.

"You said you wanted to talk about what to write for your victim impact statement. You have some questions." Kelly brings the folder to her lap, away from my prying eyes. "It says here that your father, Jeffrey Parker, assaulted you on the night of . . ."

I stop listening because I'm back in my room, that night when dad *assaulted* me. His eyes are angry and red, his mouth turned in a grimace. The whiskey on his breath burns my nostrils. His hands grope my pajama pants, before his fingers dip into them, probing relentlessly as I try to fight back, his other hand on my throat, squeezing.

I blink. I'm back in the fluorescent light of this office, with Kelly watching me.

"Miss Parker," she says, "are you all right?"

I swallow, fumble for the glass in front of me and pour some water into it. Feel the condensation wet on my hands but don't lift the glass to my lips. "Look, it's true that my dad attacked me that night. And he . . . but I think . . ." Tears start to well up, and I'm stammering. My phone buzzes and I grab it, grateful for the distraction. Until I see that it's Tiffany. I hit the dismiss button and push it away from me, sliding the phone on the table.

"Take your time," Kelly says softly before jotting down some notes.

I swallow again. My throat feels raw. After the missed call, a text appears on my phone. From my stepmother.

Your aunt emailed me.

I avoid Kelly's concerned stare and grab the phone to read the rest of the message.

She asked if she could talk to me about Sarah's statement. She told me you are going to tell the district attorney's office what happened with your dad wasn't as big of a deal as you made it seem. I know this can't be true. You wouldn't do that to Sarah. I can't believe that you would lie about everything that you two went through to get here. What is going on?

I shove my phone in my bag, shaking my head. Of course

Tiffany would be upset, but I hadn't thought she'd find out like this. And Sarah. *Sarah.*

I see Sarah that day I tried to help her escape Dad. Her fear, how she trembled at the sight of him. How she screamed.

I remember holding her all the times we've talked about our nightmares. The way we remember what Dad did during waking dreams too. He's everywhere, still, even though he's locked up.

"I . . . I can't," I breathe, and then a sob comes out. I grab my bag. "I'm so sorry." I run from the conference room, not stopping when I hear Kelly call my name. I rush past the cubicles, where lawyers stare at me from their desks. I run from the DA's office, past other gray government buildings, bumping a man with a briefcase as he tries to walk past me on the sidewalk. "Hey!" he shouts as his briefcase falls to the ground, papers spewing onto the street. I don't stop. I'm running, running, running, but I don't know where I can run to without my dad finding me.

CHAPTER
SEVENTEEN

I text Tiffany to tell her I didn't tell the DA's office anything. She wants to know what's going on, but I tell her I can't. Not that I can't talk now. Or I'll explain later. Just *I can't*.

I can't.

My phone rings. She's calling. I don't answer.

I stare at my phone, mind racing. How can I help Dad, keep him from being beat up and probably even *raped* in jail, if doing so will hurt Sarah? If doing so will hurt me?

Please don't tell Sarah, I finally text Tiffany back. She responds that she won't as long as I explain myself. I tell her I will, but I need time.

To breathe.

To figure this out.

I sit at my small kitchen table, the two-seater Tiffany bought for me before I started school, and open my laptop. Maybe I can type the damn thing rather than write it in that stupid notebook.

So, I type. The words *Victim Impact Statement* stare at me from the mostly blank screen.

My dad hurt me, my fingers clack at the keys. *But he didn't—*

I slam my laptop shut. Heat rushes to my face, my ears pounding.

I open my computer again and close the file, instead

clicking on some English homework. I can't focus on Dad. Audrey texts me to ask how I'm doing with my statement. I ignore her messages.

Homework keeps me occupied for about an hour before I get another message. I almost don't bother to look at it because I'm tired of feeling like a disappointment to everyone, but Trey's name catches my eye.

He's calling, I realize.

"Hey." I hold the phone to my ear, surprised he didn't text me.

"Victoria," Trey breathes. Something is wrong; I can tell by the tone of his voice. "I . . . I'm sorry . . ." He hesitates. "Blake wrote about what's going on with you and your dad on Twitter . . ."

The pounding in my ears returns ten-fold. I can't hear what Trey is saying. I can't breathe.

I gasp. "What . . ." I don't finish my sentence, though, because I'm bringing up Twitter on my laptop. Blake's posted a thread with pictures of notes from his phone. *SASAH club eating itself,* it says. *Club secretary Lana Tyler turns on newest member Victoria Parker.*

At first, I almost want to laugh. Blake knows my name is Victoria and not Valerie after all. But I realize the laugh bubbling up is me turning hysterical, because none of this is funny. "I gotta go," I tell Trey, ignoring his pleas for me to wait as I hang up to read the rest of the post.

You thought the so-called Students Against Sexual Assault and Harassment had enough drama surrounding it? What, with members spreading false accusations that can't be proven, with them being called out on campus as being a man-hating group? Well, you'd be wrong, friends. Victoria Parker, TMCC freshman and SASAH member, is planning to tell the district attorney her father didn't assault her last year because she's afraid of the treatment he'll get in prison for being a child molester.

One might think this is her business, and it is.

My eyes are full of tears. It is my business to share or not to, but Blake doesn't care. He's doing this to hurt me, to hurt the club. My hands are shaking, but I keep reading the next note on his Twitter thread.

Victoria's BFF Lana—the girl behind the "Patriarchy Pounder" blog that allows disgruntled people who've been rejected to call rape—seems to disagree. Seems Lana is fine running the libelous so-called whisper network for students to accuse people of sexual assault or harassment, without any proof, but not with her friend telling her truth to the district attorney.

My stomach clenches.

I continue to read. *Well, Lana's at it again, it seems. Because word on the street is she and a few other SASAH members are hosting a rally to encourage victims to not protect their so-called abusers. Sounds like a load of horseshit to me. If they can't keep it together even within their own club, how can the school allow them to keep up their antics on campus? Defunding them is not enough. #BanSASAH*

My mouth falls open. Blake's been retweeted hundreds of times.

My phone buzzes with another text. This one is from Lana.

Saw what Blake tweeted. Victoria, are you okay?

My hand shakes as I start to answer. *Is it true, Lana? Are you hosting a rally about me?*

The three dots show Lana is typing. But then they stop. I hold my breath. The three dots reappear.

I haven't told anyone about you. It's about survivors. It's why I'm in this club, to spread the word about how we shouldn't perpetuate rape culture. It's not my fault Blake—

I stop reading Lana's message. Red heat pounds in my ears, my face, my chest. I turn the phone off, rather than throw it across the room.

I grab a pillow and scream into it until my throat is raw. Throw the covers over my head and stay there, crying all night, drifting in and out of nightmares starring Dad in my bedroom coming for me or Dad in prison with faceless men coming for him.

———

Nevada Day is next week, which means a three-day weekend. Everyone else is getting ready to celebrate the time off, while I sulk. Ray texts me a few times. I don't answer the first few texts until he calls and I finally message him back. I lie and tell him I'm swamped with homework. I don't want to bring him down when he's so happy.

It's easy enough ignoring Lana, as I now sit far away from her in our shared classes. I haven't returned any of her texts, but since I haven't heard anything about a rally happening, maybe she changed her mind. I can't bring myself to ask her though. During bio, I stare at the back of Lana's head. She's wearing the same Princess Leia hairstyle I saw her in that first time we hung out in the library. It feels like ages, but it hasn't even been two months.

Trey turns to look around, probably searching for me, as the teacher's assistant hands his row a stack of blue books for the test. I duck down as his eyes land on me. Trey's face falls, as he realizes I'm hiding. His eyes search mine for a moment until the TA is on my row and the person beside me hands me a blue book.

After the class period, I head for the door, feeling fine about the test. I don't spend too much time outside of class studying, not like last year when that's all I could do to feel like I had control over my life. It's not really necessary at TMCC, or at least it hasn't been for me. If I show up to class, pay attention for the most part, and take notes, I do fine. School is fine. Everything is fine.

I'm fine. Maybe if I keep telling myself that, it'll be true.

"Victoria!" A hand grabs my shoulder and I flinch. But it's Trey, I realize, when I turn around.

Trey grimaces. "Look, sometimes Lana can be a piece of work, I'll admit that, but her heart is in the right place. What with what happened with her old best friend, it really did a number on—"

"Fine, Trey." I sneer. Because why is he defending Lana to me? "I get it."

I stomp away, grateful that Trey doesn't follow me.

I call Christina that night. She doesn't answer.

Thinking of you, I text her.

I pull up some old pictures on my phone and land on one of my favorites. Kale's arm is around me, and we look happy. His piercing blue eyes seem to smile as big as the rest of his face.

Maybe I should call Kale. Tell him I've been a jerk and I'm sorry. He'll ask why I needed space in the first place, though, and I can't tell him it's because he doesn't get what's going on with me and my dad and I'm tired of everyone telling me how to feel and what to do about it.

I can't tell him I was mad at him for having fun and living his life without me in Silver Valley. And I *really can't tell him* I was pulling away from him as I grew closer to Trey.

I shove my phone aside. When I ignored Ray's messages, he couldn't exactly walk down the stairs to check up on me. He's in Los Angeles checking out the office for the advertising company he wants to intern for after graduation. "Somewhere I can get my *Mad Men* on," he joked as he said goodbye before heading to the airport. Originally, he told me he wants to move to LA for a change of pace. "Because it's bigger, with more culture," he said to me even before Jake ever mentioned applying to law schools there. Of course, I want Ray to be happy, even though I'll miss him if they leave for good. Then I'll *really* have no one.

I pull up Blake's stupid Twitter thread and read it again like the masochist I am.

If I hadn't told Lana and Trey what was going on, Blake wouldn't have overheard Lana and me fighting, and maybe I wouldn't be in this mess. Because he already knew something about what happened with Dad and me and, for whatever reason, hadn't said anything about it. But Lana and me fighting was just too good of an opportunity for him to pass up. I snap my laptop shut, longing for the days when I didn't let people in, people who would only disappoint me.

Kale's face comes to mind and I shoot him a text on a whim. *I know I've been MIA, and I'm sorry. You deserve better.*

My phone buzzes. Kale's calling me. I suppress a sob and turn my phone off. Because hearing his voice will make me break down. Hearing and feeling his love for me and being afraid that it's not enough. Telling him how I feel won't fix things. It won't fix us.

When I turn my phone back on, there's a voicemail from Kale. His voice is strained, worried, and angry, I realize.

"Victoria," he says, "why are you doing this? To us? To me? This isn't how you treat people you love."

He's right, I think, putting my head in my hands. But I'm still not going to call him back.

Thursday after my last test, I'm about to leave campus when I get a text from Jasmine.

Lana and some other SASAH members are hosting a rally outside in front of the Student Center. I'm so sorry. I tried to stop them.

Dread fills my gut. I thought Lana had changed her mind. I rush through the double doors and race outside.

A group of around forty people stand on the grass, some holding signs recycled from the walk, the signs I wrote.

Candace holds a megaphone at her side, while Lana

shouts. I guess they gave up on a workable microphone. Several people stare as I approach.

"Victims should protect victims." Lana's voice strains on the last word. "Being an ally and being a survivor is more than just paying lip service to the things we talk about; it's about *doing* them. Activism isn't just to post online and look cool to your friends. It's about helping people."

Her eyes land on mine. I bite my lip to stop it from shaking. "That's why protecting abusers is wrong." She looks right at me. Heads start to turn. Angry stares follow.

Lana finally looks away and I gasp for breath. She starts to chant. "Victims not abusers. Victims not abusers."

Candace raises the bullhorn. "Victims not abusers," Candace chants and so does everyone around me.

I stare in shock. Candace is angry, and I get why. What happened to her is terrible. But I'm not the one who did it, and my not knowing what to do about my dad is not about her.

A swirl of black braids rushes to the front where Lana and Candace stand. Jasmine grabs the horn from Candace, shaking her head in disgust. "This is not how we do things," Jasmine shouts. "You should all be ashamed of yourselves!"

"Victims not abusers! Victims not abusers!" The crowd chants over Jasmine. Lana shrugs at her, before pumping her fist and chanting along.

Tears roll down my cheeks. I start as a finger taps my shoulder. I look and see long black hair and a worried face.

"Lance," I breathe.

Lance's voice comes out softer than I've ever heard it.

"Let's get you out of here," he says. He shakes his head at Candace and Lana. "I can't believe them."

I'm shaking as we reach the parking lot. "Can I give you a ride home?" Lance looks uncomfortable as I shake and sob in front of him. He drags a hand through his curly hair.

I hear running footsteps hit the pavement behind me and I turn, half expecting an angry mob, but it's only Trey. His mouth twists in a grimace. "She promised me and Jasmine she wouldn't go through with this."

He reaches for me, but I flinch away, wiping my tears off. "I'll take that ride home, Lance."

Lance opens the door for me, sparing an apologetic look at Trey.

Lance and I don't talk the entire ride to my place. Once in front of my building, Lance breaks the silence. "I'm . . . I don't know what to say." He shakes his head. "That sucks . . . Lana and Candace. That really sucks that they did that."

I try to make my voice sound stronger than I feel. "Thanks, Lance. You're a good guy."

I shut his car door behind me. Once I'm inside my apartment, I crumple to the floor. It's hours before I rise again.

———————————

I wake to the sound of my phone buzzing near my head on the couch. I didn't make it to bed once I finally got up from the floor.

It's Christina.

I wipe my eyes and answer. "Hey," I sniff.

"Are you okay?" Christina wastes no time. "I heard about Twitter."

I groan and heave myself up to a sitting position. "How?"

Christina inhales and pauses for what seems like a long time. I'm not quite ready for what she says next.

"Kale. He follows a hashtag about your club. He told me there are a bunch of comments about some rally that happened at school . . ." Her sentence ends as if it's a question.

I stare at my closed blinds, blocking out sunlight. It's dark in the apartment. I can't tell what time it is, how long I've been asleep for, or how long it's been since Lance drove me home from the rally.

"Why didn't Kale . . ." I trail off.

Christina sighs. "He wasn't sure if you'd want to hear from him."

And the floodgates open. I'm sobbing, clutching my side because it hurts all of a sudden. My chest throbs.

"Oh, Victoria," Christina whispers. "I'm so sorry."

"I am, too, Christina." I push through my tears. "I'm sorry about everything. About . . . about . . ."

"Shhh," Christina says. And though I'm not with her, I imagine my best friend waving an arm as if to dismiss my apology. "You have so much on your mind. I can't even imagine."

I cough and sputter. "It's not fine. Kale, Kale." A new flood of tears pours out. "I hurt him. I'm still hurting him, and I don't know why."

Christina is quiet again before she says, "Sometimes we push the people we love away when we're hurting."

"I don't know what to do, Christina."

"About what? The asshole who blasted you on Twitter? Those so-called friends of yours who put that rally on?" Christina's voice hardens.

I put my head in my hands. "No. I don't know what to do about my dad."

"Oh."

We're both quiet for a long time.

"I wish I were there to hug you," Christina says softly.

I squeeze my eyes shut, wanting that so badly too. "Who would think I'd actually miss last year? That I'd wish I was back in Silver Valley?"

But then a thought pops into my head. I know what I need to do, so I tell Christina.

"I'm going to Connie's."

CHAPTER
EIGHTEEN

Friday afternoon, Connie arrives at my front door. I called her and asked if I could come for the three-day weekend, and she said she'd pick me up.

Connie wraps me in her arms the second she's inside. "Girl, when I said don't be a stranger, I meant it. I'm so glad to see you." I let Connie hold me, sinking into her soft but tight embrace. Right now, I feel like there's nowhere safer than being wrapped in her arms. What a change a few months makes.

Connie pulls away and takes in my disheveled appearance. Her thin eyebrows furrow. "You haven't been eating enough. And," she pauses and sniffs, "you could use a shower."

I haven't exactly bothered to brush my teeth or put on deodorant since the rally.

Connie smiles at me. "I'll cook something. That your kitchen over there?" She nods behind me. "You go get cleaned up. I'll make you a sandwich or something."

After my shower, I find Connie sitting at the small dining room table. She shifts in her seat, which is a little small for her. "Come on and eat."

Connie slides a grilled cheese sandwich to my side of the table. "And tell me what's going on."

"No kids with you?" I change the subject.

Connie gives me the side eye as I sit and bite into my sandwich. "I left them at my mom's for respite care. Annie loves spending time with her grandma, and little Johnny likes getting to know her too."

Johnny is the six-year-old that Connie's working on fostering to adopt. She told me about him a couple months ago.

"What about the new girl—Lilly, right? The one you were short-term fostering who was missing her mom?"

Connie blinks, her expression pinched. "Baby girl has gone on to a more permanent placement. I knew it was going to happen, but I'll still hold a place in my heart for that little one. Annie's devastated she's gone. Never thought she would go from hating to share her room with another little girl, to loving her so much."

My eyes widen. That's a change I didn't expect to hear from Connie about her toddler who used to refer to Jamie, Lizzie, and me as "the foster kids," while treating us like servants.

"I'm sorry I had to miss your walk, though," Connie says.

Connie stares at me, likely waiting for me to explain myself.

"Thank you for coming," I say, my voice starting to shake. "I just, I'm going to tell you what happened, but I'm . . ." I don't want to cry right now. "Can we just drive and talk about it later?"

Connie nods, her face falling as she watches my lip tremble. I bite it, trying so hard to control myself.

"Sure thing, Victoria." She pats my back softly. "Let's getta move on then."

Once on the freeway, I stare out the window as a beam of sunlight cuts through the clouds, warming my face. Now that we're out of Reno, there's open space all around us. Hills, dirt, grass. Cattle and horses, grazing in their pens or pastures as we get closer to Silver Valley. Connie's front lawn is still yellowing but now missing the lawn gnome and some of the broken children's toys that were here last time I was. I think of how kids came and went while I lived here, first Lizzie, then Jamie, and me, Samantha not long after. The grass is still brittle and yellow, though.

It's strange being at my old foster home in Silver Valley, with no one here but Connie and me. With all other foster kids gone. Once inside, Connie tells me to get settled while she makes us some tea.

"You make tea?"

Connie rolls her eyes. "Just go drop your bag and meet me out here."

In the room, the dormitory as Connie used to call it, I stop. Because the two bunk beds are gone. Connie took a break from fostering when her home went under investigation after she lied to CPS to keep me out of trouble. She told my social worker she gave me permission to go see Sarah last year. I knew after the investigation cleared her that Connie still hasn't fostered much, other than an emergency placement here or there, but I didn't expect this.

Connie clears her throat behind me. I start. I wasn't expecting her in the doorway.

"This is Johnny's room now." She points to the bed in the corner, where Lizzie's bunk used to be. "Like I said, he's with Annie at my mom's, but he was happy to hear you'd be staying in his room. I told him all about you." She gestures to the bed. "I changed the sheets for you."

I drag my bag to the floor beside the bed and plop down. Without knowing why, I start crying. Hard.

Connie comes to my side, the bed sinking under our weight.

She wraps her arms around me. "Shhh, shhh." Connie squeezes my shoulders softly. "It's going to be all right, Victoria. It really is. I promise."

———————————

A few minutes later, we're both seated at the dining room table, tea in front of us.

"Chamomile." Connie nods at the mug in front of me. "To calm your nerves."

Steam rises from the mug as the tea steeps. I wrap my fingers around the handle and stare at it.

"Want to tell me what's going on now?"

"Kale," I begin, but then I stop, trying to figure out how to even explain any of this. "I've been pushing him away and now I've just about ghosted him."

Connie gives me a perplexed look at "ghosted" but doesn't say anything. "I don't even know where to start, maybe when my"—I make air quotes with my fingers—"'long-lost aunt' came into town, a woman I'd never known existed until recently. And she told me she and my dad were molested by their grandpa as kids and it messed them up, my dad especially."

Connie's eyes pop, round as saucers. But she doesn't ask why I didn't tell her before. Connie, better than anyone, knows how speaking these things aloud makes them feel real, and sometimes that's too much. Connie waits, listening.

I stare into the greenish brown of my tea and continue, because once I've started, the words come pouring out. "She wanted me to visit my dad in jail, and I did. I hoped he would apologize . . ." The tears are back now and I'm stammering. "But he really only asked me there because he wanted me to tell the DA that what he did wasn't as big of a deal as I made it, to ask them to go easy on his charges."

"Oh, Victoria." Connie reaches for my hand and holds it.

My hand trembles in hers. "And my aunt came to the walk, the fundraiser, and told me other inmates in jail found out what Dad did to me and they were beating him up every day. She said that it was only going to get worse, that . . . that . . ." I'm gasping for air now and I can't fill my lungs. Tears are pouring down my cheeks, into my mouth.

Connie scoots her chair closer to mine and puts her arm around me. "Breathe, girl. Breathe. In and out."

I inhale deeply, in through my nose, let it out through my mouth. Until my breath slows.

"I don't want him to get raped in there because of me," I whisper. And it's like a thousand shards of glass cut my insides, my heart. How can he still hurt me this much, even from jail?

Connie's lips become a thin line. "Whatever happens to your dad in jail, that's not your concern. He's the one . . ." Connie's voice strengthens. "It's not your faul—"

I cut her off. "I tried to talk to someone at the DA's office, to ask about how they weigh the victim impact statement. I wanted to feel them out about how it would go if I were to downplay my story and ask for leniency. But it was just too hard." I squeeze my hand into a fist on the table in front of me.

Connie nods, her face full of compassion.

And that's not even the worst of it. I stare at Connie's hand, still holding mine. "But before I went, I told a couple of my friends from the club and then this awful guy overheard. He's mad because one of our members outed him as a rapist, and he started tweeting about me to try to make our club look bad."

Connie starts to say something, but I keep talking. "He wrote about what was going on with me to show that there was club infighting, to show what a mess we are. And then there was a rally at school, that my friend—someone I thought I could trust—put on about not protecting the people who hurt us . . ."

Connie inhales sharply. "Your friend talked about you . . . at school, *in front of everyone*?"

I nod. Even though Lana didn't name me, of course everyone knew after Blake's stupid Twitter storm.

"What are you gonna do?" Connie finally asks.

I shake my head, saying nothing. Because what can I say?

After more crying and hugging, I tell Connie that's all the talking about my problems I can do for the day. We head into the kitchen to make dinner together. A first for us. That night I go to bed early, wiped from all the crying, all the worrying. Sleep seems like it can be my only reprieve, if not for the nightmares.

The next morning, I wake in Johnny's bed, light streaming in through the open blinds. There aren't bars on the window anymore. Connie really has made changes to her home.

I sit up and grab my phone to see that Trey's texted me. *I talked to Lana,* he writes. *She thinks she did what she had to do, but you have to know I don't agree with her. I begged her not to do the rally and the only reason I didn't warn you is because I thought Jasmine and I changed her mind.*

I text him back, letting him know I'm in Silver Valley and that I'll talk to him when I get back.

I'm sorry. I should have done more.

I stare at Trey's words for a moment, unsure how to respond, but Trey sends one more message.

I miss you.

I miss him too, I realize. I hardly know him, but I feel like he knows me. I feel like we could really care about each other, like he could really care about me, if I let him.

I stare at my phone. Think about responding that I miss him too. But instead I text Kale, tell him I'm in Silver Valley, and ask if he'll meet me.

Kale texts back that after lunch he was planning to go to the movies with his family but that he'll stay behind so we can have his house to ourselves.

The walk to Kale's house is a familiar one. We used to stroll past his place, hand in hand, on the way to Connie's after school. Kale always insisted on walking me. Now, outside his white picket fence, I survey his manicured grass—no doubt Kale's the one who cut it himself. Kale's dad's usually out of town for work and when he is home, he can't be bothered to help with anything unless it's at the bottom of a beer bottle. It hurts that Kale said the way I've treated him reminds him of that man. But I guess probably not as much as it hurts for Kale to feel that way.

I push the gate open and walk past the small toy jungle gym for Kale's youngest sister. The way Kale is with them, his three sisters, so loving and kind, is one of the things that made me first fall for him.

Kale opens the door before I get a chance to knock. His hair is wet and ruffled, as if he's just gotten out of the shower. The light gray T-shirt he's wearing is damp around the neck.

I hesitate. Instinctively wanting to touch him, for him to wrap me in his arms.

Kale seems awkward too. The smile he usually has for me, the one that lights up his face, is noticeably absent. "Come in," he says, his eyes serious.

Kale doesn't lead me back to his room, like he normally would after I turned eighteen and Connie allowed me to hang out with friends. Instead, he heads for the brown sectional in the living room and sits on the edge. I consider sitting on the other side, to be farthest away, but I can't. *He's Kale.*

I sit about a foot away from him, a lump lodged in my

throat. "I miss you." I hadn't planned on saying it, but it's true. I look up at Kale and his eyes are distant, his jaw set.

"I miss you too. But . . ."

But.

I squirm in my seat but force myself to hold his gaze. He looks so mad. *So hurt.*

"I'm sorry." I grasp my hands in my lap. "I know it was awful, what I did, pushing you out like that. It's just . . ." I trail off.

Kale doesn't say anything. Silence stretches between us. How did I create such a big divide between him and me?

"Things have been hard. My aunt told me . . . my dad's been getting beaten up in jail, and he asked me to write in my victim impact statement that I want them to be lenient on him." The words start pouring out of me, just like they did with Connie. Even though he knows about the rally, I want him to hear it from me. "And when I told a few people in the club, Blake overheard and tweeted about it, and then there was a rally. Lana did it; she didn't even care. I thought she was my friend." I'm crying, hard now, tears streaming down my face.

Kale's mouth parts and his shoulders sag, some of his anger seeming to fade. "I'm sorry about your dad." He pauses and closes his eyes, pinches his nose. "I feel sick even saying this, but what does that have to do with us? You'd been pushing me away before. You've been ignoring me, won't answer any calls. Why, Victoria?"

Kale releases his nose and looks at me.

My chest tightens. He's right, I know he's right. "Even

before that," I begin, voice shaky, "I couldn't . . . with the victim impact statement . . . I didn't think you'd understand—"

"That's crap, Victoria," Kale interrupts, his voice coming out harder than I expected. "I wouldn't understand? We went through this last year with everything with your dad and you being in foster care. I went with you to save Sarah. I'm here, I've always been here. And you were supposed to be done with secrets."

Back to one of our favorite arguments. My nostrils flare. "Kale, it's not that simple. Yes, you've been great. *You're always great.*" I narrow my eyes. "But that doesn't mean you get what it would feel like to see my dad suffering, for him to ask for help. He was molested by his grandpa. He's broken too."

"Broken?" Kale's eyes bore into mine. "*You're* not broken, Victoria. Bad stuff happened, sure—"

Now it's my turn to interrupt. "You say that like it's something I can just get over, like I can just put it behind me." My hands clench and I look away from Kale to the mantel above his fireplace lined with family pictures. Kale doesn't get it. He'll never get it.

My jaw clenches as I look back at Kale, and I change tactics.

"It's not like your dad's perfect, but you don't hate him."

Kale's eyes widen in shock. To compare his dad—a mean drunk, sure, but someone who has never raised a hand to hurt anyone in his family— to my father, who assaulted me, that was low.

I hurriedly add, "I didn't mean to compare them. Your dad's nothing like . . . what I mean is . . ." I stop and collect myself. "It's not like the moment I realized what my dad did was wrong, I could just hate him. The man who raised me, the only family I have."

Kale seems to move on from my comment about his father. He stands and starts pacing the living room. "You have Sarah. What about her? How does she feel about this?"

She would hate it. Not that I would know because she's not speaking to me. She hasn't replied to any of my texts in weeks. And it hurts even worse that Kale would use her against me, knowing how much of a stab to the gut it is.

"You know," my voice comes out cold, and I pull my gaze away from Kale as he stands over me, "this is why I've been hanging out with people from the club, because they actually get it."

The second the words come out of my mouth, I regret them.

Kale looks down at me, his gaze hardening. "The ones who held that rally?"

I blink, but don't say anything.

Kale's eyes flash. "You mean that Trey guy."

I shake my head half-heartedly, staring at the beige carpet at my feet.

Kale scoffs. "If he's so great, if he understands you so well, why are you here talking to me? Why aren't you crying in his arms right now? That's all I ever was to you, right, a shoulder to cry on? And now I'm not even good at that."

Kale heads for the door. My chest heaves. I don't know how we got here so fast. I don't know how it all went wrong.

"Kale," I whisper.

Kale turns around at the door, facing me. "You know, Victoria, I'm sorry." He closes his eyes and takes a shaky breath, bringing his voice back down. "This isn't me. Mad, jealous. I hate it." He shakes his head. "But I'm tired of giving you all I've got to only get scraps back from you. I can't . . ."

I'm up off the couch, walking slowly toward Kale. We're about a foot apart and I so badly want to reach out for him, touch his face. Kiss him softly. Tell him I take it all back.

"I love you, Victoria." He slowly reaches to cup my cheek, and I close my eyes, leaning into his hand. Craving his touch.

Kale takes his hand back and I open my eyes.

"I've always loved you," he says, frowning. "But I can't take you jerking me around, pushing me away, pulling me in, and then ignoring me. I won't be like my mom and keep running back for more punishment." He shakes his head quickly to stop me from interrupting. "I know you're not my dad. You'd never scream at me or call me names. But I can't help but think that this, whatever we have, it's not right." Kale looks down at his feet. "I think you should go."

A tear that had been clinging to Kale's long eyelashes finally falls and slides down his flushed cheek. I blink back my own. "I love you, too, Kale," I whisper. "Does this mean . . . are you saying we're over? This is it?"

Kale quickly jerks his head away from me. Like looking at me will break his resolve. After a moment, he forces his eyes back to me, and I can see that he's trying so hard to hold back more tears. "I think we've been over for a while now."

Kale's angry and he's sad and he's breaking up with me.

I did this. I did this to him. To us. "I'm so sorry," I say. Too little. Too late.

It's not until Kale closes the door behind me that my tears really start to fall, so fast that I think they'll never stop.

CHAPTER
NINETEEN

Connie's in the kitchen when I open the door to her house. "Dinner's almost ready," she says cheerfully. "I hope you like—"

Connie stops, her mouth agape when she catches sight of me. My face is probably blotchy, my eyes red and swollen from crying. That's all I've done lately. Cry. Weak—I'm weak. And I don't care what Kale says. I'm broken.

"Oh, honey." Connie sets the spatula on the counter and closes the space between us, wrapping me in a hug. I cough out a sob. "I-I," I sputter, "I'm sorry, Connie, but I just want to be alone right now."

Connie stills. "Okay." She pauses. "Food will be in the fridge if you get hungry."

I pull away from her and dart to the dormitory. I sit on a fiery red rocket ship on Johnny's white and blue bedspread.

I see Kale's face, angry and hurt. No love in those blue eyes anymore, not for me. I ruined everything. He was right. I've been so selfish. I've taken him for granted.

I think back to all the times I didn't text him, all the times I was cagey on the phone about Trey. No wonder Kale is done with me.

I wipe my face, sit up in bed. I've treated Kale terribly, but maybe he's right. I've always worried I don't feel the way about him that I should. I care for him, love him, but I don't seem to want him the way he wants me. It's more like I *need* him around, for comfort, security.

For someone to actually love me.

My throat throbs, sore. That's not fair to Kale, and I know it. Would I have been so interested in Trey if I had felt the way I should have about Kale? I can't keep lying to myself, like I did to Kale. There's something there, something between Trey and me.

I stare at my phone for a long time. I'm not going to call Trey, not after what just happened with Kale. My gut twists. I might not have looked at Kale the way Ray looks at Jake, but I do love him, I really do. And I've hurt him, again and again.

I don't want to keep pushing away people who care about me. But I don't know how not to.

Lana's face comes to mind. Our friendship is the one thing I can't take credit for messing up. If it weren't for her, I wouldn't be sitting here. I wouldn't have run from TMCC in shame. She calls herself an ally, but she threw me under the bus to make a point.

And she won't even admit it was wrong.

I pick up my phone. Dial her number.

Lana answers on the third ring.

"Hey." Her voice sounds awkward, unsure.

I grit my teeth as I picture her at the rally, yelling about victims, a thinly veiled attempt to call me out. "It was messed up what you did, Lana."

Lana's quiet for a moment before she mutters, "I disagree."

I bolt out of bed, heat flooding my ears, my face. I stare

at the wall across from me, the wall above my and Jamie's old bunk bed, where Jamie hung her boy band posters. Now it's just plain white space. But the holes from the tacks that held the pictures are still there, proof of what once was. "You could at least admit it, Lana. You owe me that much."

Lana is quiet for a moment. She sighs. "I won't, Victoria. I'm sorry you're upset but I had to do something, because after what Blake was saying, people were talking. They were calling us hypocrites—"

"That's exactly what Blake wanted," I roar. "And now you've played right into his ridiculous plan to hurt the club. But you didn't just hurt the club." My voice falters. "You hurt me."

I hear Lana inhale sharply. Her words come out fast. "All I wanted was to make sure something like what happened to Michelle didn't happen to anyone else. That's why I'm in the club. That's why I made the whisper network." She hesitates. And I can feel her realizing what a hypocrite *she* is.

"You get why people want to report their attacks anonymously for the whisper network, but I don't get that same respect? How is that okay?"

"I didn't tell anyone," Lana speaks loudly over me, "Blake did—"

"But you held that rally after and everyone knew why!" I'm yelling. Connie can for sure hear me from the kitchen or wherever she is, but that doesn't stop me. "You're supposed to be an ally! You're supposed to care about victims." I slam my hand against the wall near the window. "I'm a vic—a survivor. And you threw me to the wolves! You hosted a rally about me!"

I'm shaking. Shaking with rage.

"This is exactly why people get away with what they do. It's why Michelle didn't press charges and why she left," Lana spits. "If you help your dad, you could be helping him get out of jail, pretty much gift-wrapping other victims for him. How can you not see that, Victoria? How can you not agree with me? Is SASAH all just a game to you? How could you be so selfish?"

I run a hand through my hair, not seeing the walls or the room around me. Lana yelling, chanting, to a crowd about me. That's what I see.

"This. Is. My. Life," I sputter. "You blasted my abuse to make a point."

Rage makes me go quiet before I scoff. "We were never friends. Someone like you can't have friends."

I stab the end button and toss my phone at the bed.

A second later, I get a text from Lana. *Trey agrees with me, you know. He just won't say it to your face. And so does everyone at SASAH. Stop kidding yourself.*

And there it is, that familiar sinking feeling. Everyone knowing my secrets again. Whispering about me. Forming opinions without knowing the whole story. Except this time, I have no one in my corner.

Kale hates me.

Everyone in the club probably thinks I'm a traitor. So will Sarah when she finds out, if she doesn't already know.

And Dad. He's in jail right now, black and blue. In danger of being sexually assaulted, if he hasn't been already.

My chest hurts; it's squeezing tight. I think back to the monkey bars, him teaching me how to ride a bike. Playing beach volleyball with Mom.

He hurt me, but he's still my father. My dad.

I close my eyes, and I'm not in my old room in Connie's house anymore. I'm back home with Dad. The smell of his whiskey makes me gag. His fingers are digging into my pajama pants, into my underwear.

No.

I shake my head. I can't go there. I can't go back. I thought I had gotten better; I thought things were getting better. I sink into the bed and throw the covers over my head. Not wanting to see anything. Not wanting to feel anything. Not wanting to exist at all. Until I finally doze off.

Dad's on top of me. He's breathing hard, his eyes closed, pushing up against me.

I try to scream, but he covers my mouth. I buck, kick, bite. But he's too heavy. He's choking me, choking me, and I can't breathe, I can't see, my vision's going black.

"Victoria!"

My shoulders are shaking and I'm fighting, pulling away.

"Victoria!" It's Connie's voice. "It's me. It's just a nightmare."

I open my eyes, and it's Connie kneeling next to my bed. Not Dad. He's not here. He's not trying to hurt me. My whole body shakes and I'm sobbing and I can't breathe I can't breathe I can't breathe.

Connie wraps me in her arms. "It's okay, baby." She strokes my hair softly. "You're safe. I got you."

I cry into her arms until my eyes hurt. Until the blazing sun peeks out from behind the mountains outside of the window. My eyes start to close, worn out from all the crying.

Connie gently nudges me back into Johnny's sheets. "Get some rest. Breakfast will be ready when you wake."

When I wake up, my body hurts, like I ran a marathon. It feels heavy. My eyes are sore.

I drag myself up. Not sure how I can face today, never mind next week. As for going back to school, seeing everyone who read that blog post or worse, went to the rally? There's no way.

But I have to.

I sit at the table as Connie sets a serving bowl of scrambled eggs in front of me, next to a plate of toast. "Eat up. You skipped dinner last night, don't think I forgot."

I sigh. I know how Connie is about food. When she was a teen and didn't know how to cope with being raped by her stepdad, she threw up her meals in secret. After I vomited at school when I was stressed about Dad last year, she became extra watchful of my eating habits.

I scoop myself some eggs and butter a piece of toast. Connie gestures at the orange juice in front of me.

"Thanks, Connie."

"Don't mention it," she says, with a mouth full of eggs. We eat in silence. I start to clear our plates, but Connie stops me. "Nope, you're a guest. Go sit in the living room. I'll be there in a minute."

Connie hasn't let me clean up since I got here. I used to do the cooking and cleaning in this house, when I was a foster kid. So much has gone down between me and Connie—me hating her, her treating me terribly because of what I reminded her of and then finally telling me the truth about her past, not to mention her covering for me when I broke the rules to go with Christina and Kale to save Sarah. We've been through a whirlwind together.

I sink into the loveseat and wait for Connie to finish up in the kitchen. Annie's toy chest is still overflowing by the TV, but some of the toys are new. Toy trucks, dragons, G.I. Joes. Connie's biological kid Annie, last I knew, prefers dolls and noisemaking toys. Maybe they're Johnny's. The thought makes me smile. Things really have changed around here.

Connie joins me in the living room, on her favorite spot on the other couch. She leans forward, her elbows on her knees. "All right, girl, it's time you tell me what's going on with you."

"I told you about my dad and aunt already, about the kids at school."

Connie raises an eyebrow. "That doesn't explain why you came home from Kale's last night crying your pretty little eyes out, went to bed with no supper."

I look at my shoes, breathe deeply. I don't want to cry

anymore but it feels like if I look at Connie the dam of tears will break.

Connie leans closer to put a hand on my knee. "You can tell me, Victoria. I'm here for you."

I slump down in my seat. "I told you I've been pushing him away. I've been avoiding him, not answering his calls or texts. And he's had enough. Enough of my drama. It's over between us. I just . . . he doesn't understand. He never will."

Connie leans back in her seat. She sighs heavily. "Victoria, I don't know if that can be helped. Not a lot of people, thank the good Lord, are going to understand what it's like to be abused like we have. I don't know if you can fault him for that."

I blink.

Connie tilts her head at me and frowns.

"It's not just that," I say. "I mean, he's so nice to me and I felt like I was coming apart at the seams and I couldn't take it. I wanted him to . . . I don't know . . . be different or something, because I was. And then I resented him for having a life here, without me, even though I made friends and had stuff going on in Reno too." I look away, unable to watch Connie as I say the next part. "And then there's this guy in the club, not one of the jerks who did that stupid rally, but my friend. He's been through what I have, with his uncle. And when I'm with him, I just feel more . . ."

I look at Connie, who's staring at me with understanding in her brown eyes. "It's not just what he's been through. It's just easier with him. Happier, even though we've both had it so rough. I can't explain it, I—"

Connie laughs softly. She smiles. "You're falling in love."

My eyes pop. "That might be a little extreme."

Connie crosses her legs. "It's normal, you know. To change. And when you do, relationships change."

I swallow. "But I wasn't good to Kale." I twist my hands in my lap. "I hurt him."

Connie nods. "That's normal too." She pauses as she gauges my expression. "Not that it's good or that you shouldn't apologize. But it's hard going through all you've gone through. No one has shown you how to be in a healthy relationship. This is all new."

I stare at her, not understanding.

Connie chuckles. "I know Kale was your first boyfriend, but kids learn how to be in loving relationships way before they ever date. Their parents are supposed to model how to treat people, with love and respect and boundaries. They're supposed to show you how to work out differences in a healthy way. You didn't get none of that from that lousy father of yours."

I nod. Dad only showed me chaos. His mood swings. His gaslighting. All of it a ploy to control me, to get what he wanted.

My heart constricts. I know I'm not my father, but I took out my emotions, my confusion and hurt, on Kale. And he didn't deserve it.

"So, Kale might not be the right person for you," Connie begins. "After all, you're young. You said you've changed and you might want different things now, but you can still try to make it right with him. And maybe be friends again."

Friends with Kale. I don't know if I can do that. There are still feelings there, between us. But I want to try.

"Thanks, Connie." I nod. "I, uh, that's good advice. I'm going to talk to him. After he's had some time. I think he needs that. Maybe we both do."

Connie stares at me quietly for a moment.

Even though I knew something wasn't right with me and Kale, especially when I saw Ray and Jake together, I pushed my uncomfortable feelings down and tried to ignore them. It hurt Kale. I don't want to hurt the people I care about.

"If what you say is true, that I don't know how to have a healthy relationship because of what I learned from my dad, what do I do to fix that? So I don't do the same thing . . . next time?"

I swallow. It's hard to think about moving on from Kale, because I still love him, in my own way. But Trey's smile comes to mind.

Connie tilts her head at me. "Therapy could be good. It helped me loads after what happened with my stepdad. I went every week for a year, then twice a month until I thought I got a handle on things. I still go sometimes, when I need perspective."

Audrey says going to therapy helped her come to terms with what happened to her as a kid and that she wished my dad had gone. That if he had, maybe he wouldn't have done what he did. Dad always told me therapy was for people who liked to hear themselves talk and that therapists weren't real doctors. That they just liked to revel in others' misery.

But we've seen where believing my father has gotten me.

"I'll think about it. About going to therapy, that is," I tell Connie. I'm about to get up to go shower, when she starts up again.

"Now, what are you going to do about the kids at school?"

Heat rushes to my face. Another problem that I have no idea how to solve.

Connie fidgets in her seat. "I know you don't want to hear this, but I understand why the kids in your club were upset." She jerks her head to stop me from interrupting. "I don't agree with what they did—it was terrible, immature, and damn right abusive. But they're kids and they're angry. Hurt even. Some of them may have been hurt by others, and they are probably reliving it in some ways when they see you trying to help your father."

I clench my fist. Lana feels guilty she wasn't there to stop Blake from assaulting her friend.

She's suffered from watching someone she loves go through the trauma of not only being raped but then not being believed. She's experienced the pain of not being able to do anything to help. And when her friend couldn't deal, her friend didn't just move away but pretty much left her entire life behind. I know Lana misses her.

And Candace was raped. I should have known before. I saw it in the way she looked when she hung that poster up in the hall across from us. The way her face fell the second Lana told her about my dad, before she told me what happened to her.

But that still didn't give them the right to do what they did.

I grit my teeth. "It's none of their business. It's my life."

Connie nods fervently. "Absolutely. I just wanted you to think about that before you respond."

"Respond? How can I? What could I even do?"

Connie blows a raspberry. She chews on her lip, as if she's thinking. "Let me ask you something. Why do you want to help your dad?"

My body tenses. Images of him being abused in jail flood my mind. "Because my aunt says he's being hurt in jail. Because people don't like . . ." I hold my breath, exhaling as I finally say the words I have been holding back this entire time.

"Child molesters. Because the other inmates hurt child molesters."

Connie scoots forward in her seat. "Exactly. And that's what your dad is, right?"

"But that doesn't mean he deserves—"

"I didn't say that," Connie interrupts, "and I know you feel for your dad, especially now that you know he was molested as a kid, but I want you to really think about this. You want to help your dad so he doesn't get hurt, right?"

I nod.

Connie continues, "Why is your dad in jail?"

I roll my eyes. "You know why."

Connie scoots closer to me so our knees are touching as she's on the edge of the opposite couch.

"Right. Because he chose to hurt you. And that's why he's in jail. And it's possible that other men will hurt him in there. Why? Because *they* choose to." She gets off the couch and kneels on the floor next to me. "And you know who's responsible for that?"

My nostrils flare. If she says my dad—

"The men who hurt him. And the people in charge of security at the jail. But you know who isn't responsible? You."

Connie takes my hands in hers.

"Your dad, and your mom before she died, trained you since you were a little girl to take care of your father. It's not your job. And I know this is hard to believe but you've got to—this isn't your fault."

My chest rises and falls quickly, and my hands shake in Connie's.

"But I can stop it," I whisper.

Connie shakes her head. "You don't know that." She squeezes my hands. "But listen, I'm not here to tell you what to do. I just wanted to make sure you know that taking care of your dad and his well-being has never been and is especially not your job now. Okay, baby?"

A tear rolls down my cheek.

Connie wraps me in her arms, and I sob silently into her chest. She caresses my hair.

"And that goes for those little demons at school too. It's your life, your choice. Not theirs. You just gotta show them they can't push you around."

I lean into Connie's embrace and let myself cry.

"It seems to me you've spent a lot of time these past few months worrying about what you thought you could do to help *other* people," she says softly into my hair. "Maybe you could send some of that love your own way."

I start to shake my head, but no argument comes out as I think over Connie's words. I haven't wanted to hurt Dad, and that's why my victim impact statement has been such a struggle for me. I didn't want to write something that could get him more time. But I didn't want writing something that downplayed his abuse to hurt Sarah either.

The tears are really flowing now as my insides ache from all the pain that's going around. Pain I never wanted to cause anyone.

I didn't want Lana and other people in the club to be angry about me struggling over whether to help my dad.

This whole time, all I've wanted was to help other people, like Connie said.

I didn't stop to think about me.

I've been running from how I feel. Yet my problems still caught up to me.

After a moment, I pull away from Connie and stare into her brown eyes, and her thin lips pull into a smile.

I take a deep breath. "You're right," I say. "And I think I know how I'm going to do that."

CHAPTER
TWENTY

The next day, after breakfast, I get a surprise visitor. Connie opens the door to reveal Christina. I leap from the couch and rush over, pulling Christina into a hug.

"What are you doing here? I didn't know you were coming home!" I smile, big, for the first time in a while.

Christina laughs. "Surprise! I wanted to surprise my parents and then I thought I could do the same thing to you and Kale."

My face falls at the mention of Kale.

Christina's full eyebrows furrow as she pulls away from me. "Want to take a walk?"

I look back at Connie. "I'll be back in a little while."

Connie waves me off. "You girls have fun."

Christina and I start heading in the direction of Kale's house. I kick pebbles in front of me on the sidewalk as we walk through the residential neighborhood. The sun hides behind the clouds, giving today a gray overcast fitting for my mood.

I fill Christina in on what happened when I saw Kale.

Christina twists the end of her French braid. "I was hoping you two would have made up by now."

My shoulders slump. I'm a disappointment to her too. "We're not getting back together, Christina." I can't bring myself to look at her. "I love Kale, but not the way he loves me. Not the way he deserves. Every time I try to talk to him, I hurt him."

I stop to look at my friend, worry creasing her face. Christina loves us both. She's known Kale most of her life.

"I wish I could apologize, explain . . ." I trail off because my explanations don't do anything for Kale. "To tell him I know he deserves someone who looks at him the way he looks at me. Or used to." My voice breaks on the last word.

Christina puts a hand on my shoulder. "I didn't mean to make you feel . . . you're not a bad person just because you aren't in love with him."

I melt under her arm, under those words I so desperately needed to hear from my best friend. I hug her again, and Christina laughs softly into my shoulder.

"This is the most hugs I've gotten from you, like, ever." She squeezes me.

I let her go. "I'm so glad you're here."

We decide to walk back to Connie's, get into Christina's car, and drive to a diner downtown. We have milkshakes and catch up on the things we've missed. Such as Christina winning the election for freshman class president.

My mouth goes slack around my straw. "Oh my gosh, and you're just telling me now?"

Christina beams. "I wanted to tell you in person."

Christina tells me about all the support she's getting on campus. Events she's planning, policies she wants to enact. And despite what's going on in my life, I feel happy seeing her so happy.

Christina is here, and I feel like I'm going to be okay. I even tell her what I'm planning to do about Lana.

Christina grins, dropping her spoon in her milkshake. "Devious. I love it."

As I say goodbye to Christina that night, I feel strong enough to do what I have to do. To show Lana she can't mess with survivors like she did. To show the club. To show my aunt.

But most importantly, to show me.

———————————

I text Trey that afternoon, letting him know my plan. It was a risk, asking him to trick Lana so that he could help me. But he agreed, right away.

I can't relax, knowing Trey is with Lana at her family's house, knowing he's asking to borrow her laptop for a paper he has to write. Telling her his is in the shop getting repaired.

An hour later, I get a text from Trey. It's done. I have the username and password. Lana trusted him, like I trusted her.

Sitting on Johnny's bed, I stare at the blank screen in front of me. The words don't come. I picture the guilt I felt when Audrey told me about Dad, what happened to him as a kid, and what is happening to him now. I imagine the hurt on Sarah's face when I told her I visited Audrey. The incredulous way Candace and Lana looked at me when they each realized I wanted to help my dad with the DA.

Everyone wanted something from me. And no one had a right, no one except Sarah. She's suffered enough because of Dad, and now I'm adding to it.

And suddenly the words start pouring from me, my fingers stabbing the keyboard on my laptop as fast as I can think them. As I type, I keep thinking over and over, almost like a chant: *This is my story to tell.*

I write that I know people have been talking about me. That I know they have opinions about someone from SASAH helping a perpetrator. That if they want to hear my side of things, if they want the truth, there's only one person who can tell it to them.

I end the blog post with a call to action.

Meet me at the SASAH meeting room, at 6 p.m. Monday, and I'll tell you everything.

I save what I wrote in a Word document in case Lana takes this post down when she realizes it's gone live. I screenshot it, so I can put it on my social media if I have to, but hacking her blog and posting from there gives me way more visibility. And I think it adds to the sense of drama, which is sickening, but it will get more people to come.

After I hit publish, I text Trey. *It's done.*

I send a link to my aunt, whose calls and texts I've been dodging since I ran out of the DA's office. I text Sarah that we need to talk. That I'll explain everything if I can come over tonight.

She doesn't respond. No surprise, since we haven't exactly been talking. So, I call her, and when she doesn't answer, I leave a voice message. Tell her that I know I have a lot to explain, and I want to. My voice breaks as I tell her I need her.

"Because things are falling apart around me, and I can't do this alone. *Please.*"

A minute later, I get a text from Sarah.

I'm sorry, I can't talk now, about to head into therapy. Can I call you after?

I exhale. That's the first response to a message I've gotten from her in a while.

I'm in Silver Valley and will be heading back to Reno soon. Can I come by your place?

She tells me yes.

Finally. Something might just work out for me.

Before we leave Connie's, there's one last thing I need to do. I find the email addresses for the TMCC president *and* board members. The president didn't want to hear what SASAH had to say, so I'm sure he doesn't care what I have to say, but maybe others will. Once I'm done writing the message, I hit send without giving myself a chance to second-guess myself.

And then I turn my phone off, before all the notifications can come in. Before people see my post and have questions.

I'll answer them all on Monday, at school, when *I* tell my story. The way I want to tell it. On my terms.

I'm not going to let everyone else tell me how to feel or what I should be doing about it. I'm not being quiet. Not anymore.

———————————

Connie drives me back to Reno, to Sarah and Tiffany's house. "Want me to come in with you?" my former foster mother asks as her van idles, parked in the driveway next to Tiffany's station wagon.

I shake my head. "I'll be fine. I've owed Sarah an explanation for too long."

Connie hugs me and I hold on for a little longer than necessary.

"Thanks, Connie." I sigh. "I don't know what I would have done without you."

Connie snorts. "You'd have managed just fine; you always do." She pulls away to look at me. "But I'm glad I could help."

Tiffany welcomes me inside after I've waved goodbye to Connie. Her van chugs along down the street. Sarah's sitting on the couch, waiting for me. Tiffany moves toward the kitchen, but I stop her. "You're both going to want to hear this. I mean, I need to tell you both something. And it starts with"—I hesitate—"I'm sorry."

After I explain everything about my aunt and Dad, the DA, and the club, both my and Sarah's eyes are red and puffy from crying.

"You should have told me," my stepsister says. "I had a right to know."

I scoot closer to her on the couch, and thankfully Sarah doesn't bristle or flinch away. "You're right. I should have. But I'm telling you now."

Tiffany twists a piece of her wispy blonde hair, looking uncomfortable. "You're sure you want to announce this to everyone at your school, Victoria? That's . . . it's a lot to say to people you hardly know. Once you do, once it's out there . . ." she trails off.

I swallow. I know. I won't be able to take it back.

"They've already heard one side of the story. They already

have an opinion based on the garbage Blake tweeted and from that stupid rally. At least this way, it's me controlling it."

Tiffany looks at Sarah, her light eyebrows furrowed. "Yes, you're controlling what you say, but you can't control what people think. And this is about more than just you."

Sarah interrupts, "I support her, Mom.

I whip toward Sarah, afraid to hope. "You're not mad at me?"

Sarah's eyes, still bloodshot, narrow. She crosses her legs and adjusts the gray tunic she's wearing over her leggings. "You should have told me. Because now I know what I'm going to do. I've written my victim impact statement and I've decided I'm going to read it to the judge myself, tell *my* story."

I nod. That's fair.

Tiffany gives a sad smile to her daughter.

"But," Sarah continues, looking from me to her mom and back again, "I get why you need to do this, and I'll be there for you. *We* will be."

I hold my breath as Sarah stares at her mom, who nods slowly.

It's like a brick has been lifted off my shoulders. I exhale, letting go of some of the fear I've been bottling up. It'll still be terrifying, facing Lana and everyone at school. But now that I have Sarah on my side, I feel like I can do anything.

"Let's show those so-called friends of yours who they're messing with," Sarah says.

I laugh, looking at my fierce stepsister, ready to take on the world. "They won't know what hit them."

———

I texted Trey I'm back in town, and he wants to meet before everything happens on Monday. I invite him over later Sunday night, when I'm back home.

As I meet Trey outside, I hear a familiar voice calling my name.

"Victoria!" Ray jogs down the stairs.

Trey shoots me a questioning look, as though he wants to know if it's okay to talk about our plans in front of Ray.

"Were you watching from the window or something?" I ask, before I let Ray hug me. "How was your trip?"

Ray chuckles. "Not nearly as eventful as your last week has been, I hear. That's why you've been so cagey in your texts, dodging my calls."

My shoulders slump. With Ray out of town and everything going on with me, I didn't really feel like filling him in from the beginning. I should have known he knew something was up when his texts turned into phone calls, asking me to call him back on the voicemails he left.

"Sorry, I've been—"

Ray gives me a cutting look, as if he knows I'm about to lie. He shows me Blake's Twitter account on his phone. I narrow my eyes and push it away. "How'd you find out about that?"

Ray scoffs. "Just because I don't go to school with you doesn't mean I live under a rock. Saw this posted all over Twitter this morning with some shit about you clapping back tomorrow at school. You could have told me, you know. You *should have* told me."

Ray's right, but I don't have it in me to apologize. So, I shrug. I'm just too wrecked by everything.

Ray gives me a knowing look and drops it. He types something on his phone and then shows me a hashtag: #DontShutDownSurvivors.

My eyes widen as I scroll down. Several people have been posting about SASAH turning its back on me and how messed up the rally was. There's a group of people coming to support me tomorrow.

It's her story, her say. #DontShutDownSurvivors

Allies don't dictate how survivors cope with their abuse. #DontShutDownSurvivors

I stand with Victoria. #DontShutDownSurvivors

I stare at Trey, openmouthed.

"Did you do this?"

Trey shakes his head. "Wish I had." He takes the phone from me, squinting his eyes as he reads. And then he grins. "Look, it's coming from the official SASAH Twitter account. It's Jasmine, showing people the club stands behind you!"

There's a graphic that reads *Don't Shut Down Survivors* starting this all, along with a link to the club's official website.

SASAH did not host that rally, the image reads. *Two members, acting on their own and against the wishes of the club, did. SASAH stands by survivors. We support them to tell their truths, however and whenever they see fit. We'll be at school for our member who is speaking up, and if you're an ally, you should come hear what she has to say too. #DontShutDownSurvivors*

I grab the phone and can't help but smile too. "Wow,

that's . . . wow." My stomach warms, for once in a good way. Having the club officially stand behind me—it's more than I would have expected or hoped for. I send Jasmine a quick thank-you message. My phone buzzes with Jasmine's reply. *I wish this hadn't happened in the first place. But don't worry, Victoria. We've got your back.*

Ray takes his phone back from Trey. "So, are you two going to invite me in?" he asks. "Tell me what you're planning to do about this shit show?"

Trey and Ray follow me inside. I offer them sodas and sit across from them on the floor, the two of them on the couch. I give Ray a quick rundown of my plan, filling in the gaps he didn't pick up from Twitter.

Ray takes a pull from his soda, balancing Sasha on his opposite knee. "You're a superhero for doing this, Victoria. All we gotta do is get you a cape."

I smile, but my stomach starts to knot as I imagine talking to people I don't know at school about something so personal. Like Tiffany said, I can't control any of this once I do so. But I can't just sit by without doing anything either.

Ray scoots forward and reaches a hand down to my shoulder. "It's going to be okay. We'll both be there."

After his phone buzzes, Ray replies quickly to a text. He looks up at me. "Jake's really sorry about all of this too. I didn't tell him anything you've told me, of course. Wanted to respect your privacy. But he's got Twitter."

I nod. "How are things going with him?" Kale and I might have come apart at the seams, but at least someone's in a happy relationship. Ever since Ray met Jake's parents and it went amazingly, according to Ray, they've been spending more and more time together. Even saying the L-word back and forth.

"They're good. But let's not focus on me; I'm here for you."

I shake my head as I try to hold back tears. "I'm happy for you, Ray." Despite my jealousy and unease watching Ray fall in love—because it's shown me how very differently I feel about Kale—that doesn't change how much I care about Ray and how I want the best for him. "I really am."

Trey's been quiet, but now he sets his soda on the table beside him. He flicks its aluminum tab. "You don't have to do this, you know."

Ray glares at him incredulously and Sasha reacts by actually hissing at Trey. He withers.

"It's not that I think you should or shouldn't, it's just . . ." He fidgets in his seat. "No one should ask this of a survivor. Lana shouldn't have put you in this position. It's no one's business—"

I get up from the floor and step toward Trey. "I know. I shouldn't have to." I put my hand on the armrest beside him, searching for the words. "But I feel like I have to make a stand. Like I need to show everyone Blake didn't silence me. I need to show Lana that what she did wasn't okay. I need to show my aunt, my dad even, that they can't make me do what they think I should." I take a deep breath.

Ray is nodding along with me, like I'm preaching to the choir.

"I'm not doing this for any of them." I step back, rising

to my full height before looking back at Trey. "I'm doing this for me."

CHAPTER
TWENTY-ONE

Monday, I skip class. I'm too nervous about the meeting later, plus I don't really feel like dealing with awkward stares or whispers. I arrive at the SASAH room about an hour early and stand at the podium, imagining the space filled with people watching me. My hands start to sweat. I've already asked school facilities workers to come in and move the conference table out, and once they do, I set up rows of chairs facing the podium.

I don't know how many people will come. Part of me hopes no one will, but I know that's not what I *really* want.

I check my phone and notice a direct message from someone I don't follow. I accept. Melanie's picture appears.

I heard what happened, about what Blake did and then that rally. You deserve better than that. You gave me a chance, even when I was so wrong. You didn't call me out or try to embarrass me. Thank you for that.

I take a deep breath. Gratitude filling me. Another message pops up from Melanie.

I broke up with Ross.

I think about sending a thumbs-up emoji, but that doesn't express what I want to say. I need to talk to her when I don't have what feels like the world already sitting on my shoulders.

Thank you for messaging me, Melanie, I reply. *I really needed that right now. Let's talk soon.*

I turn around, consider writing my name along with that hashtag on the white board, #DontShutDownSurvivors, but decide against it. The broken microphone, discarded on the floor behind the podium, catches my eye. I sit down beside it, imagining Candace or Lana banging the thing trying to get it to work.

I run my finger along the edges of frayed paint on the bottom, my thumb catching on something. I turn it over. There's a latch.

A latch for batteries. A smile spreads across my face and I actually laugh out loud as I pop it open. Empty. There are no batteries in it. This microphone may be broken—it doesn't work when plugged in—but if I use batteries, then it should go cordless just fine. If the others had just taken the time to look at it, really look at it, they would have seen.

My phone lights up with a message from Trey. He's about to head over to help me set up for the meeting and wants to know if I need anything. *Chairs are already set up*, I type. *But can you bring some AA batteries?*

I clutch the microphone to my chest, leaning back against the wall as I wait. This is not something I wanted but now I'm sure I have to do this. People are going to hear me. I twirl the microphone in my hand. *Loud and clear.*

A few minutes later, Trey opens the door. He closes the distance between us until he's about a foot away and then fidgets with the sleeve on his blue and gray flannel.

"Look, I know I said this before, but I don't know if you

and Ray understood what I meant. It's not that I don't think you have every right to want to do this. I get it, you know, and I support this, if it's really what you want. I just don't want you to think you *have* to." He lets go of his shirt and takes my hand. I hold my breath for a second.

"You don't owe anyone an explanation. You don't owe anyone—"

I tug on his hand, pulling him closer, so our noses are just a couple of inches apart. "Thank you," I whisper, "for saying that. For being here."

I take a step back and Trey blinks several times. "But I got this," I say.

Jasmine is next to arrive. Her braids swing as she rushes toward me, wrapping me in her arms. "Gah, I know I texted you, but I still have to say I should have done something. I should have stopped Lana." She pulls away to look at me as her deep voice breaks. "I'm so sorry."

I shake my head. "You couldn't have done anything. Lana's a force. When she has her mind set on something . . ." I don't finish the thought. Instead, my eyes water at my gratitude for Jasmine. "Thank you for supporting me, for showing people SASAH supports me. For tweeting about this."

Jasmine tilts her head at me and smiles. "You're not alone," she says.

My chest tightens as I look at her and then Trey. "Thanks. It means a lot."

More people file into the space over the next twenty minutes. Jake and Ray stand in the back near the door, holding hands. Ray's other arm is occupied holding up a giant foam finger. I can't help but laugh. From here, it looks like he wrote my name on it along with the hashtag in big black letters. I make eye contact with him and mouth *thanks.*

Audrey is sitting in the second to the last row, shifting uncomfortably next to two girls who are talking to each other loudly. I don't know either of them, so I assume they saw my hacked blog post on Patriarchy Pounder or the hashtag on Twitter. Beside one of the girls sit two older women, talking in hushed tones. I don't recognize them either. Looking around, I notice there are a lot of people here who I don't know. I swallow.

Audrey catches my eye and gives me an awkward wave. I wave back. She's not going to like what I'm going to say. A lot of people here won't.

But I don't care.

Connie walks in, followed by Tiffany and Sarah. Connie hugs me quickly and then bounces slightly on her feet. "This is wild, Victoria. I'm proud of you."

I smile at her and then look at Sarah. "You're sure you're okay with this?"

Sarah makes a show of cracking her knuckles. "Where's this Lana chick? I think we should have a talk with her."

Tiffany rolls her eyes with a smile at her daughter, before she puts a hand on my arm. I don't flinch or move away. "We're here for you," she says.

They take three open seats in the row behind Audrey.

I'm about to start talking when Lana and Candace slip in, Lance trailing behind them. My eyes widen at him and he quickly shakes his head, like he's trying to tell me something.

Behind them comes Melanie, her head full of blonde curls covering her face. I meet her eye. She smiles. I give her the thumbs-up, in real life.

I didn't expect so many people. It's standing room only. I look to Jasmine and Trey, sitting in a couple chairs set aside near the podium, facing the audience. Behind me, with me. Jasmine's nodding, telling me to go ahead.

Trey looks at me and I look at him and we stay like that for a moment, not saying anything, until he breaks the silence. "You're going to be great."

I look to the back, at Lana standing next to Ray, him giving her the side-eye. I guess he figured out it was her, somehow. I stare straight at Lana and Candace as I grab the microphone, newly equipped with batteries, and turn it on. My voice booms into the speakers at the edges of the room. "Thank you for coming, everyone."

Lana's eyes widen in surprise and Candace whispers something in her ear. I smile.

"For those of you who don't know me, I'm Victoria. I'm a freshman. A member of SASAH, TMCC's group for Students Against Sexual Assault and Harassment. I'm a sexual assault *survivor*."

Survivor. Not a victim.

The door opens once more. Lance steps out of the way to make room for the assistant DA who interviewed me, Kelly. I swallow. I don't know how she heard about this—maybe Tiffany told her—but I'm glad she's here.

I clear my throat and clutch the microphone to my chest. The crowd watches me silently.

"My dad attacked me last year and is in jail for it now, awaiting sentencing."

Audrey sits up in her seat, panic overcoming her features. I continue. "I was recently approached by a family member, asking me to go easy on him when I write a statement about what happened. She has become more and more worried about my dad, because he's been getting hurt in jail." The crowd starts to murmur. One person calls out, "So what, let him get what he deserves!" A few people start clapping until Jasmine calls from the front, "Shut up and show some respect!"

Suddenly I'm hot all over. Beads of sweat pool at my hairline, yet my hands are clammy. So many faces are staring at me. And I'm telling them the most personal things, and I can't take it back after this, like Tiffany said. She catches my eye and nods for me to go on. Sarah gives me a thumbs-up, and Connie smiles warmly at me.

I clear my throat. "It might not make sense to many of you, but I still love my dad and when I recently learned about some of the abuse he suffered as a kid, I felt bad for him. I was worried about him." My heart hammers, and I start talking faster. "I decided to try to help him, to see if I could help my dad get a lesser sentence. To make it seem like it wasn't as bad as I said before, what he did to me."

"Boo!" a girl in the crowd jeers. My eyes dart to her, and I'm about to say something when Ray shouts from the back, "No one asked you, troll!"

Laughter ripples through the room, and I can't help

but grin. Jake smiles proudly and pecks Ray on the cheek. Nervous energy electrifies me. I stand taller.

"So, here's when things got even more messed up. Someone in student body government, Blake Rexby, wrote a Twitter thread about this, sharing my most personal business to make a point." I make a face, showing everyone exactly what I think of Blake.

"And then a few people in SASAH hosted a rally, also calling me out. Even if they never said my name." I meet Lana's eye and she stares at me, hard. That's why she's here. Because I'm the one calling her out now.

Candace whispers something to Lance, as Lana shifts on her feet. Lance steps away from Candace, nodding at me to go on. He's here for me, in case Lana and Candace try something. That's what he was trying to tell me with that look when they all walked in together. I can feel it.

I look over the faces of the crowd. Strangers, so many of them. Here for the spectacle, or to support Lana's cause or mine. I can't be sure. But it doesn't matter, because I've got the microphone now.

I pause to stare at Lana for a long moment.

"SASAH is supposed to be about supporting survivors. That's why I joined anyway. But it's pretty obvious not all of us agree on what we're about. I don't support calling out people who have suffered abuse in any way. Telling us how to process, how to tell our stories. How to share our deepest pain in hopes of changing things, even for the better." I look at Audrey. "And even more than that, I see now it's also not the survivor's job to help our abusers avoid consequences they earned or even to forgive them."

At my words, Audrey looks stricken, and I care, but not enough to let it stop me.

My eyes find Lana's. "We shouldn't burden survivors with the mandate to cut themselves open and bleed for the greater good. It's not the survivors' responsibility to fix things that are broken. Sure, if that's something we want to tackle, we absolutely should be empowered to get involved in a way that makes us comfortable. But no one should try to force their way on us."

I continue, looking around the room at so many familiar and unfamiliar faces. "Changing the culture isn't the responsibility of someone who has been hurt. That's on all of us. That's on all of you."

I'm quiet for a moment as I return Lana's gaze, her mouth in a firm line, before I look back around at the crowd. Watching me quietly, attentively.

"For those of you who want to know what our club is really about, let me tell you. It's about changing rape culture on campus and in our community. It's about supporting survivors, letting them know what happened to them matters," —my voice breaks—"that *they* matter."

The two older women sitting a couple seats away from Audrey are staring at me, as if they are holding on to every word. "People who have been abused don't come forward for a lot of reasons. Many survivors feel shame for what happened to them. Many are in denial or want to minimize the abuse." My eyes start to water and my voice falters again.

I take a deep breath and resume control. "Many of us are afraid of what will happen to us, that people will call us liars if we come forward, which I can say is something I have experience with when no one believed me initially."

Someone in the crowd stands, and immediately I recognize her beautiful smile. Rosa. She holds both hands to her heart, nods at me, and sits back down. I didn't see her before, but she keeps eye contact and I know that she supports me in this. I'm so grateful for that.

"Some of us are afraid we won't be believed. So, you may be wondering, after all of this, why I would even consider dialing back what I said. Why would I do something that could undo everything I went through to get my dad behind bars?"

I can see a few people nodding in the audience. They want to know. It's a hard answer to give, one I'm not sure I understand myself.

"Survivors, or some of us anyway—I can't speak for everyone —we suffer from low self-esteem. We feel hopeless. We have a history of being violated, and for some of us that's all we know. Being made to feel small. Being so confused. And the person who hurt us, also loved us. Or we felt that they did."

Rosa nods, pulling her bright-red lips together in agreement. She understands. My voice strengthens.

"Just because someone has hurt us doesn't mean we all want them to hurt too. Some of us also believe in forgiveness. And second chances. I had to believe there was good in my dad, somewhere, because he's the person who raised me."

Lana shouts over me, "That's all well and good, but what

about the others he could hurt if he gets out of jail because of you? What about the message you'd be sending by lying to the DA? What about—"

"Lana," Jasmine calls, "could you do us all a favor and for once—"

I hit the microphone with the top of my hand, sending feedback through the speakers. Several people groan. That got their attention.

I cover the microphone for a second and turn to Jasmine. "Thanks," I whisper, "but I've got this."

I look at Candace, at her big blue eyes that make her seem younger than she is. "Survivors have a high rate of anxiety and depression, and many unfortunately end up taking their own lives."

I think of Jamie and the letters we send back and forth to each other from her new group home. How she tried to kill herself last year when she felt hopeless, but how she's finally getting better, seeing light and love in the world. Hope. If I had lost her last year, I don't know what I would have done. I look at my stepsister, sitting behind Audrey. She's so strong, but if she ever hurt herself—I couldn't take it.

I shake my head. "No one, no matter how good intentioned, has a right to tell survivors what to do or how to do it when it comes to sharing their stories."

Candace's lip quivers, and I hurt for her.

"So many of us have secret scars, silent pain." I hold the microphone tighter. "If you stand for survivors, you don't just do it when they act the way you think they should. I'm done being quiet. I won't be quiet about what my dad did to me, but I also won't be quiet about what Blake did either, or what the people"—I pause, and look right at them—"what Lana and Candace did when they hosted that rally to try to make a point but used my deepest pain to do it."

Lana's eyes widen and Candace looks at the ground, as if she's ashamed.

"I'm tired of everyone having an expectation of what I should be doing," I say to the crowd, "of how I should be handling this."

I hold the microphone down at my waist and look at my aunt. Her green eyes are wet. Maybe she knows what I'm about to do. I'm sorry, not for telling the truth, but for the hurt it causes her.

But that's not my fault.

I meet my stepsister's eyes. Sarah sweeps her long blonde bangs out of her face and smiles, nodding at me. I love her so much. I think of what she's gone through, what I've gone through.

I bring the microphone back to my mouth. "One thing this whole fiasco showed me is I can't make everyone happy. My dad wants me to help him and so does my aunt. Some people in SASAH want me to throw the book at my dad. The DA wants the truth." I look at Kelly, the assistant DA, and she stares back at me, unblinking.

"Well, I guess I can do that part. I can tell the truth. But I'm not doing it to make the angry club members happy, and I'm not doing it for anyone else. I'm doing it for me."

I pause, scanning the crowd. Wanting to remember

this moment. "Thank you all for being here. Thank you for listening."

The speakers squeak as I turn the microphone off. Jake and Ray cheer and Connie, Sarah, and Tiffany stand to clap. Slowly, so does everyone else. They're all clapping.

Even Candace.

Even Lana. Sort of. She claps a few times and keeps staring at me.

Lance hollers, "Go, Victoria!"

Well, not *everyone* is clapping. My eyes land on Audrey, who is covering her mouth with her hand as tears trickle down her cheeks. She looks away from me and rushes for the door. A little part of my heart breaks for her, seeing her pain.

I turn away from that part of me, away from Audrey, as I hand Jasmine the microphone and she congratulates me.

I look to Trey. "I gotta get out of here." That's about my quota for a lifetime of public speaking. I can't stand the thought of having to chat with everyone after. "Can you make sure the room is cleaned up before heading out?"

"I can give you a ride." Trey stands.

I shake my head. "I need some time alone. I'll text you later."

He nods and I head for the exit, waving to Sarah, Tiffany, and Connie as I pass their row and mouthing that I'll call them. I stop by the assistant DA. Within earshot of Lana, I'm sure.

I tell her, "Call me and let me know when a good time is to come by again, please. I'll drop off my statement in person ahead of sentencing, so we're all on the same page."

Kelly reaches out to shake my hand. I take it. "See you soon, Victoria."

As I start to walk away, I feel an arm behind me. "Melanie," I say when I see her. She smiles.

"That was incredible," she says, her eyes wide with what could be awe.

I thank her. "If you want, we can get together sometime, after all of this"—I wave an arm around me—"calms down."

Melanie nods. "Actually, I'd like to join SASAH. I mean, if they'll have me, you know, after I—"

I interrupt. "We'd love to have you with us. Text me if you want to meet up before the next meeting." I smile at her. "I gotta go."

I walk through the door and into the hallway, when I hear rushing footsteps behind me. I turn to see one of the older women I didn't recognize in the crowd.

"Victoria," she breathes. Composing herself, the gray-haired woman stands up straighter as her friend from earlier catches up behind her. "My name is Evelyn, and this is Gemma." The woman gestures to her slightly younger, brown-haired friend. "We're members of the board of trustees. Thank you for inviting us."

Evelyn beams at me. "That was one of the bravest things I've ever seen." She reaches out to shake my hand and when I let her, she holds on, not letting go for several seconds. "You brave, brave girl."

The other woman, Gemma, clears her throat. "We received the link you sent us to Blake Rexby's Twitter posts about what happened to you, and we take that breach of privacy, especially concerning an ongoing investigation, very seriously. Not to mention that a little digging showed us Blake's motives for that petition might not have been sound."

I raise an eyebrow.

Evelyn nods. "We've interviewed a few people on campus who seem to think so anyway. Maybe even a couple from student government," she adds. Gemma gives her a pointed look, and Evelyn folds her lips on themselves.

I look back and forth between them. "So, what are you saying?"

"We're saying we will speak to the school president. We will encourage him to intervene with the recent, possibly very biased choice of student government leadership to deny funding to your club on the basis of it being a"—Gemma raises her eyebrows incredulously—"*hate group*."

I blink several times. Adrenaline still pumping through my veins, I could hug them. But instead I simply reply, "Thank you."

Evelyn looks at Gemma. "I think we're done here," Evelyn says before turning to me. "Thank you, Victoria. We appreciate your courage and honesty. We'll be in touch."

I watch the women's retreating backs before I continue down the hallway, people now filling in around me as they leave the conference room. Not wanting to talk to anyone, I speed past those around me and send a group message to Sarah, Tiffany, and Connie. I tell them again that I'll call them later, and I appreciate them coming but I want to take the bus. My thoughts are swirling with everything that has just happened. I want to clear my head.

But once I'm outside of the building, I realize Audrey is out here, waiting for me.

"Victoria," Audrey says, tears in her eyes, "I never wanted to hurt you. I just wanted to help my brother."

"I know you didn't mean to hurt me," I say, staring at her wide green eyes that are so much like mine and Dad's. Thinking a silent goodbye. "But that doesn't mean you didn't."

And I walk away.

CHAPTER
TWENTY-TWO

I keep replaying and replaying everything I said in my head on the bus ride home.

My phone has been blowing up.

Tiffany telling me she was glad the assistant DA took her up on the invitation to hear me speak.

Trey, Jasmine, Lance, Ray, Sarah, Connie. All telling me how great I did and how proud they are of me.

Audrey. Saying she's sorry.

I tuck my phone back in my pocket and round the corner, the old brick apartment building there to greet me. What I see, or rather, *who* I see outside my door makes my breath catch.

Kale.

He's staring at his phone, his light eyebrows furrowed.

I walk faster.

"What are you doing here?"

Kale sucks in a breath at the sight of me. "I saw your speech."

"I didn't see you there."

Kale steps away from the door as I fumble my keys out. He closes the door behind us, and I have no idea what to do now.

"I was there," Kale says. "In the back, behind the guy with the foam finger."

I gesture for Kale to sit and hesitate as I consider whether I should join him on the small loveseat. Kale gives me a pained look and I plop down next to him, quickly.

We're only inches from each other on this couch, but the awkwardness between Kale and me makes it seem like we're thousands of miles away.

Kale looks down through his long eyelashes at his hands.

"I'm sorry, Kale." That's it, that's all I've got. *I'm sorry.*

"Me, too," he replies. "I knew you were going through a lot, and I should have been more supportive. I shouldn't have let . . ." Kale looks up at me. "I shouldn't have let jealousy get in the way of us."

I shake my head quickly. "No, you were right to be upset. I'd been pushing you away."

Kale's Adam's apple bobs as he swallows, his blue eyes piercing me with their intensity.

"I let myself get closer to Trey than I should have," I admit. "Nothing ever happened with him, like, ever." I enunciate the last word. "But I felt close to him, understood."

Kale's shoulders slump and I hate that telling the truth hurts him so much. But he deserves to know that none of this was ever on him.

The couch squishes underneath my fidgeting. "I love you, Kale," I murmur.

Kale lets out a breath. "I love you, too, Victoria. Sometimes I wonder if . . . if we could have worked it out. But . . ."

But.

We let that word hang between us for what seems like a long time.

"You've been so good to me," I finally say.

Helping me through last year when I was in foster care, helping me face my dad. Kale has been nothing short of wonderful.

My eyes start to well up. "You deserve to be loved the way you love, wholly. And I do love you, Kale, but not the way I want to. Not the way you love me." A tear runs down my nose as I remember all the times Kale has looked at me the way Ray and Jake look at each other and how much I hurt for not being able to give that back to him.

Kale gently wipes my tear off with his finger.

My voice shakes. "I should have been honest. I've known something was missing for a while and rather than tell you I ignored it. And then when my feelings got more complicated, not just about you but about my dad and everything else, I treated you badly. I'm so sorry."

Kale nods solemnly, staring at his jeans. "I think I've known that deep down, for a while. I just didn't want to admit it to myself."

He looks back up at me and his blue eyes are bright with tears clinging to his long lashes.

My throat is tight and my tears are coming and Kale's eyes widen and he shakes his head quickly. "No, Victoria. Don't cry about this. It isn't your fault." He wraps me in his arms and I cry and he cries for our past and our broken hearts and a future where we won't be together.

When we finally let each other go, Kale softly pushes a piece of my hair, damp and stuck against my cheek, away from my face. "You'll always be my first love, Victoria. I'll need some time, but I hope we can . . . be friends again. Maybe by next year, when I'm at UNR?"

I almost smile at him. "It's settled, then? You're for sure going to UNR, not TMCC?"

Kale chuckles. "A wise person once said that I shouldn't choose a school based on a girl."

I laugh at that. "I *am* pretty wise."

I walk Kale to the door, and we hug one last time. "See you around, Victoria."

I nod, unable to speak without releasing another round of waterworks.

I watch Kale as he walks away, and even though it hurts, it also feels like a weight has been lifted off my entire body.

And I can breathe.

Despite Christina's incessant texting that I should tell Lana what a traitorous bitch she is in bio on Tuesday, I don't say a word to her when I see her. Lana's black hair is pulled into a loose ponytail and she's wearing a characteristic graphic tee.

Lana must feel me staring as I approach a seat toward the back of the room. She turns and meets my eye before grabbing her phone. A moment later, I get a text from her.

Meet me after class? Please.

Lana's watching me when I set my phone down. I nod and her features ease into a tentative smile.

The period runs long. What could Lana have to say to me after what she did?

We meet in the hallway, other students bustling around us. As we walk toward the double doors, my hands are in my pockets and Lana's mouth is pursed. It's like we don't know how to be around each other anymore.

I open the door for Lana and follow her outside. Once out of the way of most of the foot traffic, standing near a bench on the side of the building, we both stop. Looking anywhere but at each other.

"I'm sorry, Victoria. What I did was messed up." Lana meets my eye. "I was pissed at you. I felt so betrayed. Like you were helping the Blakes of the world by helping your dad."

My lips become a thin line. "It wasn't your call, Lana. It never was."

Lana nods. "I know that now." She recoils under my glare. "Okay, I knew that, then too. I made it about me, about what happened to Michelle and how it affected me. I wanted to save other people from that pain, but I put it on you. I shouldn't have."

I swallow the lump in my throat. "You're right, you shouldn't have."

Lana's shoulders slump; she looks defeated. I think about how I felt when she had that bullhorn in hand, yelling. But I also remember everything else, all the good stuff with the club. How she makes me laugh. And how I miss her.

"I want to forgive you," I finally say, even though I know our friendship will never be the same after what she did. "And I'm going to try to."

Lana's head shoots up, surprise all over her face.

"As long as you never pull anything like that again. And

maybe we need to work on our conflict resolution skills, you and me both."

Lana grins. "Fair enough."

I surprise us both by hugging her. It lasts about a second.

"I'm not much of a hugger," Lana chuckles, pulling away.

"Yeah, that was weird." I laugh.

We start walking in step toward the parking lot, stopping at Lana's car.

I'm about to say goodbye when Lana's jaw clenches. "Why can't he just leave us alone?"

I turn to see Blake heading in our direction.

"You two finished with your lovers' quarrel?" Blake saunters over so he's just a few feet from us.

Lana cringes. "Isn't there something, anything, better you could do with your time? Like read a book, or several?"

"Or turn yourself in to the police?" I add.

Blake scowls at me. "You believe this bitch? You think I'm a rapist because Michelle wanted this"—he gestures at his body like the idiot he is—"and then was mad when I wouldn't date her? You know how much trouble I've gotten into because of her lies? My dad has some shit to deal with on the board of trustees because a couple of chicks went to your stupid speech." He glares at me, before turning his attention to Lana.

"They told him *I've* been bullying your club, harassing *you!*" He sneers at Lana and steps closer, anger lining every inch of his face. "Now I've got to shut my club down, and my dad's resigning from the board. You happy now?"

Lana stands very still next to me.

Blake takes another step toward Lana, knocking me aside with his shoulder. Lana stops breathing. He's so close to her, and I can see my friend is afraid.

"I'm talking to you, bitch." Blake glowers down at her. "You're mad because you hate men and no one else cares?"

I grab Blake by his shoulder and yank him away from Lana. He whirls, hate in his eyes, and lunges toward me. Instinct takes over. I grab him by both shoulders and knee him in the groin as hard as I can. A move I saw on TV, but apparently effective.

Blake gasps and hunches over, hands on his knees. He wheezes. "Bitch!"

"You're right about one thing," I say quietly, with control. "Lana is angry, and so am I. And we have every right to be. Because you're a rapist and a liar and a bully."

Blake coughs as he struggles, unsuccessfully, to right himself. Lana lifts her chin and pushes him over. A few people from class stand several cars away watching us. Not one person makes a move toward helping Blake.

Blake writhes on the pavement for a moment before Lana steps around him. "Want a ride?" she asks me, as though there isn't a rapist moaning at our feet.

Feet pound the pavement, running behind me. I whirl around and exhale when I realize it's only Trey.

"What happened?" He looks down at Blake, who has now gotten to his knees. Trey steps in between us, as if he's trying to shield Lana and me from him. "Are you two okay?"

"We should go," I say, eyeing Blake warily. After the

trouble he said he and his dad have gotten into, I hope he won't try anything else. But better to be safe than sorry.

Trey slips into Lana's backseat and I settle in the front. A now upright Blake slams his hand against my door. Lana hits the gas so fast, it's all Blake can do to get out of the way before he gets run over.

"I'm going to report that," Trey says. "Not whatever happened that landed him on the ground"—he looks at the back of Lana's head, likely assuming she's the one who did it—"but that he got threatening and hit your car."

"Good idea," Lana replies. We both look at each other, grinning. We doubt Blake will say he got his ass handed to him by a couple of girls.

Lana drops me off at my apartment and Trey gets out of the car when I do.

"Can we talk?" he asks.

I nod at Lana, letting her know it's okay. Trey smiles. "I'm glad you two made up."

Lana laughs. "Lucky for me, forgiveness is in the air." She shoots Trey a pointed look. "I might even consider forgiving you for tricking me into lending you my computer so Victoria could hack my blog."

Trey's eyes flit back and forth comically. "I'm glad we're all so forgiving."

All three of us laugh at that.

After Lana drops us off, I lead Trey inside my apartment. Trey sits on the loveseat, right next to me. I have a hard time focusing on any coherent thoughts with Trey's knee so close to mine. His hand inches closer to my hand on my own knee.

"This has been . . . it's been a lot, I know," Trey says softly. He takes a piece of my wavy hair in his hands and I shiver involuntarily. "But I just want you to know, I admire you. It was brave what you did yesterday."

I think about Trey telling me about his past, him understanding mine better than almost anyone. Except Sarah. And maybe Connie. I think about how I've grown this year, how I've pushed myself to do things I wouldn't have in the past, like canvass and speak up for survivors. To speak up for myself. All with Trey by my side. I feel drawn toward him.

"I broke up with Kale," I blurt.

Trey's lips part, and his hand lets go of my hair and moves to my hand.

"I want to," I tell him. We both know what I'm saying even though I don't spell it out. "But I can't. It's too soon. With everything with me and Kale, and . . ."

Trey's face falls slightly but he quickly turns his expression into a smile. "I get it. It's—"

"No," I interrupt, "I need to say this." I move my hand away from his, even though it almost physically hurts to do so.

Trey scoots back, not like he wants to get away from me, but like he's being respectful. I continue, "Since everything with my dad happened last year, I've been running from dealing with things, in one way or another. First it was not wanting to admit what happened, then it was just trying to move on. I was so focused on coping. Even after he went to jail, I didn't ever pause to think about how this has all affected me. How I don't trust people. How I keep secrets and push away those who care about me."

My stomach pinches as I think of Kale. How I pushed him away when things got hard, when I didn't know what I wanted. I didn't know how to open up to him and Christina about what was going on with my dad and the victim impact statement, even after all they went through with me last year. Especially Kale.

And even still, I couldn't let him go. Even though it was selfish. Even though it hurt both of us. I was too afraid of being alone.

I take Trey's hand in mind. Trey smiles, cautiously.

"I don't want to do that with you," I say. "And as much as I'd like to see if this thing between us can go anywhere, I'm not ready. I have to work on myself first."

Trey pats my leg gently. "Say no more."

He rubs my shoulder once with his other hand and then lets go. "Friends it is." We both look down at our hands that are no longer holding each other's.

"And as your friend," Trey says, "I will be sure to fill you in on the emergency leadership meeting Jasmine called where the two of us will rip Lana and Candace a new one for that rally."

Trey arches an eyebrow at me. I may be working on forgiving Lana but I'm glad her crimes aren't going unanswered. I smile, thinking that makes me a little like her.

"That sounds great. The play-by-play, that is. Can't wait to hear all about it." I laugh as I lead Trey to the door. Because as much as I love having him here, I know it's not what I need. Not yet, anyway.

"And there's no way Lana can become SASAH president next year, not after what she pulled. Jasmine and I were talking, and we think it would be great if you thought about it. We'll have an open spot with Jasmine transferring to UNR."

I lift an eyebrow at him. "You're vice president. Wouldn't you want to fill that role?"

Trey shrugs. "If there was no one better to do it. And I think there might be."

Smiling, I walk Trey to his car.

Trey hugs me, and I breathe in his scent before I let him go and practically push him into his seat, both of us grinning.

As I turn and head back for my place, I don't feel like I'm walking away from a relationship, leaving something or someone behind, but more like I'm going toward something.

Something important. *Someone* important.

Me.

CHAPTER
TWENTY-THREE

After giving the speech at school, making up with Lana, and talking to Trey about working on myself, I felt ready to sit down and finally write what *I* had to say for my victim impact statement.

Not what Audrey wanted me to.

Not what Tiffany or Sarah wanted me to.

Not what Lana wanted me to.

My words. My feelings. My story.

Like I promised, I made an appointment to go see Kelly.

But before I can really say goodbye to this chapter of my life, there's still one person who needs to hear my side of things.

I follow the guard through the narrow hallway after getting through jail security.

I find myself in the same long room, full of telephones with computer screens in front of them.

The guard resumes his station at the end of the room where he can keep an eye on things. There are around the same amount of people here as when I came to see my dad last time. An elderly woman clutching a phone as she stares at a screen showing a young man. Maybe her son or grandson. A young couple placing each of their hands on their respective screens, so it's as if their hands are touching.

My dad's face is on the screen waiting for me. I take the phone.

"After hearing from your aunt about that show you pulled at school, I'm surprised you came."

My dad's face is hard, his eyes narrowed, jaw set. The look reminds me of one he'd give when he was talking about one of his clients at the law office, judging them. Like he was above their problems. It makes my stomach curl.

"I did what I had to do," I reply simply.

Dad shakes his head at me. "You know what that makes me look like? Do you even care that I'm going up for sentencing soon?"

I keep my lips pursed. I do care, but it's not my job to lie for him.

When I don't respond, my dad's voice comes out low and hateful. "You have no idea what it's like in here. The trouble you caused me—"

"I didn't cause you any trouble," I cut him off. "You're in here because of what *you* did."

Dad slams his hand down on the desk in front of him. On his side of the screen, I hear a guard call out.

"Is there a problem here?" the guard barks. "Because if there is, you can go back to your cell, inmate."

Dad shakes his head at the guard slowly, his features slackening. Until he looks back at me. Eyes narrowed.

We stare at each other for a long time without saying anything. This is my dad in here, in a jumpsuit. He's got a gash on the top of his left eyebrow, I realize, pink and swollen. He doesn't look like he's in as bad shape as Audrey made him out to be, but I guess his wounds could have healed.

Or they were exaggerated so she and my dad could manipulate me.

I pull a folded piece of paper out of my pocket. "I need to read this to you," I tell my father. The paper shakes in my hands. I've imagined this moment, talked myself up for it, for days.

But being here, seeing him, knowing after I read this, I am going straight to the DA's office to drop the statement off. It's different. After this, there's no going back.

"Dad," I say, making my voice as firm and calm as I can. "This is my victim impact statement. I'm giving this to the DA's office before I have Tiffany hand it to the judge on my behalf. I'm not going to read it to him like Sarah is going to read hers. But I am going to read it to you."

Dad appears to stop breathing as he watches me. I continue. "I want you to know what I'm going to say because I want you to know how what you did affected me. You seem to think that the only person who feels the ramifications of your actions is you. But you're wrong."

Dad starts, "Victoria, I—"

"I'm reading this now," I interrupt. And then I look down at my victim impact statement and begin.

"My name is Victoria Parker, and I'm writing to provide my victim impact statement. I don't like that it's called that. I don't like that what my dad did to me made me feel like a victim. I choose to be a survivor."

My dad huffs but I silence him with a look.

"My statement is as follows. My dad sexually assaulted me last year when I was seventeen years old."

Dad interrupts, "You can't say that, Vic—"

I give him a withering glare. I'm tired of being silenced. "Look, this is what is going to end up with the judge. You can either listen to it and know what it says beforehand or not. Choice is yours."

Dad blinks. His mouth forms a thin line, his jaw is clenched, eyes are blazing, but he doesn't say anything.

I go back to reading. "He came into my room late at night. He kissed me and shoved his hand down my pajama pants, touching me where no father should ever even think about touching his daughter." My voice breaks. I don't look up to see how my words land. Instead, I inhale deeply and continue.

"I tried to push him away, but he made it clear he'd force me. He choked me until I couldn't breathe. I was so scared." The paper shakes in my hands as I remember that night. Remember the terror. The confusion. The pain.

"But my stepmom walked in and he said I was making a pass at him." The words blur as my eyes well up. I wipe my face quickly and sniff. I have to get through this. He has to know what he did. I have to tell him.

My voice strengthens as I stare at the words on the white page, separated by the familiar thin blue lines. This is just a piece of paper. These are just words. They are more than that, of course, but I have to tell myself whatever I can right now to be able to get through the statement. I can do this.

"It was a lie. He'd been grooming me, or trying to, for ages. He had been manipulating me, making comments about my body, staring at me, touching me in a way that didn't seem normal."

I have this next part of the statement memorized, because it cuts so deep into how I feel. How I've felt all along. I look up at my dad's face, which shows a mixture of disgust, judging by the look of his scowl, and fear, by his wide eyes. I stare right at him as I recite the statement from memory.

"Back then, I thought there was something wrong with *me*." I enunciate that word because of how ridiculous it is. It's Dad's fault. He's the one with the problem.

I take a shaky breath. Close my eyes for a second before opening them and continuing reading.

"Even though I know better now, sometimes I still feel like it's my fault he's in jail because I told the truth. Even though I know it was him, that he made his choices. Learning he was abused as a child complicated my feelings too. But that doesn't change how he hurt me."

I look into my dad's green eyes. "Dad." I put the statement down and keep talking, even though this paragraph isn't in the statement.

"I have nightmares about that night, still. I don't know that they'll ever go away. I hate that you got me to blame myself last year. I hate that it took me so long to unlearn that. I hate that I lost so much when you assaulted me. I lost a part of myself I'll never get back." Tears rush down my cheeks and I don't bother to wipe them away.

Dad's eyes start to well, too, whether for me or for the prison time he is most certainly going to serve for this, I don't know. But I keep talking.

"I will never be the same after what *you* did to me. I'll

always have a hard time trusting people. I'll always blame myself, feel responsible, for things that aren't my fault."

Dad opens his mouth to say something, but I don't think I can stand to hear him beg or make excuses. I grab my victim impact statement and go back to reading, before he gets the chance.

"My dad lied about what he did to me and what he did to my stepsister. He wanted me to lie for him in my victim impact statement, but I won't. The fact that he wants me to lie to help him shows he hasn't changed. Maybe he'll get rehabilitated in prison, or maybe he won't. But that's not my concern. Now you know what he's done and how it's affected me. What to do with him is your choice."

I carefully fold the paper and return it to my pocket. Dad and I look at each other, and he shakes his head. A tear rolls down his cheek.

"Victoria,"—his chin shakes—"I'm sorry."

My heart hurts. It actually aches as I hear the words I wanted to hear for so long. Even still, they don't change my mind.

I stand and put the phone on the receiver.

On his screen, my dad's eyes widen with panic and he calls out to me. Against my better judgment, I pick the phone back up.

"Please, Victoria, you can't do this. I need your help. I need—"

I hang the phone up again.

And I walk away.

EPILOGUE

A week later, after I gave a copy of my victim impact statement to Kelly at the DA's office, things are starting to feel like they could go back to normal again. Things are going well with the club. We've been through the wringer together and have come out whole, still a group, still wanting the same thing.

Jasmine confirmed to us that Evelyn and Gemma went to bat for our club after talking to me. They got the school president to step in to get Ross's ruling to deny us funding next year overturned. Also, they did some digging and asked around about Blake. Turns out Gabby Garcia had a lot to tell them. About Blake threatening her and Thomas with derailing their other leadership efforts in student government to get their vote, and it working on Thomas but not on her. About how Blake uses fear and intimidation to get what he wants, and how a lot of girls on campus are afraid of him. Ross and Blake both resigned from student government, and after Trey reported him to the school authorities for harassing us, Blake's under strict orders to stay away.

I smile, thinking about Gabby's bravery. She'll be a great student body president next year, when she runs and wins. She's got my vote, and everyone's from the club. If the last few months have taught me anything, it's that we need to support each other.

"Victoria?" The door to the lobby where I sit on a

faux-leather couch opens. The woman who opened it smiles at me. "I'm ready for you."

I follow the woman, Breanna's her name, into her office. She tucks a wisp of her dark brown hair out of her face before gesturing for me to sit. "Wherever makes you comfortable."

I'd thought about going to therapy before, back when I graduated and was starting fresh in Reno. But I wasn't ready to face everything head-on. Audrey told me how therapy helped her work through being abused by her grandfather. Then, too, I thought about it.

The people I know who have come out on the other side of abuse have faced their trauma. Like Connie, Trey, and Audrey—even if she has more work to do when it comes to how she sees her brother.

Tiffany and Sarah are trying to heal themselves. And they seem to be making progress. But really, it was that heart-to-heart I had with Connie that made me pick up the phone and make an appointment.

I survey the therapist's office. A small blue loveseat and a beige recliner are on one side, with a desk and an office chair on the other. I choose the beige recliner, keeping it upright, and Breanna, my potential new therapist, takes the seat at her desk.

"It's nice to meet you in person, Victoria." She smiles warmly at me. "After talking on the phone, I thought you might change your mind about coming in."

I lift my chin, look up at the paintings on the wall of beaches and sunsets.

"I wasn't sure, at first, that I was going to come in.

But . . ." I hesitate, thinking not just about Kale and wanting healthy relationships with others moving forward, but about myself. I want to heal from what my dad did to me, rather than ignore it by throwing myself into helping others, like I did with SASAH. I want to keep doing advocacy, but I don't want to use it as a way to bury my feelings.

I want to be brave.

"I think, after everything I've been through, I have a lot I could learn here."

Breanna nods knowingly. "I agree. Everyone can benefit from therapy, at some time or another, especially after experiencing something so traumatic." She grabs a notepad and a pen from her desk. "Tell me about what brings you in today."

Tiffany recommended Breanna to me, because the therapist she and Sarah see recommended her.

I take a deep breath, summoning the brave person I promised Sarah I would be.

"As you know, my dad is in jail for sexually assaulting me," I begin, "and even though I've written my victim impact statement about what he did for the judge, I don't think I've dealt with it yet, emotionally speaking."

A copy of the letter is in my backpack. I don't want to read it here, not until I know how I feel about therapy, if I decide I can trust it.

But I can remember what it says, word for word.

I hope that what I told my dad about not being able to trust people again isn't true, even though I feel like it is. I hope that I won't always blame myself for things that aren't my fault, like the possibility of Dad getting a longer sentence because I told the truth. That's part of why I'm here, in therapy. I want to get better.

I twist my hands in my lap, not able to meet Breanna's understanding gaze. "I'm scared to be here, scared of having to talk about everything that's happened. But if I've learned anything, it's that I can't run from things. And I can't help anyone else until I help myself."

I look up to see Breanna studying me, not with judgment but with what seems like compassion. "Well, you came to the right place. I'm glad you're here, Victoria."

"Me too." A tear slides down my face as I exhale. "Me too."

ACKNOWLEDGMENTS

It's surreal to me that I keep getting to live my dream as an author, and I have many people to thank for this special gift.

Thank you to my wonderful editor Kelsy Thompson. Kelsy, you understood what I was trying to accomplish, and with your editing magic, you helped me bring it out in the best possible way. You are a lovely person all around, and it's been an honor to work with you.

In addition, my sincere gratitude goes to the incredible people at Flux—including but not limited to: Mari Kesselring, Megan Naidl, Sarah Taplin, Jake Nordby, Sam Temple, Joe Riley, Emily Temple, Meg Gaertner, and Meredith Madyda.

Thank you to my fabulous literary agents, Elizabeth Harding and Sarah Gerton. Elizabeth, I am grateful for your guidance and belief in me. Sarah, you helped me talk through my thoughts on this book so many times and revise it almost as many. *Quiet No More* wouldn't be a book if not for you.

Thank you to Nikki Grimes for being a great mentor and friend. Nikki, I'm honored you not only blurbed *The Quiet You Carry* but also allowed me to use your wonderful words as the title of this book!

I'm grateful for the support of many friends in the publishing community, especially Autumn Krause, for being an inspiration to me as an author, wife, and mom; Eric Smith, for loving *TQYC* and shouting about it to the world; and Christina Tucker Wise, for understanding the intersection of grief and writing and for always being a listening ear. Thank you to everyone in Class of 2K19 Books, especially Kelly Coon and Lillian Clark for their remarkable kindness and encouragement, as well as Novel Nineteens and Las Musas. Although it's exciting, debut year can be challenging (especially when you're writing a sequel!), and I'm grateful for the people who helped me enjoy it.

Thank you hugs to my many friends who have encouraged me through all of this book stuff, including Rachel Breithaupt and the rest of the Breithaupt family (with a special hug for Erin!), Jason-on-Vacation Wilkins, Holly Cheek, Carolyn Bolton, Katie Watson, Laura Maher, Hannah Rael, Angel Pacheco, Matt Scott, Alicia Paige, Rita Chang, Marilyn McMahon, Amy Albano, Michael Tachco, Devlin Durkin, Erin Nicole Smith, Joel Nolette, Michael Munoz, Ari Volpe, Elizabeth Oberan, Andrew Henley, Nick Frontera, Matt Lewis, Erin DeLullo, and more (apologies to those who aren't mentioned—I blame "pregnancy brain"). Additionally, many thanks are owed to Ray Martinez for encouraging me to write a character who is one of my favorites!

So much love goes to those in my Reno family who continue to support my writing journey, particularly Barb and Sara. Thank you both for always showing up.

All the hugs to my sister Rachelle for her social media marketing help with my debut. It meant a lot to me!

The biggest possible thank you to my grandma, Carmen, for being my biggest fan. Grandma, seeing how proud you are of me makes me so happy. Te quiero mucho, Abuelita. In addition, I'm thankful for other members of the Almanza family—Yvonne, Diane, and Rudy—for the support you have given me and our growing relationship over the past few years. To many more!

All the thanks to my in-laws! I am over the moon because of the continued encouragement of Tina, as well as Sue and Tom, the Gs, and more. Carol, I joke that you're my publicist because you have gotten the word out about *The Quiet You Carry* more than anyone who isn't paid to work on it! Whenever you compliment my work, I'm thrilled because I know you mean it. Your encouragement has meant the world to me. Don, thank you for saying the most sincere, heartfelt things about my writing. I will cherish that piece of art you gave me to commemorate my first novel for my whole life. And DeeDee, it made me smile super big when I saw my book on display at your house!

Thank you to Corgus for being the cutest, most high-maintenance writing "assistant" that anyone could ask for. And though you haven't made your big debut as of this writing, Hadley, you were with me as I revised *Quiet No More* and deserve to be in here. I am thankful to you for things I can't express in these acknowledgments, so I will only say I'm excited for all of our adventures to come.

There is not one person in the world who I should thank more than my husband. Robby, your belief in me helps me believe in myself. Your love for me has made me better than I was, and your support helps me do this writing thing I adore so much. Whether it's by saying something kind or telling a silly joke, making sure I eat when I can't be bothered to cook, or missing work or attending a conference on your birthday to hear me give a speech, your actions show me what I mean to you. You are my everything.

It is a miracle I am not only alive but thriving and living my dream. For that, I am grateful to God.

Finally, I appreciate every reader, blogger, reviewer, bookseller, librarian, and anyone who has championed my work. To those who have written to me to share their stories or told me how meaningful my writing has been to them, your words keep me going when I doubt myself. Your strength motivates me to keep trying, no matter how sad or tired I am in the moment. From the bottom of my heart, thank you.

RESOURCES

Crisis Text Line
Text HOME to 741741 anytime, from anywhere in the United States, to talk about any type of crisis.
www.crisistextline.org

National Domestic Violence Hotline
1-800-799-7233
1-800-787-3224 (TTY)

National Suicide Prevention Lifeline
1-800-273-8255
suicidepreventionlifeline.org

RAINN (Rape, Abuse & Incest National Network)
www.rainn.org
   National Sexual Assault Telephone Hotline
   1-800-656-HOPE (4673)

ABOUT THE AUTHOR

Nikki Barthelmess is an author of young adult books, including *The Quiet You Carry, Quiet No More,* and *Everything Within and In Between* (HarperChildren's, Fall 2021). Nikki entered foster care in Nevada at twelve and spent the next six years living in six different towns. During this time, Nikki found solace in books, her journal, and the teachers who encouraged her as a writer. A graduate of the University of Nevada, Nikki lives in Santa Barbara with her husband, daughter, and pride-and-joy Corgi pup.